Praise for THE DEVIL WEARS SPURS

"It's no gamble to bet on cowboy Ryder King. Soraya Lane's *The Devil Wears Spurs* is hot as a Texas summer. It's a wild ride you don't want to miss."
—*New York Times* and *USA Today* bestselling author Jennifer Ryan

"Watch out, the Devil has met his match! Sit back with Soraya Lane's *The Devil Wears Spurs* and enjoy the sparks that fly between champion bull rider Ryder and Chloe, a barmaid with a few aces up her sleeve. You won't want their story to end!" —Laura Moore, bestselling author of *Once Tasted*

"Sassy, sexy, and so much fun, *The Devil Wears Spurs* is a cowboy fantasy come to life. With this rowdy, romantic ride from the ranches of Texas to the casinos of Las Vegas, Soraya Lane proves herself a bright new voice in western romance." —Melissa Cutler, author of *The Trouble with Cowboys*

GORDONSVILLE BRANCH LIBRARY
WITHDRAWN
GORDONSVILLE, VA 22942

W9-CEA-957

WITHDRAWN

The Devil Wears Spurs

Soraya Lane

St. Martin's Paperbacks

NOTE: If you purchased this book without a cover you should be aware that this book is stolen property. It was reported as "unsold and destroyed" to the publisher, and neither the author nor the publisher has received any payment for this "stripped book."

This is a work of fiction. All of the characters, organizations, and events portrayed in this novel are either products of the author's imagination or are used fictitiously.

THE DEVIL WEARS SPURS

Copyright © 2015 by Soraya Lane.

All rights reserved.

For information address St. Martin's Press, 175 Fifth Avenue, New York, NY 10010.

ISBN: 978-1-250-06008-2

Printed in the United States of America

St. Martin's Paperbacks edition / July 2015

St. Martin's Paperbacks are published by St. Martin's Press, 175 Fifth Avenue, New York, NY 10010.

10 9 8 7 6 5 4 3 2 1

For Holly & Laura. Without you both, this series wouldn't even exist!

Acknowledgments

The most terrifying thing about being an author is knowing that once you finish a book, you have to turn around and do it all over again! I often give myself only a few days to bask in the enjoyment of finishing one book before I start another, so it can be very daunting to have to brainstorm something entirely new again so soon. That was one of the reasons this series was so enjoyable to write, because I was able to complete all three books back-to-back, and stay in the same "world" for the better part of a year.

Being incredibly busy writing so many books, in addition to being a busy stay-at-home mom to two young boys, means that surrounding myself with supportive people is hugely important.

My amazing mother is an equally amazing grandma to my boys, and helps me so much on a daily basis. Without her I'd be unable to put the time and effort into my career, and I'm forever thankful for her "granny nanny" duties!

Thank you to Hamish, my husband and biggest supporter. Talk about being a fantastic cheerleader, encouraging me and always believing in whatever goals I set my mind to.

I'm also incredibly lucky to have a core group of author friends, and I'd be so lost without them. Natalie Anderson, Nicola Marsh, and Yvonne Lindsay are not only accomplished authors, they are also amazing friends and provide daily encouragement.

There is also my talented literary agent, the fabulous Laura Bradford. Signing with you was one of my best career decisions, and I love that you always have my back.

And finally to Holly Ingraham, editor extraordinaire. You had a vision for this series, and somehow I managed to create what you were looking for. Thank you for the opportunity to work with St. Martin's Press; it has been not only a privilege, but a very enjoyable experience. Working with a new editor is always nerve wracking, but I have thoroughly enjoyed working on these books with you!

Chapter 1

Chloe knew she was being a hypocrite. Only months ago she was on campus campaigning for animal rights, and now here she was sitting front and center at a rodeo, and loving every minute of it.

She raised her beer and took a sip, laughing when her friend grabbed the hat off the guy next to them and dropped it onto her head.

"Yee-haw!" Shelly giggled.

Chloe smiled an apology and gave the hat back, wishing she was drunk. Shelly had always been able to drink her under the table back when they were in college together, and today Chloe wasn't even close to keeping up with her. The last thing she wanted was to face work with a thumping headache, so she'd been nursing the same beer for over an hour.

"Who is *that*?"

She looked up and followed Shelly's gaze. They were standing near where the riders were waiting, and had ogled plenty of the Wrangler-clad cowboys, but this guy was . . . Chloe gulped as he glanced over at them. His bright blue eyes locked on hers through the crowd. It was impossible to look away. He raised his hat, slowly, still watching her, a lazy grin kicking the corners of his mouth into a smile that almost turned her to liquid.

"Is he looking straight at you?" Shelly hissed.

"Um," Chloe murmured, tongue darting out to moisten lips that had turned as dry as the dirt beneath her boots. "Yeah. I think he is." She knew he was, because he still hadn't looked away.

The cowboy touched the corner of his hat, with the barest hint of a nod, before he looped his thumbs into his jeans and strode off. Chloe blew out a breath and laughed when Shelly fanned at her face with her hand.

"Is it hot out here or is it just me?"

"Hot," Chloe replied, sipping her now lukewarm beer for something to do. "So freaking hot."

It may as well have been a hundred degrees—her whole body felt clammy, and her skin flushed from the burning intensity of the cowboy, who was now climbing over the metal railings, brushing some powder onto his hands, and settling onto the back of a huge black bull. She watched as he joked with the guys gathered around, settling himself in the seconds before they opened the gate.

"And getting even hotter with that bucking bull between his thighs," Shelly said with a grin. "Hot, hot, hot."

"Our next rider is competing to retain the title belt." The speakers crackled, the voice fading, then audible again. "Give a round of applause for our current title holder, Ryder King!"

King. She knew that name. Then the penny dropped. She might not have grown up in Texas, but she'd heard about the King family, had met a couple of the brothers in the bar she worked at. But she definitely hadn't met this brother. The other guys had been dark haired and handsome, but this one . . . *damn.* His blond hair had been messy before he'd put his hat on, his eyes as bright as the ocean on a summer's day. The way his jeans hung low on his hips, and his muscled forearms were on show with his shirt rolled to his elbows, was enough to make her heart beat overtime.

"We need more beer."

Chloe ignored Shelly. She couldn't take her eyes off the bull rider, and besides, she wasn't interested in drinking anything other than soda for the rest of the afternoon. The massive beast was charging around the ring, head down, and Ryder was holding on with one hand, the other flung out in the air behind him as he rode out each buck, body jerking one way, then the other. Until one big buck in the middle of a 180-degree spin sent him flying through the air.

Shit!

Chloe's heart was pounding as she pushed through the crowd, grabbing hold of the fence and trying to see where he'd fallen, if he was okay. She searched the ring frantically, and cringed as the furious bull careened in her direction then charged off toward the center of the ring again. That's when she saw Ryder, stumbling backward fast, and launching himself up on the railings, a grin on his face so wide it made her furious.

"Damn idiot could have killed himself," she muttered.

"What was that, darlin'?"

She glanced at a man standing beside her, only noticing him now that she wasn't in tunnel-vision mode over Ryder. She must have practically knocked the man over to get past.

"Nothing, sorry."

Chloe dragged her eyes from the ring and headed back to wait for Shelly. *Stupid cowboy.* She didn't know if it was the frenzied crowd or the burning hot sun, but something was making her crazy enough to even look at the cowboy like he was someone she could be interested in.

"You looked thirsty," Shelly said, laughing as she passed Chloe a cold beer and banged the bottles together.

Chloe jumped back but still managed to get sprayed with beer foam. Shelly was starting to get so drunk she wouldn't even notice if Chloe nursed the beer without drinking it.

"Damn." She wiped at her jeans before giving up. They'd dry and it wasn't like it mattered—they were almost ready to leave. Which meant it was almost time for her shift at Joe's.

"You know that guy we were watching? Absolute idiot," she muttered to Shelly. "I mean, he jumped on that crazy big beast, fell off, and just about got his head stomped in, then the next minute he was laughing and everyone's clapping like he's a—"

"Chlo," Shelly said, interrupting her. *"Chloe."* Louder this time.

"What?" she mumbled, looking up. Shelly's eyes looked like they were about to pop out of her head. She didn't answer, just cleared her throat too loudly and made a weird gesture with her head. What the hell was going on?

"Shel—"

Chloe's voice died in her throat when a too-husky voice sounded out behind her.

"Maybe you should try it sometime."

A full-body shiver worked its way from her shoulders down her back and to the very tips of her toes, the deep voice lazy and sexy all rolled into one. She glanced at Shelly before turning slowly, knowing there was only one man who could have a voice so deliciously sinful. Because there was only one man she'd seen here today who *looked* that sinful.

"Try what?" she managed, fighting to keep her composure as she came face-to-face with the handsome cowboy.

"Riding a crazy big beast," he said, raising one eyebrow as a slow smile spread across his lips. "Your terminology, not mine."

Chloe's face flushed, the heat burning like fire across her skin. She wasn't embarrassed, but she sure as hell was attracted to the man standing less than two feet away from her. Everything—from his full lips to his stubbled jaw to the long dark lashes framing bright blue eyes—made her think about having his mouth and his hands all over her.

"Shouldn't you be icing your injuries?" It was the best she could come up with, her brain suddenly going into lockdown.

"After that little tumble?" His grin was matched with a wink that had her heart racing way too fast to be healthy.

She swallowed, hard, trying to think of something witty to say. She'd grown up surrounded by brash men and she wasn't going to be the pathetic girl going all goofy over any guy, even if this one was a super hot cowboy.

"If you think flying through the air and having a bull almost crush you is a little tumble, then you're crazier than you look." She glanced at Shelly, her confidence slowly seeping back as she saw her friend's grin. "I stand by my comment."

"Crazy, huh?" He chuckled, folding his arms across his big chest, icy blue eyes never leaving hers.

She shrugged, trying to act uninterested. And she should be uninterested. The purpose of her being in Dallas was to work and save money. No complications and no men. *And definitely no sexy-as-hell cowboys.* If there was ever a time to stick to her good-girl mantra, it was now.

"So I was thinking we could go get a drink tonight."

The way he asked, all chilled out and self-assured, told her that he wasn't used to women turning him down. She got it—he was gorgeous to look at and she knew his family was insanely wealthy—but that didn't mean she was going to melt into a puddle at his feet.

"I'm busy, sorry," she said, folding her own arms across her chest as he pushed his hands into his pockets, a surprised look on his face.

"Tomorrow, then?"

Chloe bit down on her lower lip, trying not to laugh. She wasn't usually so standoffish, but there was something about the sexy cowboy that was pushing all her buttons. If he hadn't been so arrogant she'd have said yes, but there was something satisfying about turning him down. Even if she did want to go out with him.

"Sorry, busy again. But maybe I'll see you around."

A look passed over his face, a frown hovering before kicking back up into a grin, as if he'd decided she was playing a game instead of actually turning him down. *Smart boy.* Even if she did want to think she was in control, the desire thumping through her body was telling a different story. From the way he was watching her, she could tell he liked that she was screwing with him. Maybe he liked the fact that someone actually had the balls to say no to him.

"How about you give me your number and we can talk about this in private some time?"

She laughed, refusing to make eye contact with Shelly. Her friend would be in hysterics by now, and she didn't want to cave in. Flirting like this was fun, even if she was the one breaking out in a sweat from their bantering.

"I don't have a pen."

He bent in, too close, his lips brushing her ear. She'd thought about that mouth of his from the moment he'd smiled at her from across the way, and she was so close to giving in and just saying yes to going out with him. Or turning her head a few inches so that his full mouth brushed her lips instead of her ear.

"Give me your digits. I won't forget them."

Chloe swallowed and raised a hand between them, placing it on Ryder's chest and pushing him back. Her hand hovered, her fingertips gripping his shirt briefly before letting go. Guys like Ryder were used to yes, and she wanted to break the mold. Sure, she might say yes to him eventually, but she was going to let him sweat it out a bit first.

Just as she was about to tell him no again, Shelly called out Chloe's number before bursting into laughter. Chloe turned, furious with her drunken friend. She'd pay for this big-time.

"I'll call you," he said, grinning as he took a few steps backward.

"Fine. Play your cards right and I might say yes next time," she replied, unable to stop herself from smiling at him, slipping her hands into her pockets and trying hard not to cringe at the cliché.

Ryder laughed and turned, and she found it impossible not to check out his butt. His jeans, faded and worn, hugged his frame, and she only dragged her eyes away when Shelly's fingers dug into her arm. Then she remembered that she had to kill her friend.

"Are you insane?"

Chloe glared at her. "Me insane? You're the one who gave him my number."

Shelly shook her head. "Uh-uh, I'm not the bad guy here. You just turned down the hottest man you've probably ever met, and I did you a favor."

Chloe turned to look at him one more time, then shrugged, deciding it was stupid to make a big deal out of it when Shelly had had so much to drink. She could just say no to him when he called, and she'd find a way to punish her friend another time.

"You need to sober up before work."

Shelly groaned. "Can't we just call in sick?"

Chloe shook her head and linked their arms. "Not all of us have parents footing the bill for our law school tuition," she said. "So let's go eat some greasy fries and you can tell me what an idiot I was for trying to act like I wasn't interested in the hottest cowboy in Texas."

"In Texas?" Shelly giggled. "Hell, he was the hottest goddamn cowboy in the country."

Chloe groaned again. Next time she wouldn't try so hard to be coy. Next time? If there was a next time she'd just say *hell yes* if he asked her out. Her phone buzzed and she slipped her hand into her back pocket to pull it out. She stared at the screen, chewing the inside of her mouth and trying not to laugh.

Shelly nudged her and tried to peer over her shoulder. "It's him, isn't it?"

"I could kill you," she muttered.

"Or you could just say yes."

Ryder grinned as he stared at the screen of his iPhone. He didn't even know her name, but he'd never had a woman turn him down before and it was hot. And the way she'd been looking at him? He could tell when a woman was playing hard to get, or at least he hoped he could. It had been a long time since he'd had to chase and he liked it.

"You've got that look about you."

He pushed his phone into his jeans pocket and looked up at his brother. Nate didn't look impressed, his dark brows pulled together as he stared at Ryder.

"What look?" Ryder gave his best innocent face, but there was no fooling his big brother.

"Is it a girl or a game?"

Ryder laughed. He could get away with lying to anyone, except his brothers. "Both."

Nate as good as growled, the rumble in his throat signaling he was about to grab Ryder and try to march him home.

"A girl," Ryder clarified, walking slowly alongside Nate toward the beer stand. "Wanna get a drink? Then you can laugh when I tell you that a hot-as-hell filly just had the nerve to turn me down."

Nate grinned. "And I bet you're real hard for her now, huh?"

Ryder smiled wickedly. "Fuck yeah."

Nate stopped walking and dropped a hand to Ryder's shoulder, forcing him to stop. "Then how about you tell me all about her while the doctor checks you over." His face looked like a thundercloud about to wreak havoc on an unsuspecting city.

"I'm fine," Ryder muttered. "Just let it go."

Nate was still staring at him, jaw like stone. Ryder shrugged, not giving a damn what his brother thought. He kept walking. What he wanted to do was drink, watch some rodeo, collect his title belt, and figure out how to get this mystery woman to give him the time of day. Dealing with his overprotective brother telling him for the umpteenth time that he needed a new vocation could wait.

"Don't walk away from me, Ryder," Nate demanded.

"Shut the hell up and come get a drink with me," Ryder called back.

"You won't be saying that when you're brain damaged from all the falls."

Ryder stopped walking, bunched his fists, and spun around. "I'll give up rodeo when they take me away in a casket. So when I tell you to shut the hell up, I mean it."

They faced off, staring at each other, neither ready to give in. Ryder was sick of both his brothers getting on his back about retiring—the more they told him to give it up, the more determined he became. Nate was getting prepped to take over the family business, managing a nationwide property portfolio that rivaled Trump's, and Chase was running the ranches, which left Ryder with fuck all if he didn't stick to doing what he was good at. It wasn't that his grandfather hadn't wanted him involved, but he just didn't fit the same molds his brothers did.

"Ryder . . ."

He spun around and strode toward the temporary bar. Nate would follow—eventually—but right now Ryder needed a whiskey. Three pours over ice. Or maybe even the entire bottle.

"Wait up!"

Ryder grinned when his brother called out. They might argue all the time, but when it came to drinking or women, they were always on the same page. Ryder slowed so Nate could catch up, and then they fell into an easy step side by side.

"So where did you meet her?"

"She was watching the title ride."

Nate groaned. "Seriously? You're all ruffled up over a rodeo groupie?"

Ryder nudged him hard in the shoulder. "She's no groupie. I only managed to get her number because I wrangled it out of her friend."

"You're kidding me?" Nate's shoulders shook as he laughed. "You're losing your touch. Need some pointers from your big bro?"

"Ha ha, real funny," Ryder muttered. The truth was he wasn't used to hearing the word no, not when it came to women, which was why he was even more determined to hear her say yes.

"Hey look, it's Ryder King!"

He glanced sideways and saw a group of girls squealing and laughing, hurrying toward him. He didn't mind the fuss, usually loved it, but right now he just wanted a drink.

"Looks like you could take your pick here," Nate murmured, low enough for only Ryder to hear.

"Will you sign my T-shirt?" a cute blonde asked.

He turned on the charm, smiling and hitching a thumb into his belt loop as he looked down at them. They were young, maybe eighteen or nineteen, but it was still flattering. And he'd never said no to signing across any woman's breasts before, even if they were covered in a tight white tee with a bucking bronc on the front rather than bare.

"Any of you gorgeous ladies have a pen?" he drawled.

They all giggled again before a brunette plucked one from her purse and passed it to him. Ryder signed each of their T-shirts before folding his arms, standing back to look at the group. They were all beautiful. He should have invited them for a drink and enjoyed the view, but the only woman he wanted to entertain tonight had turned him down flat.

"Now y'all go and have a good night," he said, taking a few steps back before turning away. "And don't forget to come watch me ride a bronc later on."

"A bronc ride?" Nate growled out. "You're out of your fucking mind. The doctor said . . ."

Ryder walked off and left his brother talking to the dust in his wake. He knew exactly what the doctor had said—that he had to be careful—and he was. But he also wasn't giving up the one thing in his life he loved, no matter how dangerous it was. He'd started wearing protective gear at the big rodeos, but the rest was down to being smart—and lucky.

He pulled his phone from his pocket to check if the mystery woman had sent him a text back, frowning when he saw the screen was empty. It was time to put in the hard yards—she might want to play hard to get, but he was a King, and Kings never turned down a challenge. *And they always won.*

Chapter 2

Cool beads of sweat broke out across Ryder's top lip. Not wanting to give himself away, he calmly reached for his beer and took a long, slow sip, his gaze traveling to each of the men seated at the table around him. The smoke filling the small room was starting to make his eyes sting, but he hardly blinked, staying still and silent as he decided what to do. It had been an exhilarating weekend, and he wanted to end on a high. Since he'd been back in Texas he'd been trying so hard to toe the line, but damn, he still needed to have a little fun sometimes. After the three years he'd had on his own, living rough half the time, gambling, riding . . . it was hard to stay on the straight and narrow.

Ryder looked at his hand, fingers playing across the slightly worn edges of the cards, before leaning back in his seat at the same time as he pushed his money to the center of the table.

"All in," he said, folding his arms across his chest and waiting for the other men to make their play.

"I'll see your fifty thousand dollars."

A couple of the guys folded, leaving only three of them in the game. Ryder's heart was pounding loud, adrenaline racing through his body. He lived for moments like this. Card games, horse races, bronc or bull rides—it was the thrill of the win that made him tick.

"You're bluffing," the man seated across from him growled out.

Ryder shrugged and matched his stare, refusing to be intimidated. He was the youngest player at the table by at least a decade, but it took a lot more than a bully with a couple of thugs on the payroll to intimidate him. *Especially when it came to gambling.* And he'd been dealing with Parker since he was a boy—the bad blood between their families stretched back decades, and the tension still hadn't eased any.

"Fast game's a good game, isn't that right, boys?" Ryder grinned as a few of the men glared at him, the others too interested in their drinks to care. He pushed his chair back on two legs and reached for his beer again, tipping it back and finishing the bottle.

"Fuck you. I'm all in, too."

Ryder watched the other player's face, knew his tell, and had that unmistakable gut feeling that he'd just won a shitload of money. Brent Parker had the toughest reputation in town, was notorious for gambling big and shafting people out of everything from their land to the bank balance. *But not tonight.*

Ryder placed all his cards facedown on the table, one eyebrow raised as he slowly leaned forward, scooped all the money to his side of the table, and winked. "Looks like I win."

He was expecting a punch to be thrown or the table knocked over, but instead he received a slow smile laced with hatred from Parker. Neither broke the stare, Ryder not moving a muscle as he held his ground. He rode two-thousand-pound bulls for the fun of it—he wasn't about to let this jackass get one up on him.

"So the kid wants to join the big boys, huh?"

Ryder laughed, waving over a waitress for another drink. "It took me taking all your money for you to realize that? I think I've well and truly earned my spot at the table."

Parker liked to taunt him, thought he was going to piss him off with a little name calling, but Ryder didn't give a damn. They could call him whatever they wanted—he was here to play cards and the more shit they talked, the more he wanted to win.

He ignored Parker's reaction and turned to the blond waitress standing beside him, winking as he took the beer from her. *Damn.* It was her, the hot girl from the rodeo, only tonight she wasn't wearing her tiny cut-off denim shorts. Ryder turned around properly, suddenly a whole lot more interested in her than the table.

"Thanks," he said, pushing a few bills from the pile in front of him toward her. "Fancy seeing you here, huh? I thought your friend had given me the wrong number." He'd given up texting after she'd ignored him, so he'd tried calling her a couple times, too.

From the way her eyes were shining, he was guessing she was trying hard not to smile straight back at him. "Sorry, it's been a busy, ah, day or so."

He stood and held out his hand. "I'm Ryder, but if

you've listened to the voice mail I left you, I'm guessing you already know that."

"Chloe," she replied, slipping her hand into his and letting him shake it.

Ryder didn't let go, stroked his fingers across the back of her hand as he stared at her. "Pleased to meet you, Chloe."

She raised her eyebrows, one side of her mouth kicking up into a smile that commanded all his attention. He loved the thrill of gambling, but nothing kept his attention like a beautiful woman, especially one wearing a tight white T-shirt and even tighter jeans. Although he wasn't sure if her smile was from the amount of money he'd just tipped her or the fact that he was so obviously trying to impress her. He didn't care what he was doing that was making her smile, so long as she didn't stop.

"I take it you're having a good night," she said, retrieving her hand and folding the bills in half, pushing them into her pocket.

"Maybe you're my good-luck charm," he said, turning around to see the expression on Parker's face and realizing the table had gone quiet. But the silence didn't make up for the look Parker was giving Chloe—he looked like a drooling dog, which pissed Ryder off.

Chloe laughed, oblivious to what was going on, hand closing over his shoulder and fingers playing across his shirt as she turned to leave. "Well, good luck, *Ryder.* Let me know if you want another beer."

Ryder leaned into her touch, catching her gaze again. "How about we head out for a drink after your shift?"

Chloe looked away then back again, her tongue

darting out to moisten lips he was already focused on. "I don't finish for a while."

He nodded at the table. "Me neither."

Her smile crept back and he knew she was going to give in and say yes.

"Okay. I finish at eleven," she said, reaching over for the empty bottles and giving him the perfect view of her ass. Her jeans were tight, hugging curves that dipped into long lean legs. "But just one drink, okay?"

Ryder winked as she turned to go. Something about Chloe was getting him all twisted in knots, and the sooner he got her alone, the better. She was the kind of challenge he lived for; hearing her say yes was all the sweeter given the times she'd said no.

"Maybe you could have a drink with me instead, sweetheart, huh? Whadda ya say?" Parker reached out and slapped Chloe on the ass, laughing his head off and reaching for her a second time.

Ryder jumped up and shoved him back, putting himself between Chloe and Parker.

"Easy," Ryder said, glancing at Chloe to make sure she was okay. "You want to impress her? How about you play me again?"

Parker was getting drunker and drunker, which meant he was going to get lazy. Ryder had already taken most of his money, and now he wanted to make sure he bet him out of every last dollar.

"You think you can beat me again? How about we play for the girl?"

Parker's high-pitched laugh made Ryder want to smack his head in, but he didn't. His fists were bunched at his sides, anger pulsing through his veins, but he kept it in check and touched Chloe's back to gently push her away. The sooner she was out of Parker's sight, the better. He didn't mind getting into a fight to protect a girl, but he sure as hell wasn't going to initiate one with Parker if he could help it. Their bad blood ran deep, and it wasn't just Parker he'd have to knock out if things turned bad.

Ryder glanced at Chloe again as she paused a short distance away. He should have been chasing her, not another game of cards, but she didn't finish work for another couple of hours and he was high on winning. It was time to teach Parker a goddamn lesson.

"Kid?"

Chloe could wait. It was time to prove to all the assholes seated around him that no one beat him—not in the ring, not at the card table. Not ever. And anyone who talked to a woman like that deserved to be humiliated.

"Ready to play, or you sick of losing already?" Ryder asked, dragging his eyes away from Chloe and settling back into his chair. "You might need some more cash. Aren't you out already?"

There were a few nervous chuckles around the table, then a series of scraping sounds as a few chairs were pushed out, a couple of the guys leaving before things got too heated.

"Sorry guys, I'm done," one of the men said.

"Yeah, I'm out, too. Good luck."

A few of them just shook their heads but stayed seated.

Ryder grinned "Let's play."

"Hey, pretty one," Parker called out, banging his fist

on the table and waving his arm. "New pack of cards and another whiskey. Now."

Ryder was pissed about the way Parker had just spoken to Chloe, but called out for a drink, too, downing the whiskey in one swig when she brought it over, the liquor burning a fiery path down his throat and into his stomach. He could make it up to her later—once he'd won. It was time to win some big cash and send this idiot packing.

"Let's do this." Adrenaline pumped through his body, more toxic than a drug in his veins.

Parker broke the plastic and took the box out, sliding out the cards and starting to shuffle them.

"No," Ryder said, motioning for Chloe not to leave and touching her wrist. "Let her shuffle and deal."

Parker shrugged. "Know how to shuffle some cards, sweetheart?"

"Sure." Her voice was soft as she glanced at Ryder, calming him like only a woman could. She didn't seem to care about Parker, or if she did she was good at ignoring him. "How do you want me to deal?"

"Five each, we're playing straight," Ryder told her, not taking his eyes off his rival. For all he knew Parker was trying to play him, had asked Chloe to shuffle as a distraction, and he wasn't going to be duped. After he won this game, Chloe was his next conquest. He could already imagine her naked, tangled in his sheets, skin slick with sweat, but even she wasn't going to take his mind off the task at hand now. "How about we get started with thirty grand."

The other guys nodded, faces serious. There was serious money on the table right from the start now—no more joking around.

The cards were dealt and Ryder ran his fingers across them, breathing steady, not even looking at them straightaway. He forced all thoughts of Chloe from his mind and focused only on the game, on the cards that he had to play that would decide his fate. There were four of them playing, and he watched each man's face, took his time to study them.

Ryder fought the urge to grin as he slowly lifted the corners of his cards up, relief hitting him like a ton of bricks. He'd been confident, but now he was starting to relax. The hand wasn't a home run, but it wasn't half bad either. It wasn't about the desire to take another man's money, for him it was all about the thrill of the game, it always was. Although tonight it was also about knocking Parker down a peg.

"I raise ten grand," Ryder said, staring Parker straight in the eye, not letting anything else distract him. He blocked out everything else—the noise of the bar, the beautiful woman standing beside the table—his eyes on Parker's.

"That all you got?" Parker asked.

"I don't see you offering more."

Parker nodded, thrumming his fingers across his own cards. But Ryder could see the sweat beading across the other man's face, knew the bastard was panicking already. Still he sat there, though, not wanting to rush, wanting to draw the game out for as long as he could.

Parker pushed a wad of cash into the center of the table, alongside Ryder's money. "Ten grand it is then."

One of the others folded, which just left Tom. His face was blank. "Fifteen."

Ryder had to fight not to grin. He loved this. There were three of them left and he knew he was going to smoke them. He watched, never taking his eyes from Parker as he discarded one card. Tom threw down two. Ryder didn't blink as he pushed two of his own cards together and discarded them, pushing them facedown toward Chloe. *Damn*. If Parker had only needed to discard one . . . Ryder fought the urge to glance at Chloe—he could feel her watching him. Parker had been easier to read before, but now he wasn't so sure.

"Two," he confirmed, heart pounding like a jackhammer as she slid the cards across the table. He blew out a low breath, picked at the corner of the first one to see what he'd been dealt.

Fuck yes. It was the fourth ace. He glanced at the other card, taking no longer to look at that card than at the first one, before pushing his entire hand into one neat pile. Chloe was his good-luck charm, his hand was as good as unbeatable. He was about to win the lot, whatever the bet was.

"I think we need to up the stakes here, boys," Ryder said, drumming his fingers against his glass. "Two hundred."

Parker sniggered. "That all you got? I was thinking something more tangible."

"Like?"

Parker leaned over the table, his fat stomach stopping him from coming too close, cigarette hanging from between his lips. "How about the deed to that pretty little ranch of yours? Didn't your granddaddy carve it up for you boys?"

Tom looked between them, eyebrows raised. "I'm out," he said, throwing his cards down and pushing off. "Whatever the fuck you guys want to bet, go for it."

Ryder didn't even bother looking at Tom's cards. He never shifted his stare. It was just the two of them now. The other guys were watching, waiting to see who was going to lose a ton of money, but Ryder couldn't see anyone else except the asshole seated across from him. Even Chloe wasn't distracting him now.

"What are you offering?" Ryder kept his voice calm when all he really wanted to do was slam his fist into the table. *Or into Parker's smarmy face.* "How about the latest ranch you burgled? Or maybe your own."

Parker laughed. "I'm in. My ranch against yours."

Ryder was going to win, there wasn't a doubt in his mind. Whatever the stakes, he was playing. Parker swindled locals out of property all the time, men who couldn't afford to keep a roof over their families' heads, which in Ryder's books meant he needed to be knocked down a peg or two. And Ryder was just the man to do it.

He reached for his drink, took a sip while he thought about what he was about to do, swallowed away his nerves. His third of the ranch meant everything to him, and if his brothers found out that he'd even thought about gambling the property he'd just inherited . . . *but he had four aces.* It wasn't unbeatable, but it was damn close to it.

"I'm in," he replied, "so long as your ranch is on the table, too." There was no chance he was going to lose, not after the run he'd had. Hell, not after the weekend he'd had. He'd win the game, take Parker's ranch, and then call it a night. Satisfaction was sweet, and winning was beyond describable, a pure hit of adrenaline to the part of him that was insanely competitive. And he was about to take it all.

Ryder gave in and glanced at Chloe, saw her swallow, recognized the worried expression on her face as he turned his focus back to the game, downed the rest of his drink, and flicked his cards over faceup on the table. She had nothing to worry about—it was one of the best hands he'd ever been dealt, and he had her to thank for that.

"Four aces," he announced, leaning his chair back on two legs.

Parker shook his head, looking down before slowly raising his gaze again. Ryder sat still, his breath catching in his throat as he recognized the smirk spreading across the other man's face.

"Well played, *boy*, but I think you'll find that a king-high straight beats your aces. No?"

Ryder dug his fingers into the table, never taking his eyes off Parker's cards as he watched them flutter to the table. *He never lost.* All these years he'd ridden the toughest bulls, jumped on horses no one else would, hell, the only consistent thing he'd done in his life was gamble, and now . . .

"Fuck." The word was barely a whisper as his eyes shut, hand closing around his glass almost tight enough to turn it into splinters. "Fuck!"

A hand fell on his shoulder and he shrugged it away, stalking toward the bar before he ended up with Parker's goddamn neck in his hands. The fucking asshole had won, *the one time he'd had the balls to put everything on the line*, and now he'd lost the only thing that meant something to him. Parker had probably been fucking with him all night, making him think he was the better player. And he'd been the stupid asshole who'd fallen for it.

"Send over the keys and the deed," Parker yelled out, his voice backed by laughter from the other men they'd been playing earlier. "And don't take too long, you hear me?"

"Give me a full glass of whiskey," Ryder ordered, pulling his wallet out and dumping a wad of cash on the bar. "Or the bottle."

The girl was taking too long—he wanted the drink now. "Hurry up," he ground out, "and fill it to the top."

She did as she was told and he stalked off, heading straight for the door. For the first time in his life, emotion choked in his throat, tears burning fiercer than the straight liquor making its way to his gut. The only things he really, truly cared about were his family and his ranch, and now that he'd gambled away his share of the property, he'd lose everything. His brothers would never forgive him, his grandfather would disown him, and he couldn't blame them. He was an idiot and he knew it. Maybe they would have all been better off if he'd never come back.

Chloe finishing serving a table and put down her tray, heading for the back door. She'd seen Ryder disappear after the game and she was worried. What the hell had made him bet the deed to his ranch? Maybe he was just stupid, and god only knew she shouldn't have given a crap about a man who was prepared to gamble that big. Yet here she was with her arms wrapped around herself, goose bumps spreading across her skin, looking for him. Because from the moment she'd set eyes upon him at the rodeo, something had made it impossible for her to stop thinking about him. She might not have returned his phone calls but it didn't mean she hadn't been thinking about him.

And there he was.

She stopped, looking at the forlorn figure hunched over against the side of the building, before sighing and heading toward him. The clever thing would have been to walk back inside and finish her shift, but instead she was out in the cold, using her ten-minute break to comfort a drunk gambler. Sounded like her childhood all over again.

"Hey," she called out, not wanting to startle him.

She received a grunt in reply, bloodshot eyes meeting hers when she stood over him. He was sitting on his butt, knees drawn up, elbows resting on them. His head had been hanging and now it was pushed back, tilted up to look at her. In the time since she'd seen him stumble from the card table, he'd drunk a lot of liquor. And he looked nothing like the guy she'd met at the rodeo. That guy had been confident, cocky, and powerful. This version of him didn't remind her at all of the bull-riding cowboy who'd so brazenly caught her eye then come over and asked her out.

"Did you bring the bottle?" He squinted up at her and held out a glass.

"No," she replied, dropping to her haunches to get a

closer look at him. "But I can go back and get a water for you."

He shook his head and shut his eyes. "Need whiskey. Or bourbon. I'm not fussy so long as I can stay drunk."

Chloe sucked in a deep breath and told herself to walk away, to just head back to the bar and forget all about him. But she knew who he was, had always liked his older brothers the few times she'd met them, and she did kind of feel sorry for him. The King boys were notorious through Texas from what she'd heard, as much for their money as their reputations. They owned more land than any other family in the state.

She studied Ryder's face. And the Kings were known for their looks. He might have bet too big tonight and lost even bigger, but for some stupid reason she was still attracted to him. And the way he watched her when he talked? It sent a shiver through her that had nothing to do with the cold and everything to do with the sexual heat in his gaze. Tonight and yesterday, the effect had been the same, although his lusty expression had been replaced with a defeated one from the moment he'd lost.

"I'm going to call one of your brothers," she said, moving closer until she was sitting beside him. Chloe was careful not to let her thigh brush his, not wanting to give him the wrong idea. She felt sorry for him. That was it. She was not going to get involved and she wasn't going to act on her attraction. "Can I have your phone?"

"Hell no," he said, banging his head back and clenching his fists into tight balls.

"You need someone to come pick you up," she said, never taking her eyes off his hands. She was pretty sure he'd slam his fist into something solid rather than her, but she wasn't taking her chances.

"They'll kill me," he said, voice low as he dropped his head between his knees again. "They're going to fucking kill me and I deserve it."

"They're not going to kill you and I need your phone." She held her hand out. "Otherwise I can just head back in and call from there. Your oldest brother's Nate, right?"

Ryder jumped up, boots thumping loud as he stumbled. She rose and reached for his arm, fingers closing around his forearm to steady him as his wild eyes met hers. This was why she always preferred to be sober— she hated the idea of not being in control, or being vulnerable.

"Not Nate," he mumbled. "Not Chase. Just you."

She sighed and let him lean on her, cringing at his whiskey-laced breath. She was as sober as a nun, hadn't had anything to drink since her one beer at the rodeo, but right now she was ready to down a shot just to take the edge off what she was about to say.

"I finish my shift in an hour," she told him.

He stumbled and looked at her, his gaze meeting hers then traveling down, resting way too obviously on her breasts. She hooked a finger under his chin and jerked his head back up so he was staring into her eyes again, trying not to laugh at the goofy expression on his face.

"You don't get to check me out," she told him. "Now you either sit tight and drink some water until my shift is over, or I'm calling your brother. Your choice."

He groaned as she walked with him a few steps and then gave up. Ryder was way too heavy to be leaning on her; he must have been six foot four and he wasn't exactly a lightweight.

"Just one more drink," he mumbled.

"No," she said, surprising herself by how firm she sounded. "Sit here, I'll bring you a water, and you're not to move."

"So you'll take me home?" he asked, gazing up at her like a lost puppy dog. Gone was the lusty expression—now he was just plain drunk.

She sighed, wishing she'd just kicked back and had a soda instead of spending her break looking for him. "Yeah, I'll take you home."

"To your place," he mumbled.

"We'll see," she told him. There was no way she was taking him back to her place, but she would make sure he got home safe.

There wasn't a doubt in her mind that she'd regret helping him, but the poor guy had just bet away the deed to his ranch, and if anyone could help him, she could. If he gave her what she needed, she could solve all his problems.

She grimaced as she pushed open the door and walked into the noisy bar. Yesterday she'd been playing hard to get, with no intention of holding out for long where Ryder King was concerned. Now she was about to spend the evening with him because she felt sorry for him, and let him in on a secret she'd long buried. Now it had nothing to do with pleasure and everything to do with business.

If only she were still in law school, none of this would have happened. But then if she were still in law school, she wouldn't need Ryder's help to get her back there.

And having a little fun with him wouldn't be the worst thing in the world. All her life she'd been the good girl, done the right thing, been the grown-up when she should have just been a kid. So long as she could still get what she needed, she wasn't going to say no to a good time. At least until she was back studying. *Then* she could go back to being the good girl.

Chapter 3

Ryder's head was pounding as he waited for Chloe. If she'd let him keep drinking he'd at least still be numb, but he was sobering up fast and reality was hanging over him like the Grim Reaper. He'd lost it all.

He dropped his head between his knees and shut his eyes. His family had worked for generations to create an empire, his grandfather had made theirs one of the wealthiest families in Texas, and now he'd gambled the biggest portion of his inheritance away before the ink had even dried on the paperwork. No amount of bull riding or borrowing could make up the cash difference, either—his only salvation was that his part of the ranch wasn't on their oil land. His big brother was custodian to all of their joint property now, and Nate would never jeopardize even one blade of grass when it came to King land. Which was why Nate, not him, was named successor to the empire.

"Still feeling sorry for yourself?"

Ryder forced his head up. It was like raising a lead

balloon. "Yeah," he said. He was feeling more like a complete idiot than sorry.

"That's the problem with gamblers," Chloe continued, slipping on a leather jacket that made her look like a cute biker girl, her purse under her arm as she stopped beside him and offered him a hand. "The highs are high and the lows are very, very low."

Ryder clasped her palm and pulled himself up, letting her take more of his weight than he ever would have if he were sober. His head might be throbbing but he was still drunk enough to be unsteady on his feet.

"I'm not a gambler." Her words grated, rubbed him the wrong way.

She made a noise that sounded like laughter, only she wasn't smiling. "Says the guy who just lost his property in a poker game."

Ouch. "I might be an idiot, but I'm not a problem gambler," he told her, keeping hold of her hand as he walked on unsteady feet out to the parking lot. "I usually only bet on horses. And I'm damn good at it."

"So you're not a poker player?" she asked, stopping beside his SUV.

"I guess not," he admitted, fishing his keys from his back pocket when she held out her hand. "How did you know this was my SUV and why aren't we taking your car?"

She took the keys and left him on the passenger side, leaning on the door trying to steady himself. The driver's door slammed shut and he forced himself to yank his open and join her.

"Because it's the only Range Rover Sport in the lot, and my car's a heap of junk. I could leave it unlocked and still no one would bother stealing it." She laughed. "I know you have money, but I still would have picked you as more of a pickup truck kinda guy."

Ryder shrugged. "I've got both. But this drives like a demon."

They were silent as she started the SUV, adjusted her seat, and revved it into life. He stifled a grin as she eased off the gas—his V8 engine was hot and ready to go as she exited the lot.

"So let me get this straight," she said, turning her attention back to him. "You're telling me you're not even a regular poker player and yet you were prepared to put everything on the line over one game?"

He shrugged. So she thought he was stupid—he did too—but talking it to death wasn't exactly helping. "I'd taken his money all night and I wanted to teach the asshole a lesson. If you knew him, you'd understand."

She made that half-laugh noise again that was starting to really piss him off. "He was playing you, Ryder. A good poker player knows their limits. That was just stupid."

Now his back was up, like prickles tearing along the spine of a dog about to pick a fight. "And you know a whole lot about poker all of a sudden?"

She glanced across at him, her gaze piercing. "You'd be surprised."

Ryder stayed silent, too busy nursing his wounds to argue with her over something he was already pissed about. What the hell could she possibly know about poker anyway?

"Left or right?" she asked, braking.

"Left," he said, leaning forward to turn the radio on. "Then keep going straight and take the second exit."

"So what are you going to do about it?" Chloe asked, using the control on the steering wheel to turn the music down.

She'd gone from hot to pain in the ass pretty damn quick. "I'm going to feel sorry for myself, drink some more, then worry about it in the morning."

She sighed, loudly. "So you're happy to bet everything and lose it, but you haven't even thought about doing the same to win it back?"

Ryder pushed up from his slouched position, turning in the seat to face her. "I don't have anything else left to bet." Well, technically he did, but he wasn't putting anything else on the line. "And why the hell are you so damn nosy anyway?"

She glanced at him again, her eyes darting from the road to him and back.

"What you have is an arrogant son of a bitch who thinks he's the shit right now," Chloe told him, her voice low. "Which means you have something to work with."

"Are you talking about me or Parker?"

She sighed again, clearly frustrated with him. Only she was sober and he was just starting to sober up—or at least that was his excuse for being one step behind her.

"*Parker,*" she clarified. "He'll be expecting you to run with your tail between your legs, and if you go back to him, especially in front of the same set of guys, there's no chance he won't say yes to a rematch. It was stupid but he's an arrogant douchebag and he can be baited."

Ryder grunted, slouching again and staring out the

window, everything a murky blur in the darkness. "You make it sound so easy."

She accelerated past a slow vehicle, foot heavy on the gas.

"You drive pretty well," he said, watching as she flicked through the electronic controls on the steering wheel. "How did you know how to use the command system?"

Chloe stayed silent, leaning back deep into the seat, one hand resting on the top of the wheel, the other on her thigh. When she finally spoke her voice was low, quiet.

"When my dad was on a high, we had the best cars and rented the flashiest houses," she told him, staring straight ahead, the line of her jaw hard where before her face had been so soft. "And every time we lost the lot, we'd go back to having nothing all over again. So even though I drive a heap of junk now, there's been the odd time I've been behind the wheel of something decent."

Ryder ignored the headache that was clawing through his brain and turned to face her again. "Your dad was a poker player?"

"Sure was," she said, voice almost a whisper now. "If it was a card game he played it. Didn't matter what it was, so long as there was money on the table."

He started to sober up real fast, her pain vivid as she spoke. "So when I asked you if you knew how to deal earlier . . ."

When she laughed her entire face changed, eyes softening at the same time as her mouth. "You were asking a pro who's very good at bluffing."

This time he was chuckling. "If you're so good at poker, why the hell are you working for tips at a bar?"

She made a noise that was impossible to decipher, but he got that he'd pissed her off. "Because I know the gambling trap and what kind of life it leads to."

"I take it your dad's long gone?"

She raised her other hand and gripped the steering wheel tight, knuckles going white. "Along with my college fund and the money my mom left me when she died. I stuck with him for years but he's as good as dead to me now."

"Shit."

She took her eyes off the road for a second to look at him. "Yeah, *shit*. That's why seeing what you did tonight pissed me off so much."

Now he was confused. "Yet here you are helping me."

She gave him a look that made him shut his mouth. It wasn't often he was brought into line by a woman, but given the fact that she'd saved his ass by driving him home, he didn't have a choice other than to behave. Ryder groaned. If he'd only chased Chloe instead of another game, they'd probably be holed up somewhere together having a drink, and he'd be trying to talk her into going back to his place for an entirely different purpose. Instead she felt sorry for him and was giving him a lift home.

"If I could help you win your ranch back, would you say yes?" she asked, her voice lower than it had been, a deeper tone that commanded his attention.

"Sure," he said, not having to think about his answer. "Right now I'd do anything to win it back."

"Anything?" she asked with a smirk.

"Prostitution, drug smuggling, murder . . ." He cleared his throat and glanced at her. "Okay, so maybe just the first one."

"I'm serious," she said, glancing at him as they approached a turnoff. He gestured left again and she slowed. "I can help you."

"How?" Ryder asked, pushing his thumbs against his temple and rubbing, trying to ease his headache. "Because I'm pretty sure they're not just going to let you walk in and ask nicely for it."

"I can win it back for you the same way you lost it. Only this time I'd be the one holding the cards," she said wryly, like it was the most logical explanation in the world. "No offense."

"Hold up," he said, hiding his smile behind his hand. He might be drunk but he still had a brain. "You think those guys are going to let a girl just walk in and join the game? You've got to be kidding me."

Her sigh was audible. "I'm not stupid."

"Never said you were." He opened his glove box, searched for something to drink, and found nothing. "But you'd have to be an idiot . . ."

"They let you play," she snapped.

"Take the next right then keep driving straight," he told her, refusing to acknowledge what she'd just said.

They were silent, the only noises the thrum of the engine and the music playing on low. Ryder shut his eyes. His only consolation was that the alternative to being in the car with Chloe was being anywhere alone with his brothers. They'd have beaten the shit out of him by now, not giving a damn how crappy he felt about what had happened.

"What do you want?" he finally asked, pissed off and tired of playing games.

A slow smile spread across Chloe's face. She was enjoying every second of this, he was sure of it.

"I win the deed to your ranch back, but I get something in return. Otherwise I drive straight to your big bad brother tonight and tell him what you've done."

"Are you trying to blackmail me?" he asked, folding his arms across his chest, leaning back against the door so he could watch her.

"Yes," she said, matter-of-factly. "I want somewhere nice to live for the next few months, and when I win it back I want you to pay my law school tuition. In full. It's only blackmail if you say no, right?"

"Can I trust you to keep your mouth shut?" he asked, trying to read her face and failing. She was almost expressionless; the only tell that she was serious was the way her brows were drawn slightly closer together than before. "If I do what you ask?"

"I won't tell your brothers, but word travels. It won't be long before everyone around here knows what you've done. I give your family a couple of days, maybe a week tops. But I can win it back for you, so yeah, you can trust me."

Chloe slowed and he waved her on.

"That's our driveway there."

She turned in, then stopped, the car grinding to a halt on the gravel. She put it in park and angled her body so they were staring at each other.

"The way I see it you've only got one option," she said. "Unless you think someone's going to bail you out and buy the land back, you need me more than I need you."

She was right. Damn. "Do you realize this is the first time in my life anyone has been able to say that to me?" He'd done some pretty stupid things before, but never anything he couldn't talk his way out of or fix with money. He'd never *needed* anyone.

"Say yes to me, Ryder, and your ranch will be yours again in a few weeks."

"No." He shook his head, still not taking his eyes off her. "I need it back now."

"And I need time to play some poker, study these guys, make them think I know just enough not to be a pain in the ass if they let me join the table. I can get it back, but it's not going to happen overnight."

Ryder raised an eyebrow as he studied her face, deciding that agreeing to her terms wasn't exactly going to be difficult. "If I let you stay, will you be in my bed?"

"Sure," she said, her smile sweet. "So long as you're not in it."

"Ouch." And there she went again, turning him down and just making him want her even more. Those pillowy pink lips were just begging to be kissed, her long blond hair just the perfect length for him to tangle around one fist.

"So what do you say?" she asked.

Ryder looked away, didn't need to be able to see out into the blackness to know what was there. This land meant too much to him, his family meant too much to him, not to do whatever it took to right his wrongs. Every blade of grass, every post in the ground, *everything*, had belonged to Kings for generations, and he wasn't going to be known as the idiot youngest heir who lost what others had worked so hard for. If only he'd thought about that before instead of letting his goddamn ego do the talking. He'd always joked that he was the black sheep of the family, but it wasn't a title he wanted to be stuck with. He'd been an idiot and he needed to make the right decision now.

"I'll play along because for some crazy reason I actually believe you can do this," he told her, reaching out and stroking the hand that rested on her thigh, before closing his fingers around her wrist. "But try to fuck me over and you'll regret it, sweetheart."

"Said the wolf to the lamb," Chloe murmured, her body still as she stared at her wrist. "Now let go of my arm and don't *ever* grab hold of me like that again."

Chapter 4

Chloe hadn't been lying when she'd told Ryder about her dad. Every now and again he'd win big and they'd live extravagantly, in a beautiful house with a gorgeous car parked in the garage. And then he'd slowly start to gamble again, even though he'd promise her over and over again that he was done with poker and every other game he liked to play. It had only taken her until she was fourteen to realize that while his heart might have been in the right place, his addiction always took over, no matter what he might have promised until he was blue in the face.

She drove slowly down the driveway, lights on low as they passed what appeared to be a smaller house, then the main homestead. It was everything she'd imagined it would be even though she only had a glimpse of it as the car's lights washed over it. The house was huge, a two-story mansion that looked as welcoming as it looked imposing.

"Do I keep going?" she asked.

He frowned. "Yeah, we'll go to the guest house. It's a little bit farther down."

"Embarrassed about someone seeing me?" she asked.

"Hell no. But if we go in there I'll have to lie to my brother." He stretched his arms out in front of him, letting out a low chuckle. "Then again, you'd be a pretty good distraction. He might forget about me entirely if you're in the room."

Chloe stifled a smile. Whatever feelings she might have had for Ryder before were irrelevant, her focus purely business now that he'd seemingly agreed to her helping him in exchange for money, but she was still flattered. Ryder and his brothers were all gorgeous, guys who were no doubt used to bedding more women than she'd like to think about, so the thought that they might find her attractive was a compliment she was happy to take.

"You and your brothers are all single?" she asked.

"You've met them?" he asked back.

She nodded. "Just in passing at the bar."

"Then you know why they're single," he muttered.

Chloe laughed. Part of her wished she'd just bumped into Ryder after her shift, that they were hanging out because she'd said yes to going out with him. Then again, if she managed to win his ranch back she'd never have to work the late shift at a bar again.

"Hey, they're nice to me and they're big tippers."

"So you're studying law?" Ryder asked, suddenly sounding a whole lot more sober.

"Yes. Or at least I was." She shrugged. "I've deferred for a year."

Chloe parked the car outside the guesthouse, waiting

awhile before taking the key out of the ignition so she could study the place. It wasn't anything like the main house, but it was still pretty in its own way with a porch across the front and shutters pinned to the outside windows.

"Does anyone actually live here?" she asked.

"Yeah," he replied, jumping out and walking straight over to a rock near the base of the first porch step. She got out, too, and watched as he bent and retrieved a key. "I mean we did, until my granddad had to go into the hospital."

She walked closer to him, conscious of the fact that he was still a little unsteady on his feet. Chloe guessed he was used to drinking a lot, but she never would have forgiven herself if she'd let him drive.

"I kind of float between here and the main house. That's Nate's place now, but before we used to both live here."

So she was about to go into the infamous bachelor pad. "If only these walls could talk, huh?"

"Can I ask you something?" Ryder spun around, key in the still-closed door. He put his hands on her shoulders, hunched forward a little so he was closer to eye level with her. The night went dark around them then, the lights from the car cutting out automatically as they stood facing each other on the porch.

"Sure," she replied, sounding a whole lot more confident than she felt. In that moment, in the pitch black as her eyes adjusted, with every other sense in her body on high alert, everything that had happened between them had been erased and she was back to being the girl from the rodeo the day before. The one who only had to glance at Ryder about to climb onto a bull to make her heart race, her body on high alert at the thought of those capable, strong hands on her body as she'd watched him clap the white powder into them before his ride.

Ryder's finger brushed her cheek as his palm cupped her face. She stayed perfectly still, refused to give in to the urge to press her cheek into his touch. Instead she stared at his face until her eyes were adjusted enough to stare into his eyes.

"If I'd asked you out for dinner tonight, before the card game, would you have said yes?"

Her gaze had fallen to his lips. "Yes," she murmured back. "In case you've forgotten, I already had said yes to a drink."

He moved closer, his hand still on her face. "And now?"

She raised her eyes, meeting his stare. "Now you've got a long way to go to prove yourself to me," Chloe told him as she bent forward slightly, her mouth inches from his as she slowly raised her hand to take his fingers from her face. "So don't go getting any ideas, *cowboy*."

Ryder's smile disappeared as he cleared his throat and took a step backward.

"So what are you doing coming inside with me then?" he asked, turning and pushing open the door.

Chloe followed him as he flicked on the lights. She took a look around, bent to study a couple of photographs near the front door. Aside from the frames, the hallway was emotionless and masculine. A big rug was at the end of the hall, which led to what she guessed was the living room from what she could see.

"Once you've sobered up a bit I'm heading back to

my place," she said, still walking behind him until he disappeared through an open door into what was obviously a bedroom. She sure as hell wasn't going to follow him in there, not when it would be so easy to give in to how attracted she was to him.

And when she glanced in, she saw exactly what she hadn't wanted to see. Ryder was unbuttoning his shirt, his fingers on the last few buttons, and when he looked up she knew he was doing it for her benefit. He let the shirt fall apart then slipped his arms out, throwing it across the room. She swallowed as she stared, eyes locked on his abs, his golden brown skin with not a trace of fat, just pure muscle. His arms were the same, so strong; her fingers itched to trace across every inch of him.

"You were saying?" he asked, one eyebrow raised as he stretched and crossed the room, returning with a T-shirt and pulling it on.

Chloe looked away. So he had a great body. So what? She needed to stay in control, and more important stay focused on why she was here. This was a business arrangement, nothing more, nothing less.

"You seem pretty calm for a guy who's just lost everything," she said, checking out the living room and listening to Ryder's boots echoing on the wooden floor behind her.

"Not calm, just in denial," he said, coming up way too close behind her, his mouth next to her ear as he spoke before moving past. "Besides, I have you to distract me."

She looked at the worn sofas, a coffee table piled high with men's magazines and empty bottles strewn about. It was definitely a bachelor pad, albeit an expensive one, right down to the oversize fridge, which she was certain would be filled with beer, staring at her from the kitchen.

"You don't have *me*, you have my help."

"Same difference," he said, opening the fridge. Out came a beer. "And it's kind of hot being blackmailed by a woman. Want one?"

She shook her head. "No. I'm going home. You can drink yourself stupid, but tomorrow you're sober. No more drinking and no more gambling, for you anyway." She glanced sideways at him. "And I'm not blackmailing you, silly. We've come to a mutually beneficial agreement."

He laughed, a deep chuckle that commanded attention. Ryder was a man used to being in control, and everything about him, every movement and every word, made that clear. Only she'd glimpsed the man beneath the bravado, seen his pain at what he'd done, and no amount of cockiness now was going to make her forget that. He was hurting, but now that he wasn't as drunk as a skunk he was doing a damn good job of disguising it.

"You sure know how to boss a guy around," he said, resting his elbows on the kitchen counter as he leaned forward.

She matched his gaze, her heart beating fast enough for her to notice it. Just because she was trying to be the boss didn't mean it came naturally to her, not with a man like Ryder staring at her. She was like the mouse to his cat, somehow having the upper hand until he figured out how to snatch that power back and catch her at the same time. Only he wasn't having her. There was no way in hell she was mixing pleasure with business, not with Ryder King.

"Right now, you need me," she said, running her hand along the back of the sofa as she walked, needing to do something other than stand and have to stare back at him. "And I need you," she admitted.

"Finishing law school is pretty important to you, huh?"

She stopped moving, lifted her chin, and leveled her gaze on him once again.

"We don't all have trust funds to draw on. Some of us have to work for a living."

The smile disappeared from his face as he pushed his beer bottle away. "You must think I'm an idiot for doing what I did tonight."

There went that fragile part of him, like a hairline fracture through the strongest of bones, just a glimpse that showed her he gave a damn. Which scared her, because it only made her like him all the more.

"Yeah, I do," she told him, walking to the counter and standing opposite him. "But we all make mistakes, and we all deserve a second chance."

He slumped forward. "I fucked up, Chloe. I really fucked up tonight."

She stared at his back as he turned, his hands rising to his head, palms pressed into his face.

"Fuck!" Ryder swore.

Chloe wanted to go to him, to comfort him, because she knew how much he must be hurting, but she didn't. Because what he needed was to feel every bit of that pain if her plan was ever going to work.

"I'm going to take your car," she said softly. "I'll see you tomorrow."

His big shoulders heaved, his hands still covering his

face even though he was facing away from her. She knew he'd heard her, so she turned to go, walking slowly down the hall and shutting the door behind her. The reality of what he'd done, what he'd lost, had just hit him like a ton of bricks, which meant it was time for her to go.

Ryder opened his eyes just enough to see how painful it was going to be. They were only slits but the light was enough to burn his pupils and make his head start to pound, the alcohol from the night before like poison in his system. He shut them again and reached for the Tylenol on the bedside table, fumbling around for the container. He slipped two into his mouth, forcing his eyes back open to look for something to drink.

Bourbon. The only thing within reaching distance was an almost empty bottle of JD, and as much as he would have liked to drown his sorrows in more booze, it wasn't going to happen. He'd fucked up and now he had to pay the price, and that meant no sticking his head in the sand and imagining his shit away with alcohol.

Ryder kicked the covers off and stumbled to the bathroom, eyes still half-shut as he stuck his head under the faucet and took a big gulp of water, swallowing the tablets. When he raised his head he looked at himself, glared at the bloodshot eyes staring back at him. He'd beaten himself up enough the night before, and today he was going to have to man up to what he'd done.

His phone bleeped and he splashed some cold water on his face and brushed his teeth before checking it. Two messages, from his brothers.

Ryder read the one from Nate first. *Who's the cute*

blonde driving your truck? Chase's message was almost identical. *Hot blonde coming your way. Why the hell is she driving your truck?*

He grunted, deleting the messages without replying. Trust them to both see her coming. So long as they didn't try to stop her, he'd be fine. Neither of them would disturb him if they thought he was shacked up with a woman, which meant he'd bought himself some time without even knowing it.

But it also meant that Chloe was about to pull up outside, and he needed a shower. Bad. He pulled off his boxers, kicked them across the room, and headed into the bathroom again. The front door was unlocked and she could let herself in.

He turned the faucet on, stepping under the water when it ran hot. Ryder shut his eyes and let the water glide over his face and down his chest, running his fingers through his hair.

"Ryder?"

"In here," he called back, reaching for the shampoo and massaging it through his hair. He wanted to scrub away every reminder of the night before. Except for Chloe. That was the only positive part of the evening and he could do with scrubbing her right now in the shower beside him.

"Ryder, are you . . ."

He turned the water off and turned around, reaching out for his towel.

"I'm here," he said, rubbing his hair dry. "Come on in."

"Ryder!"

Chloe's high-pitched tone made him laugh.

"What? You weren't expecting me to be naked?" She was lucky he wasn't still hard after thinking about having her in the shower with him.

He tucked the towel around his waist, not bothering to dry his body. The look on her face was priceless, and it had cured his headache better than any pills could.

"You called me in here on purpose," she said, all shock gone from her face as she folded her arms and stared at him.

"No, I was in the shower and called back to you."

She made a noise that he couldn't decipher, but he got that she was pissed off. Although he hadn't missed the way her eyes had roamed quickly down his body then all the way back up again.

Chloe walked through the bedroom, heading straight for the almost-empty bottle of Jack Daniel's on his nightstand. She held it up.

"So you kept drinking last night?" she asked.

He shrugged, following her.

"Did it make you feel better?"

"Yeah. I guess," he replied, turning his back to her and putting on deodorant and aftershave. His reflection was looking a whole lot more human again, compared to the half-dead corpse look he'd been sporting when he'd dragged himself out of bed.

When he turned around this time, Chloe was bent over, looking at a framed photo on the other side of his bed. Ryder stopped midstride, admired the pert ass tipped up in the air, jeans like a second skin. He tucked his towel more snugly at his waist—if she kept her butt pointed in his direction for too much longer . . . He cleared his throat, getting hard all over again just looking at her. Maybe it was the fact she was bending over next to his bed, or then again it could be the fact that she was sexy as hell and he'd wanted her from the second he'd glanced at her across the ring before his ride the other day.

She turned and he crossed the room to get some underwear. He dropped his towel and pulled on a pair of boxer shorts, before going back to locate his jeans.

"Seriously, Ryder, put some goddamn clothes on," Chloe said, eyes narrowed. "I'm not just going to jump into bed with you because you're half-naked if that's your plan."

He laughed. She was even sexier when she was all hot under the collar and angry. "I didn't think you were that easy."

Her smile gave her away even though he could see she was fighting it, the slight curve on one side of her mouth telling him she'd been thinking about him in exactly the same way.

"Well, at least my reputation is intact. Now get some clothes on and let's eat breakfast."

"Breakfast?" Now she had his attention.

"Bacon-and-egg breakfast sandwiches and really strong coffee," she said over her shoulder. "I figured you'd need something as a kick start."

Damn. She looked smoking hot *and* she came bearing gifts. If he hadn't screwed up royally in front of her, right about now he'd be bending over backward to talk her pants off. Instead he had to try to prove that he wasn't a spoiled rich kid with complete disregard for his family and his inheritance. Hell, his grandfather wasn't even dead yet and he'd managed to screw up, so he got that he looked like a brat. Reckless younger brother, definitely; reformed bad boy, sure; but colossal screw-up? *No*. One bad decision wasn't going to ruin his life, he'd make sure of it, and if Little Miss Sexy could help him, then he sure as hell wasn't going to turn her away.

Chloe grinned when she was in the kitchen on her own. Seeing Ryder with his shirt off the night before had been bad enough, but naked? Damn. She guessed riding rodeo kept him super buff, all muscle and . . . She reached for her coffee and took a sip, licking away the foam that caught on her lower lip. What she needed to do was focus on the plan. Ryder might be gorgeous, and she *might* have laid awake thinking about what it would be like to walk into his house this morning, yank off his shirt, and run her mouth over his abs, to explore every delicious inch of him, but that wasn't why she was here. If she was going to stay playing cards again, she needed to get her groove back, and that meant keeping all her focus on cards, not men.

She froze when Ryder came up behind her, feeling him before she heard him. His big body was too close to hers, in her space, and his mouth was *way* too close when he spoke directly into her ear.

"The way to a man's heart," he murmured, reaching past her so that his arm brushed hers before he took one of the paper bags.

"I wasn't trying to find my way to your heart," she quipped.

Ryder turned and leaned against the counter, taking a big bite of the breakfast sandwich.

"My pants?" he asked.

This time she couldn't help but laugh, partially unwrapping her sandwich and holding the paper bag in both hands before she took a bite to keep it together.

"Not your pants, either," she muttered before eating.

He grinned through his mouthful, his wink like a burst of electricity between them. It didn't seem to matter how many times she reminded herself why she wasn't to go near him—there was something magnetic about the guy that made *not* thinking about him like that impossible.

"So tell me, Chloe," Ryder said, drawing his brows together and putting down his food to reach for his coffee, "how exactly do we convince a group of seasoned poker players to let a girl join in?"

"Short skirt, low cut blouse, high heels . . ." She shrugged. "Do you need me to keep going?"

He laughed, but she knew he wasn't buying it.

"Not gonna work," he said. "They might want to look at you, but they're not going to let you join the table. Not without asking questions or outright telling you to piss off."

She ate the rest of her sandwich, still working through the plan. She'd been awake most of the night thinking about it, but there were gray areas that she still didn't have a handle on. Chloe looked up, saw that Ryder had set his coffee down, a smile showing off a sexy-as-hell dimple on his left cheek.

"I think I know what we need to do. And it involves both of us," Ryder said.

Her last mouthful was suddenly like cobwebs resting on her tongue, hard to chew and impossible to swallow. She forced it down.

"So what exactly are you proposing?" Chloe's body was on fire, the sound of her pulse beating so loud she could hardly hear herself think.

"I'm saying that for this to work, you'll need to be my girlfriend."

Ryder looked completely at ease, his big body tipped forward so he was almost eye level with her now. She refused to look away but every part of her screamed that she should, that it was time to walk out that door instead of staying so close to him. She was playing way out of her league. Poker was easy compared to dealing with Ryder King, especially now that he was sober and firing on all cylinders.

"So what do you say?" he asked, voice barely a murmur as he ran a hand down her arm, fingers light against her skin.

"No," she managed.

"We tell them we met the night I lost, hit it off, and now I'm letting you have some fun gambling with me. They all saw us flirting," he continued, undeterred and still touching her. "You can say I've given you a decent amount of cash to play with for fun and they'll know I'm good for it."

She shrugged off his touch and took a step back. If she didn't need his money so bad, she'd have just gone with it, thought to hell with it, and had some fun in his bed. But they had a deal and she wasn't going to let her desire to let Ryder strip her naked and drag her to his bed veer her off course.

"And you expect them to believe it?" she asked. "Just like that?"

His laugh annoyed her. "Me turning up with a beautiful blonde at a bar isn't exactly going to raise any eye-brows. But yeah, if it looks real, they'll believe it."

She swallowed hard, still staring straight back into Ryder's eyes. "I'm not the kind of girl to just fall at your feet."

His smile was slow, deliberate. "Sweetheart, you've made that beyond clear from the moment I met you."

Chloe sighed. Maybe she should have invited him to her place. At least there she wouldn't feel like she'd been trapped in the lion's own den.

"So, *boyfriend*," she said, squaring her shoulders and deciding it wasn't the most stupid plan she'd ever heard. "What do you say to a trip to Vegas?"

"Vegas?"

"If I'm gonna win your ranch back, I need to get some practice in. Which means I need your cash. *A lot of your cash*."

If Ryder was surprised, he didn't show it. He dropped down onto the sofa, leaning forward with his elbows on his knees, and smiled. "Does this mean we're dating?"

She ignored his question. "I want to start with some small games, we can both play, then I want you to hang back and watch, keep an eye on things for me," Chloe told him. "There are some people I don't want to run into and I need you to keep track of all my plays, which means I need your help."

Ryder nodded but didn't say anything.

"Any questions?" she asked.

"Yeah." He chuckled. "When do we leave?"

"Depends on whether we're taking a road trip or flying."

Ryder grinned and turned around, grabbing a soda

from the fridge and passing it to her. She took it, popping the top and taking a sip.

"So car or plane?" she asked again.

He spun back around, closing the fridge door. "I thought you were kidding."

Now she paused, eyebrows raised as she watched him. "You've lost me." She had no idea why he'd found her question so weird.

"Sweetheart, my family has a jet. We can be wheels up whenever you want to be."

She stared at him, waiting for him to laugh and tell her he was joking. But he just opened his soda, checked his phone, then looked back up at her.

"What?"

"A plane? You're telling me you have a freaking plane at your disposal?" Unbelievable. If she had that kind of money she'd be so damn grateful that she'd never waste a penny, and she sure as hell wouldn't go out gambling.

"Well, I have to share it with my brothers," he said, a smirk on his face that made him look so cocky she wanted to slap him just to bring him back to reality. "And my granddad."

"I almost want to drive just to punish you."

He moved closer to her again, leaning back against the counter and stretching his long jean-clad legs out in front of him. "Twenty-two hours in a car with you wouldn't be half bad."

Heat flushed through her entire body, warmth spreading through her belly. Ryder was pure sex appeal, and no matter how hard she tried to think otherwise, she wanted him. And no matter what happened, he didn't seem able to turn it off.

"I think you'll find it's twenty-four hours." It was the only thing she could think of to say.

He shook his head. "Darlin', you obviously haven't hit the road in a Lamborghini before."

"And you've obviously forgotten that you might have a private plane and flash cars, but unless you do something damn fast you won't have a garage to park them in."

His smile died, mouth setting in a straight line. "I haven't forgotten. Don't mistake me having fun with you for me forgetting, not for a second."

"Then start acting like it." She was being snappy and she knew it, but the way he was so cavalier with his money, when he'd lost so much already, was starting to piss her off.

"Are you decent?"

A deep voice echoed down the hall and Chloe forgot all about how annoyed she was when Ryder jumped up, slamming down his soda can.

"Fuck. It's Chase." Ryder ran his hands through his hair, eyes darting to Chloe then toward the door. "In here," he called back.

Ryder swung around to face her, all bravado long gone and replaced with what looked a lot like panic.

"Don't say anything, Chloe. I meant it when I said they couldn't find out. Not a word."

And there was the real man again, the one behind the confident smile and lazy winks.

"He's probably just coming over to say hi," she said, placing a hand on Ryder's arm to calm him. "I waved at both your brothers on my way in. Won't they just be curious who you're in here with?"

"Yeah," he mumbled. "You're right. We'll just play it cool."

Chloe let go of him and slid onto one of the bar stools at the counter, trying to look relaxed, seconds before Chase walked into the room.

"Hey," Chase said, looking at her instead of his brother.

"Hey," Chloe said back.

Unlike Ryder, Chase had dark eyes, like liquid pools of chocolate that warmed when he smiled. He was obviously older, but every bit as gorgeous as his little brother. It was insane how one family could have three boys so different yet all so . . . She held his gaze. Magnetic. Charming. Hell, she didn't know what they were except damn fine.

"You going to introduce us, brother? Or are you keeping this beautiful woman hidden away from the rest of the world on purpose?"

Chloe bit down on her lower lip to stop herself from laughing. Ryder looked like he was about to rip his brother's head off.

"Chase, this is Chloe. Chloe, Chase," he said, pushing past his brother to come stand beside her. He placed a possessive hand on her thigh and she fought the urge to push it off. His big hand over her jeans sent a lick of anticipation through her.

"Pleased to meet you, Chloe," Chase said, leaning on the doorjamb as he spoke, his smile friendly. "Ryder never lets anyone drive his Range Rover, so I figured I'd better come see who'd managed to get behind the wheel."

"Really?" She tilted her head back to look up at Ryder,

noticed how tight his jaw was, body rigid. "He didn't protest one bit when I took his keys off him last night."

Chase crossed the room and helped himself to a drink. "You look familiar. Have we met?"

Ryder's hand closed around her thigh a little too firmly and she gave him a nudge with her elbow. Talk about going all alpha with his brother around!

"I work at Joe's," she said. "I think I've served you a couple of times."

"Ahh," he said, hooking a thumb into his jeans and draining a can of cola. "It explains where I've met you, but not why you'd take pity on this drunken charmer."

She put her hand over Ryder's, trying to settle him like she would a dog itching for a fight.

"Easy boys," she said, leaning back into Ryder, his chest to her back. "It just so happens we met at the rodeo the other day, and he just *happened* to swing past the bar last night."

Ryder cleared his throat. "Chloe was watching my bull ride."

"Please don't tell me you find this idiot on the back of a bull sexy," Chase said, not even bothering to glance at his brother. "We've been trying to tell him for years that he needs a new job."

"And I keep telling you I'm perfectly happy with the one I've got," Ryder growled out.

"Heroic and stupid at the same time," she joked. "But to be honest, I feel more sorry for the bulls than the riders. And if you'd heard me tell this guy what I thought of his fall the other day?" Chloe laughed. "I think you'd have been impressed."

Chase laughed and Ryder pushed his body in closer

to her, his arms wrapping around her shoulders. Her shoulders went stiff until she forced them to relax, softening into him, knowing that they were supposed to look like lovers, like they'd just spent a night hot and heavy beneath the covers. His brothers probably thought she'd just slipped out to get breakfast early, that she'd spent the entire evening with him.

"So tell me, *brother*, how is it you have this gorgeous girl in your house this morning when she never spent the night? You must be losing your touch."

Chloe hid her smile with her hand. *No fooling this one.*

"Too far, Chase. Way too fucking far," Ryder mumbled, letting go of her and stalking toward his brother.

Chloe just shook her head, watching the two of them behave like they were about to start sparring.

"Hey, just calling it how I saw it," Chase said, dropping his drink on the counter and backing away, hands in the air. "I'll leave you two lovebirds to it. You know, because some of us have real work to do today."

"Fuck off, Chase," Ryder said, arms folded across his chest as he waited for his brother to leave.

"Happy to. Now y'all go have a good day, you hear me," he drawled, eyes shining as he grinned. "And if you get bored, Chloe, come find me. I'm a whole lot more exciting than this one."

She hid her smile again as she watched Ryder escort him out. She had no idea what they were talking about, and she didn't want to know. What she did know was that having Ryder act all possessive over her had been kind of nice, his touch strong, his body even stronger. She'd never had anyone in her corner like that before, and even if wasn't real, it was amusing.

She just had to remember that for all his talk, he'd gambled away his ranch, and had complete disregard for how fortunate he was, which made him no different from her father. Kinder perhaps, and stronger in plenty of ways, but a gambler was a gambler, and those kind of leopards never changed their spots. So the last thing she needed was to get used to being his girl. *Or anyone's girl.* If she was going to have some fun with him along the way, she needed to be careful; so careful that there was no risk of her heart or any other part of her getting broken.

"Sorry about that," Ryder muttered when he appeared again.

"You're pretty similar, you know," she told him, rising and moving closer to him.

"What makes you say that?"

Ryder had looked pissed off before, but now his expression had changed. His face had softened, eyes like question marks as she stopped just in front of him.

"You're both used to getting exactly what you want," she said, sucking back a lungful of air as she placed her hands on his shoulders, running her fingertips down his tee and wishing she was touching skin instead. "And you like a challenge."

"Are you're saying that's a good thing or a bad thing?" he asked.

"I'm saying that it's about time someone took control of you."

"Hmmm, *no*," he said.

"Hmmm, *yes*." Chloe stood on tiptoe, still a foot shorter than Ryder. He had to be at least six four, which meant next time she was around him she was going to make damn sure she was wearing heels.

When he bent, Ryder's mouth was so close to hers that she could kiss him with the smallest tilt forward, could have his lips moving against hers almost instantly, but she didn't. Instead she looked from his eyes to his mouth, teasing him, thinking about it, almost giving in. Would it be so bad to enjoy him if it was only temporary? If it was clear it was just for fun?

"I thought you didn't like the idea of being my girl-friend," he said, shuffling forward an inch, his arms encircling her waist, hands firm over her hips.

"Women are fickle," she murmured, so close to kissing him. "But this is just for business, to make sure we're playing our roles right."

"So you *want* to be my bought-and-paid-for mistress?" he asked, grinning as he dipped his head and pressed a soft kiss to her neck, just below her jawline, then another even lower.

Chloe stretched her neck out and bit back the sigh that was so close to escaping, mouth parted in antici-pation. Only he didn't move up, lips caressing her collarbone instead, so gently the pleasure of it almost hurt.

"I'm not your mistress," she forced out, "because a mistress is never the one calling the shots. Rich men use mistresses then discard them like a used pack of cards."

He paused, his breath hot against her neck, his head slowly moving up so she could feel the heat against her cheek. Chloe could feel her heart slamming hard against her chest, her breathing rapid, fingers itching to claw over Ryder's skin.

"I've never had a mistress before, so I wouldn't know."

She laughed, a throaty rumble that she hardly recognized. "I doubt that very much."

Now his chest was skimming hers, his mouth even closer, his hands slipping from her hips to touch the top of her butt.

"I've had plenty of lovers, Chloe," he whispered, "just no mistresses. And I'd sure as hell remember if I'd had one like you."

Ryder stayed still, his breath warm on her skin, closer to her ear now than her lips.

"Does that mean I'm in charge, then?" she asked, turning slightly to the right, never taking her eyes from his mouth.

"It means I'm at your mercy, so do with me what you will, darlin'."

His sexy drawl rattled her, made her want to rip off his T-shirt and push him down to the floor and take him right there in the living room.

She reached up, fingers crawling up his chest, until she reached his collarbone. With all the willpower she possessed and then some, she clutched the neck of his tee and yanked him forward a little, touching her lips to his so gently it was only the barest brush of their mouths. Need swirled inside her, but she wasn't ready to give in to her lust, not yet. She wanted to stay in control.

When she pulled back, every part of her screaming out for more, his lips so pillowy and warm, she whispered against his mouth.

"We leave for Vegas in the morning."

Chapter 5

Ryder banged on the front door as he walked in, kicking off his boots and heading down the hall.

"In here!" Nate called out.

He saw both his brothers sitting at the big old oak table that'd been in the kitchen since he was a boy. They were both nursing beers, Chase leaning back and looking every inch the rancher in his worn Wranglers, and Nate with a suit jacket slung over his chair. His two older brothers might look the same, but there was nothing similar about what they did for a living. One wrangled deals and the other cattle. Nate managed the commercial property the family owned here, and in New York and L.A., and Chase ran their main ranch and oversaw the managers on their other Texas land-holdings.

"You get back last night?" Ryder asked, pulling out a chair.

"Early this morning," Nate said. "A day in New York and I'm done. Hate the place."

Ryder raised his eyebrows. "Yeah, such a hard life jetting around and going to meetings."

"Fuck you," Nate said, although he was grinning. "I have to take clients out to dinner, too, you know. Keep all our tenants on good terms and try to acquire more property."

"Give me a bucking animal any day of the week."

Nate's smile faded and was replaced by a scowl. *Damn it.* He hadn't meant to piss Nate off, not today anyway.

"Settle down you two," Chase said, leaning forward and clinking his beer bottle to Ryder's. "How's Chloe?"

Ryder sipped his beer, calmed his nerves. He half expected them both to know what he'd done, although he knew he wouldn't be sitting here now if they did.

Nate's smile returned, one of his eyebrows shooting up. "Granddad said you're taking the jet tomorrow. You're whisking the blonde away for a dirty getaway, aren't you?"

"I can't believe I didn't recognize her from Joe's. She's seriously hot," Chase said.

Ryder clenched his fists, pissed off for no good reason. Hearing his brothers talk about Chloe like that . . . It was stupid, because that's how they always talked about women, but everything about her made him go all over-protective. Maybe he'd gone too long trying not to care too much about anyone, and now he'd met someone who seriously pushed his buttons, which was driving him a little crazy.

"We're going to Vegas and her name is Chloe."

Nate slammed his elbow into Chase's side and they burst out laughing.

"Her *name*," Nate imitated, "is *Chloe*."

"Fuck off," Ryder swore.

"Settle down bro," Nate said, leaning across the table and sliding him another beer. "We're just not, hell, I don't know. It's weird seeing you all jumpy over a girl."

"Enough," Ryder snapped, grabbing the beer and finishing half of it in one long swig. "I don't want to talk about her with you two. Not now, not ever."

"Geez, he's got it bad," Chase said with a chuckle. "Have you whispered those three little words in her ear yet?"

"I said fuck off," Ryder muttered.

"What, you suddenly can't take a good ribbing about a girl?"

Ryder growled and lunged for Chase across the table, needing to take his frustration out on someone.

"Ryder!" Nate grabbed his arm at the last minute, just as he was about to connect with Chase's face, hauling him off the table so they both went tumbling.

Ryder hit the ground with a thump, Nate landing half on top of him and Chase falling sideways off his chair. *Goddamn it!* He raised a hand to his head, waiting for the blast of pain that he knew was about to hit.

"Lucky we've all had a few beers, huh?" Chase said with a grin from a few feet away.

"What, no thanks for stopping you from getting your teeth knocked out?" asked Nate, extracting himself from Ryder and standing, flexing the arm he'd landed on.

"He deserved it." Ryder stayed lying on the floor, the wood cool against his skin. He was still nursing last night's hangover and now his head was thumping.

"We're just playing around," Nate said. "What'd you

expect when we saw her driving your car? You've never even let me drive it."

"Just admit you like her," Chase said. "Simple as that. She's not just some cute girl you picked up and brought home, is she?"

"What, then you'll miraculously shut the hell up?" Ryder asked.

He watched them exchange glances.

"Yeah," said Chase. "Stop pretending like she's just some cute piece of ass and man up."

Heat rose like an angry snake through Ryder's body, creeping fast into his veins until he wanted to explode. "Goddamn it! She's not . . ."

"A piece of ass," Nate finished for him, giving him a shove. "Admit it. Just fucking admit it."

"Fine," Ryder snapped. "So I like her. Is that what you wanted to hear?"

Nate's mouth twisted into a half smile and Chase sniggered, but neither of them said a word. Ryder hauled himself up and surveyed the mess, two bottles on the ground and one tipped over on the table.

"Who would have thought, huh? Our baby brother getting all twisted in knots over a woman."

Ryder ignored him and crossed the room to the fridge, pulling out another three bottles. They could tease him all they wanted, he didn't give a damn. He had a plan with Chloe and what he needed was for his brothers to leave him the hell alone, so if that meant admitting to them that Chloe wasn't just a good-time kind of girl, then so be it. They were supposed to be dating so him being all protective over her went with the territory.

"So does she have any hot friends?" Chase asked.

"Maybe." Ryder gave Chase a beer, slapping him over the back of the head then dropping it in front of him. "Aside from one cute brunette at the rodeo the other day, I don't know yet."

"And what does she think of you riding rodeo?" Nate asked.

"What the hell do you think? I haven't met a girl yet who doesn't love seeing me ride a bull or a bronc."

Nate glared at him, his voice like a lion's growl when he spoke. "Bullshit."

"Come to my next ride and see if she's there watching."

Nate didn't look impressed with being goaded, but Ryder didn't care. He knew what they all wanted him to do, and he'd already made it clear that he was going to make his own choices about what he did and didn't do in his life. He might be back in Texas, but he wasn't going to give up the one damn thing he was good at. Besides, he knew Chase wasn't as pissed off with him as Nate was, but if their granddad had been here too—then Nate would have looked like the easy one.

"I'll stop when I need to stop. Haven't you seen the gear I'm wearing these days? There's no chance I'll hurt myself again."

"When you're dead? You're gonna be real useful to us if you stop then," Nate muttered. "You know Granddad wants you more involved in the business."

Ryder looked at Chase but just received a shrug in response. "Lay off. We've talked this to death already. Can't you just let it go?" If his granddad wanted him more involved, then he could tell him himself.

"Ah, let me think," Nate said, his glare raw anger. "*No.*"

Chase pushed back his chair, drained his beer, and stood up. "You guys wanna come see a man about a bull with me?"

"That code for something else?" Ryder asked, staying seated and watching his brothers.

"Nope. Just sayin' it like it is."

He glanced at Nate, still scowling at him, and decided he'd go with the brother who looked less likely to commit murder.

"Yeah, I'll come," Ryder said. "Lucky some of us were born capable of working on a ranch."

Nate stood, pushing up his shirtsleeves and bunching his fists. The fact that he was wearing suit pants and a dress shirt didn't make him any less intimidating, but Ryder had dealt with being the youngest all his life, knew how to keep up with his brothers. He might have been smaller once, but the only advantage Nate had on him now was a few more years' experience.

"Easy," Chase said, coming between them and putting a hand on Ryder's chest to push him out of the way.

"I've got ranch business of my own to attend," Nate told them. "Sam's coming over to show me a new horse he's been working with." Nate's childhood best friend trained all their horses, and they all liked an excuse to watch him work.

Ryder followed Chase out into the late afternoon sunshine, closing his eyes and turning his face up toward the sky for a moment. Texas was in his blood, and so was this ranch. He might scrap with his brothers all the time, but family meant everything to him—his grand-father was the most important person in his life. And he was so close to making the biggest screwup of his life, one that could cost him everything, which meant he had to keep himself in check.

"Come on, Romeo," Chase called out.

Ryder jogged the distance between them. "Coming."

"Want to go for a ride? I need some cattle moved into the pens."

He shrugged. "Yeah, I guess." He'd had only a few beers and it wasn't exactly far to ride. "What're we bringing them in for?"

Chase laughed, making a scissor motion with his fingers. "Castration. You'd know all about that though, right? Not like you to back down from a fight."

"What the fuck are you saying?" Ryder stopped walking so fast his boots sent a cloud of dust up in the air.

"That your girl might have your balls." Chase made a face and shuddered theatrically.

"Don't you . . ."

"Chloe. Her name is *Chloe*. Yeah, I heard you loud and clear the first time."

Ryder slammed his shoulder into his brother's as he passed. They might be dickheads half the time, but they were only trying to rile him up. He'd trust them with his life—although maybe not his girl. Women were fair game, survival of the fittest, but if he had it his way neither of them would be seeing Chloe at all if he could help it.

"So you're really pulling out all the stops for this one, huh?" Chase asked, catching up and falling into step beside him.

What did he say to that? That she was the one calling the shots? They'd get a damn good kick out of hearing that a woman was telling a King what to do, not to mention trying to dig him out of trouble.

"Did I mention she said no to me the first few times I asked her out?"

Chase slung his arm around Ryder's shoulder. "Look, if you need help with the ladies . . ."

Ryder laughed. "What, taking her to Vegas isn't enough?"

"Maybe you need to play hard ball. Girls want what they can't have."

Ryder chuckled. "Yeah, so do I. The second she turned me down all I wanted was her and no one else."

"Come on, let's get these cattle moved and sorted, then you can tell me all about her over a few more beers."

"Sounds good." If only he didn't feel like such a goddamn liar, it wouldn't have been a half-bad way to spend the afternoon.

Chapter 6

He stood tall as he waited for Chloe to walk down through the terminal to where he was standing. His brothers might have given him shit about taking the jet on short notice and whisking her off to Vegas, but he'd let them hassle him all they wanted if it meant keeping his secret.

Cool beads of sweat broke out across Ryder's forehead just thinking about what he was keeping from his family. *Stamp it out.* It was the only way he could deal with what had happened, pretend like he was still in control and was going to get it back. And he had to believe Chloe. His gut told him she could do it, that she could actually pull this off, but then he thought of Parker's smarmy face and he wasn't so sure all over again. But giving her a chance wasn't his problem—there was no reason not to let Chloe try to help, because she couldn't hurt him more than he'd already hurt himself anyway.

"Hey beautiful," he called out as she came near, smiling when he saw her.

"Hey," she replied, blowing away a strand of hair that had fallen forward to brush her lips.

Ryder took one of her bags from her so she had a hand free.

"You ready to go?"

"Ready as I'll ever be."

She was clutching the handle of a carry-on bag, and one glance told him that something was making her nervous. Or maybe she'd been nervous this entire time and she'd just been doing a damn good job of disguising it.

"You okay?" he asked, running his hand down her arm, stopping at her elbow when her body stiffened.

Chloe smiled even though she was still tense to the touch. "I'm fine. I just didn't think I'd be going back to Vegas ever again. It's not exactly somewhere I've been yearning to visit."

"Bad memories?" he asked, picking up their bags and walking slowly alongside her.

"Just imagine being dragged around casinos, bars, and back rooms as a kid, every night of the week sometimes, and then you'll start to get an idea."

Ryder glanced at her, saw that even though she was trying to be upbeat there was real pain behind her words.

"I had a shitty dad, too," he told her. "Everyone thinks we grew up in this amazing house with everything we wanted, but sometimes all you really want as a kid is a parent to give a crap about you, huh?"

Chloe nodded, her eyes meeting his when he glanced at her. "Did your dad pass away?" she asked.

Ryder nodded to the security guy and ushered Chloe through the door first, walking out onto the tarmac. "My mom died just after giving birth to me and my dad, well, let's just say that some men shouldn't be fathers."

Chloe stopped walking, her expression hard to read. "I'm sorry. I didn't realize."

"What? About the fact that I killed my mom or that my dad walked out?"

She frowned. "Both."

"Don't feel sorry for me," he said, clearing his throat and nodding toward the plane. "I had it way better than most and a granddad who'd have done anything for us. But if I saw my dad again right now?" He chuckled. "I'd tell him to fuck off and keep walking."

"Do you have champagne onboard?" Chloe asked, eyes wide as she stared at the jet they were approaching.

He paused, and considered how impressive the plane must have looked to someone who hadn't seen it before. He'd been traveling in it since he was a boy, although Nate did most of the airtime in it these days for business, but he never tired of seeing their family crest on the side, the rearing horse proud for all to see.

Ryder waved at the flight attendant standing at the top of the stairs, in uniform and waiting with her hands clasped behind her back. The punch of fear hit his stomach again as he realized he was so close to losing all of this, that his granddad could take everything away from him for letting the family down. Partying and not giving a damn about life was one thing, but actually fucking up like he had was unacceptable.

"Ah, sure do," he replied, gesturing for Chloe to walk ahead of him.

"I say we toast our crappy dads and then don't waste another second thinking about them."

"Cheers to that," he muttered.

She stopped when he did. "We'll leave our bags here. Just take up whatever you need onboard."

Chloe put her carry-on over her shoulder and headed for the stairs.

"I hope you brought some serious cash," she said, walking ahead of him up the stairs.

"Sure did. And I booked us at the Bellagio. If we're going to do this, I wanted to at least make sure it looked legit."

"Oh, because you'd normally whisk new girlfriends away on your jet for naughty vacations somewhere?"

He laughed. "No, if you were my real girlfriend I'd be making sure you became a member of the mile-high club first, then take you somewhere more"—he shrugged—"I don't know, more relaxing maybe. Probably an island, sure as hell not Sin City."

"Mile-high club, huh?"

Ryder grinned and enjoyed the view as she went up ahead of him. As far as fake girlfriends went, it couldn't get much better than Chloe.

"Out of curiosity, have you ever had a real girlfriend?" she asked.

That made him laugh. "When I was sixteen."

"Welcome, Mr. King," the flight attendant said. "Ma'am."

Ryder couldn't remember her name, but he was

guessing either Nate or Chase had personally selected her for the job. He winked as she spoke, holding eye contact instead of letting his gaze drop to her ample chest. If Chloe hadn't been here . . . He looked away. She was and that meant he had to be on his best behavior.

"How many times do I have to tell you ladies to call me Ryder?"

She giggled and gestured into the jet. "Please make yourselves comfortable. Once your luggage is stored we'll be cleared for takeoff as scheduled."

He turned to follow Chloe and received a smack to the back of his head.

"Ouch!" He rubbed where she'd whacked him. "What the hell was that for?"

Chloe raised an eyebrow, one hand on her hip. "My boyfriend just ogled another woman, what did you expect?"

He shrugged. "Well played. Just don't hit me again."

"Or what?" she asked, walking a step closer and letting her carry-on fall to the ground.

"Or I kiss that pretty smile from your face," he replied, wrapping an arm around her, palm to the small of her back, and pushing her forward. "Okay?"

She didn't blink, didn't pull away, just thrust her chin up defiantly. "I won't hit you, you don't threaten me."

"Sweetheart, it ain't no threat," Ryder murmured.

"I—"

He didn't let her finish her sentence. Ryder was done with talk—he wanted action and he wanted it now. He dropped the bag he was carrying and cupped her cheek, his other hand still firmly on her lower back, pushing her forward. Her breathing was shallow as he leaned in, brushing her lips softly with his.

When he thought she was going to pull away, her hand found its way between them and landed firm on his chest. Ryder drew her closer, deepening their kiss. He tasted her mouth, his tongue bold against hers when she parted her lips, unable to stay gentle any longer. Chloe's hair was soft against his fingers when he cupped the back of her head, her body supple as she slipped her fingers around his neck, no longer trying to push him back.

"Sorry to, ah, interrupt, Mr. King, but . . ."

Ryder sighed against Chloe's mouth, reluctantly breaking their kiss. He touched his forehead to hers for a second before taking a step back.

"We'll be seated in a moment," he replied without taking his eyes off Chloe. Her smile was infectious, eyes shining as she dabbed the corners of her mouth to wipe her smudged lip gloss.

"Thank you, Mr. King."

He no longer gave a damn that the attendant had forgotten to call him by his first name. The only woman he had eyes for right now was Chloe, and the sooner they were left alone the better.

"Ready to take your seat?" he asked.

Chloe's cheeks were flushed as she let him take her bag and store it before taking a seat in one of the big chairs.

"Amazing," she said, shutting her eyes and stretching out.

"The kiss or the seat?"

Her gaze was hot, her eyes like liquid fire. "Both."

Ryder settled down across from her, stretching his legs out so that his boot touched the side of her heel. He could have sat down beside her, but he wanted to watch her. *For now.*

"Two glasses of Veuve Clicquot," he called out, knowing the flight attendant would be hovering within hearing distance.

She appeared with two glasses and a bottle almost instantly, setting both champagne flutes down and pouring.

"Please let me know if you require anything else before takeoff," she said.

Ryder nodded. "I will." Although what he wanted only Chloe could give him. "So what do you think?" he asked, settling back and taking his eyes off her to glance around the interior for himself.

"I think," she said, holding up her glass and leaning forward to clink it against his, "that you've ruined any future flying experience for me. Coach will never shape up ever again."

"Play your cards right," he said with a wink, "and I might start flying you everywhere with me."

She took another sip of champagne, crossing her legs and leaning back. "You're stealing my lines."

Her legs looked even longer crossed. Her hair tumbled over one shoulder and her lips were stained slightly red from the strawberry she'd taken from her glass and eaten. He was getting hard just watching her.

"So tell me, *Mr. King*, why has a guy like you not had a girlfriend since you were a teenager?"

Ryder sipped his champagne, wishing he'd just asked for a beer. "I can't answer that."

"Can't or won't?"

He shook his head. "Let's just say I've been auditioning for the role but I haven't met anyone suitable."

"Ah," she said. "So in other words there're plenty of women good enough for your bed but not your heart?"

He laughed. She wasn't exactly being discreet in her interrogation. "Are you waiting for me to admit that I've been a man whore?"

"No." Now she was the one laughing. "I'm just trying to figure out if it's even remotely plausible that you could have fallen for me. You know, enough for anyone to believe that I'm actually your girlfriend."

Ryder slowly looked Chloe up, then down, his eyes traveling over her body. "Yeah," he told her, "you're exactly my type."

She uncrossed then crossed her legs again, fingers playing against the stem of her glass. "And what exactly is your type?"

He licked his lips, drumming his fingers against his thigh as he met her gaze. "Well, let's see," he started, studying her face. "Long hair, kissable mouth, breasts that . . ."

"Enough!" she demanded. "I get the picture."

Ryder couldn't wipe the smile off his face as he ignored her and continued. "A nice ass, just the right size for me to hold on to . . ."

"Ryder!"

He shrugged. "Just being honest."

The plane started moving then, rolling down the tarmac at the same time the pilot spoke through the speaker system.

"Welcome aboard, Mr. King, we're now cleared for

takeoff. We will be arriving as scheduled into Las Vegas, Nevada, at twelve hundred hours. Please enjoy your flight."

"So what are we going to do to kill time?" he asked, fastening his seat belt and indicating for Chloe to do the same.

"How about you tell me more about your family?"

He shook his head. "How about you come and climb onto my lap?"

She laughed at him, draining the rest of her champagne. "Settle down, cowboy. One kiss doesn't mean I'm yours. And I'm only your *pretend* girlfriend, in case you've forgotten. There's no way in hell anything's happening between us."

The jet roared down the runway and took off, lifting high into the sky. Ryder watched as Chloe shut her eyes, gripping the armrest until they were no longer on such a sharp ascent. When she opened them, her eyes found his and she didn't look away.

"No, it doesn't," he answered. "But it's a damn good start."

"Ryder, about our accommodations . . ." she started.

"What, it's not good enough?"

She smiled. "That's the problem, it's too good. We can stay there but we won't be gambling in their big game room."

Now he was the one confused. "Why the hell not?"

"We might hit the Orleans, off the main strip. The games have lower limits and I can slip under the radar. I don't need to play the pros or gamble a ton of money, I just need practice."

"You're in charge," he said, draining his champagne.

She just smiled, and it took every ounce of his restraint not to storm the distance between them and wipe that smile of her face with his mouth.

Chloe rinsed her hands and stared at her reflection in the mirror. This whole experience was insane. Everything she'd ever imagined about a private jet had been wrong—it was more luxurious and then some. The bathroom was two times as large as the one in her apartment, dark timber panels glossy and lavish. Even the white hand towels looked expensive, embossed with the same rearing horse logo that was emblazoned on the side of the plane.

She could get used to this and the thought terrified her. Because she knew how easy it was to get used to luxury, and how easily it could all disappear. Hell, if Ryder was in charge of his family's money, he might have lost the jet in a bad bet and she wouldn't be onboard right now. Unless, of course, she believed him that he wasn't a gambler. Which she didn't. Not yet. He struck her as reckless and the kind of guy who didn't think twice about putting everything on the line—until he proved himself otherwise she was going with her first impression of him.

Chloe dried her hands, refolding the towel so everything still looked perfectly in place, and let herself out. She glanced around, admiring the mahogany serving area complete with bottles of champagne and whiskey, as well as some plates of food she guessed they were to help themselves to.

She turned back around to where they'd been sitting and when she saw Ryder, every hair on her body stood on end. Chloe narrowed her eyes and marched over to her seat, placing one hand on her hip as she glared at the flight attendant half-bent over the sofa toward Ryder. In her short skirt and high heels, with a red scarf tied around her neck and long hair tumbling over one shoulder, the attendant was far too attractive for Chloe not to react. Ryder might be her pretend boyfriend but she sure as hell wasn't putting up with every woman within a hundred foot radius of them hitting on him so blatantly. And the look on his face . . . *damn*. She shouldn't have sworn to herself that she wouldn't touch him.

"Excuse me," Chloe said, voice loud and clear.

The other woman turned, gasping like the last thing she expected was to be caught. There were only three of them on the plane, except for the pilot—it wasn't like she could have forgotten Ryder was traveling with a female passenger who was clearly his partner.

"Sorry, ma'am. Can I get something for you?"

It was on the tip of her tongue to snap back that she damn well *should* be sorry. Instead she slipped past her and sat down beside Ryder, way closer than she would have otherwise. Chloe placed one hand on his thigh, stroking for a second then pausing, fingers dangerously close to his crotch.

"Another glass of champagne," Chloe said, meeting the other woman's gaze, refusing to blink as she stared the attendant down. She might not be used to flying private, but she sure as hell knew how to stake out her territory.

"And you, ah, Mr. King?"

Chloe hadn't even looked at him yet, but when she

glanced at him now she could see he was amused. The smirk on his face was impossible to ignore.

"Just a beer for me. Thanks."

When the flight attendant turned to go, Chloe dug her nails hard into Ryder's thigh.

"Ouch!" He pulled away but she kept her claws in. "You want to play rough . . ."

"I want you to myself," she hissed. "No wonder you've never had a proper girlfriend before. You have no goddamn idea how to behave."

This time he laughed when she ran her nails down his thigh before digging them in deeper. She saw the attendant coming back with their drinks and she leaned in closer to Ryder, using her other hand to push his face around so his lips were only inches from hers.

"Well you sure know how to make a guy hard," he mumbled, reaching for her hand and yanking it away from his leg. "And how to make your point."

Chloe pressed a long, slow kiss to Ryder's lips, keeping her eyes open so she could watch him. She'd met plenty of alpha men before, but she'd never been up close and personal, *intimate*, with a guy like Ryder. His hooded gaze, the calm inhale and exhale of each breath, the way he held himself—there was nothing about the man that didn't ooze confidence. But right now she was calling the shots—he might be richer and more powerful than she was, but she was in charge and she liked it. She wanted a break from being the good girl? Then this was definitely the way to do it.

"You make your point yet, or do you want to climb onboard and pin me down?"

Chloe let him murmur against her lips, aware they were being watched, then grabbed a handful of his short hair and tugged him forward.

"Kiss me," she ordered.

He obeyed, moving his lips faster against hers, his champagne-flavored mouth and warm lips making it hard for her to keep playing the boss. She would have liked to let him take charge, push her back onto the sofa and do with her what he wanted, but she was playing a different game with him, and that wasn't part of the plan. There was nothing normal about this situation and she needed to remember it.

"Still hard?" she whispered, pulling back and then kissing him again, plucking at his lips before sucking hard on the bottom one.

"Uh-huh," he grunted back.

"Good," she said, laughing as she let go of him and pushed him back into the sofa, reaching for her champagne.

"Good?" he asked, his voice an octave deeper than she'd heard it before.

Chloe smiled at him, holding her glass high. "Cheers."

"Cock tease," he muttered, adjusting his jeans and making a hasty grab for his beer, but it didn't stop him from grinning like he couldn't wait to get her back.

"A tease is someone who doesn't go through with what they started," she mused. "I haven't made my mind up yet."

"Huh. Well, make it up damn soon or I'll have to find it elsewhere, if you get my drift."

Chloe saw red. "Don't you fucking dare."

Now it was Ryder grinning. *"Gotcha."*

She turned to face him, doing a terrible job of disguising her anger as she sipped her drink again. "Don't mess with me, Ryder."

"I'm not messing with you, baby. Not a chance." His tone was more serious now.

Thinking of him with another woman made her furious. She scowled at the mental picture of him with the hot attendant, bent over in that gorgeous bathroom she'd just visited. One nod and she'd probably have been on her knees.

"If we're going to go through with this whole"—she paused—"*charade*, then we need to set some ground rules."

"Oh yeah, like what?" He leaned farther back into the sofa, hitching up a leg and propping his beer on his knee.

She mimicked his movements, slowly sipping her drink and casually leaning back. "Like the fact that while you're with me, there's no being unfaithful."

"Sweetheart, if you're not warming my bed then someone will be. I appreciate what you're doing for me, but I'm not a fucking monk."

"Funny," she said, twirling the narrow stem of her champagne glass between her fingers then meeting his gaze, "because I thought the most important thing to you right now would be getting your ranch back. Or have you forgotten about that already?"

His stare was dark. "No, I haven't forgotten. You damn well know I haven't."

"Yet you can't bear the thought of being celibate even if it gets you what you want."

"Or maybe I just can't bear the thought of being celibate with you around?" he said, his voice deep as he picked at the label on his beer bottle. When his eyes met hers, the stare was so intense she went hot all over. "I'm not sure you know quite how"—he laughed—"*fuckable* you are. But I'm also getting the feeling that you're not good at taking a joke."

She would have burst out laughing, only she wasn't convinced he was actually teasing. "If that's true then why couldn't you keep it in your pants before when *she* was over here?"

This time he roared with laughter. "Oh, I kept it in my pants. You didn't see them around my ankles, did you?" He nudged her foot with his. "Besides, it's one thing to look, right?"

She stood up, no longer wanting to engage in whatever the hell they were doing. Ryder loved to tease her, maybe he was the same with all women, but she was sick of taking the bait.

"Look, I don't know what kind of girls you're used to—" she started.

Ryder interrupted, leaning forward and waggling his eyebrows. "Pretty ones," he whispered. "But not firecrackers like you."

Chloe kept her back turned, walking a few steps until the plane jerked and she had to grab the back of a seat to stop from stumbling. "Ouch." She was super unsteady when the same thing happened again, only the lurch was much stronger second time around.

"We're experiencing a little turbulence," the pilot said, voice calm and steady through the overhead speaker. "Please ensure you stay seated with your belts on until further notice."

"You okay?"

Ryder's hand on her shoulder calmed her, his voice deep and soothing.

"Fine," she said, taking a breath and slowly turning to face him. "I'll be just fine."

"It's the bubbles," he told her, taking her hand firmly and leading her back to one of the large cream leather chairs. "One glass in the air is like three on the ground."

Chloe took the bottle of water he passed her, unscrewing the top and taking a big gulp. She did it again and started to feel less like her head was full of cotton candy. When the plane lurched for a third time she grabbed hold of Ryder's hand again, tight. His fingers interlinked with hers, his grip firm as he tugged her hand down to rest on his thigh.

"We'll be fine. It's just bad weather," he said, swapping hands so his right was holding her right hand, so he could put the other arm around her shoulders. "I shouldn't have let you have a second glass without warning you."

Chloe relaxed into him, forgetting her anger. "Thanks," she mumbled, wishing she wasn't acting like such a baby. Planes didn't just fall from the sky, but a few bouts of turbulence and she was a nervous wreck.

"Maybe we should have taken the road-trip option, huh?" Ryder said as rain started lashing the wings of the plane while they both stared out at the sky. "We could have been singing along to some country music and eating greasy burgers about now."

She leaned into him and laughed, comforted by his hold as the plane moved a little too much for her comfort. She'd gone from being furious with him to thankful he was beside her, and she did have to admit that he was kind of fun. Chloe hadn't let her hair down in a long time because life had become too serious, so maybe she needed to just enjoy Ryder's company.

"If we were in a car we'd have the wipers going flat-out and you'd be struggling to see the road."

Ryder chuckled. "Yeah, there is that."

When the weather settled and the plane hadn't lurched for a while, Chloe pulled out of Ryder's arms and picked up her bottle of water again for something to do. She took a sip.

"Could you live without all this?" she asked, looking around at their surroundings before fixing her gaze on him. "If it was all taken away, what would you do?"

Ryder didn't look at her, just grunted and stared straight ahead. "If all this was taken away from me, it'd mean my family didn't want anything to do with me. And I couldn't live with that. The luxuries, sure, but not them."

"Then why did you take that gamble on Saturday night?" she asked, wondering if she'd just seriously overstepped. "It just doesn't make sense. You might be fun and impulsive, but it's still just . . . weird."

His shoulders moved up, then down as he took a big breath and let it go. When he turned, all she saw was regret.

"I've never lost big before," he told her. "I've been on a high since coming back to Texas, but I've also been keeping a low profile, trying to keep out of trouble. Only to prove that I'm one big fuckup."

She shook her head. "I don't believe that's what you are."

"It's taken a hell of a big effort to stay on the straight

and narrow since I've been back, but maybe I'm just not supposed to be the reformed bad boy," he told her. "I was better when I didn't give a damn and I wasn't known for my family name. When I was away from home, I made a name for myself. I didn't need to drop *King* into a sentence because everything I had was self-made."

"So this is what this is about? Wanting to prove yourself?"

"Is it so bad to want to have a shot at life on your own terms? Without anyone else's expectations following you around like a shadow?" He grimaced. "I love my family, but I'm the youngest of two overachieving brothers. It felt good to show the world that I could hold my own."

"Don't you ever take what you have for granted," she said, reaching for his hand again and studying his tanned skin as she made their fingers interlace. "When I win it all back for you, I want you to promise me that you won't gamble again. You don't have to be good all the time, and you can be whoever the hell you want to be, but you do have to not be stupid."

He dipped his head. "Why are you doing this for me, Chloe?"

She was going to joke, like she always did when things became too serious, but she stopped herself. "Because I want something you can give me."

"It's not just for that," he said. "There's something you're not telling me."

Chloe stared at him. Either he was fishing for information or he actually took a lot more notice than she would have given him credit for.

"Look, I liked you when I met you, and then when I saw what happened the other night . . ." She shrugged.

"I don't know. I guess I could see that me helping you could be mutually beneficial. I don't exactly like working my ass off for minimum wage and tips."

"But you don't think I'm a complete fuckup?" he asked.

Chloe wrapped her arms around herself. "No," she said honestly. "I don't."

"So you wouldn't mind if I did this?" he asked, running a hand down her arm and at the same time raising an eyebrow, tongue seductively moistening his lower lip.

She sucked in a breath as his fingers trailed across her skin. Yes, she did mind. That's what she should have said. Only she didn't. Chloe dug her nails into the leather beneath her as Ryder explored her upper arm, across her shoulder and painstakingly slowly down her chest. All his fingers stopped at the edge of her top, except for one that dipped a little lower.

"Chloe?"

She swallowed, breathing heavily, conscious of every tiny movement of his body. His fingertips were like blasts of scorching heat against her skin, each touch making a dent in her willpower.

"What are you doing?" she choked out.

His grin was wicked. "What do you want me to be doing?"

She wasn't going to answer that. "Ryder, we shouldn't . . ."

"Why not?" he asked, his deep, husky whisper not helping her willpower any. "The way I see it, we can have some fun together and get what we both need."

She swallowed hard as he pushed down the front of

her top, so close to exposing her chest, his fingers way too close to her breast for comfort.

"So," she started, sucking back a sharp breath as he slipped one finger inside her bra and brushed her nipple. "You just want sex?"

He chuckled as he tugged her closer and pressed a wet kiss to her neck. "I want you. For as long as I can have you."

Chloe moaned, trying to find some shred of will-power, knowing she needed to pull away. But her bones were like liquid, refusing to comply, and instead of heading in the other direction she ended up climbing onto his lap, straddling him as he guided her closer, hands locked on her hips. What had happened to her steely resolve?

"You're bad, you know that?"

"So I've been told," he replied, one hand snaking around the back of her head to force her forward, tipping her down toward him.

"This is only temporary," she muttered, staying in control just enough to push him back so she could talk. "We had a deal and once it's done, I'll be heading off to school. On the other side of the state."

Ryder made a noise that sounded like a growl. She didn't know if he was angry with her words or impatient for her to shut the hell up and get back to kissing him.

"I thought you didn't want to be my mistress," he ground out, pulling her down hard so she was pinned to his big chest.

"I'm not your mistress," she murmured, her lips parting from his barely enough to get the words out. "This is just two people having fun and pretending to be in a relationship. No feelings, no strings attached."

His laugh was a throaty rumble. "Sweetheart, you might not be having feelings but I sure as hell am."

She wriggled down over his crotch, her eyebrows shooting up as she met his gaze. He was hard as a rock. "You know I wasn't talking about those kinds of feelings."

He shrugged. "I get it. No falling for you, no real relationship. Now can you stop talking and let me show you what kind of feelings I had in mind?"

"You're a devil, Ryder King," she muttered. Chloe closed her eyes as Ryder tugged her down again, one of his hands warm against her bare skin as it slipped under her top, the other tangled in her long hair and holding her in place. The little voice in her head, the one telling her she was a fool to do anything with Ryder, was starting to fade until all she could think about was how good his mouth felt against hers. His lips were painstakingly slow one minute then rough and demanding the next, his tongue clashing with hers as she explored his mouth.

Chloe heard a moan, listening to the guttural noise before realizing it had escaped from her. Ryder's hands were all over her, one on her butt, the other skimming under her T-shirt, feeling her up and sending goose bumps racing across her skin. Her body was humming, back arched as his palm pressed against her stomach and traced a path upward. But he wasn't the only one allowed to touch.

She pushed up, taking her mouth off his long enough only to yank open a few buttons of his shirt, desperate to explore his chest, to feel his muscles and taste his skin. Ryder went to move but she pressed down hard on his chest, palms flat, thighs clenching tight to lock him in place. She only hoped the flight attendant hadn't come back in—Ryder had told her the attendants knew to make themselves scarce and kept to their quarters, but still . . .

"Stay still," she ordered after a quick look around to make sure they were definitely alone.

Ryder raised one eyebrow, clearly up for the challenge. "Or what?"

She laughed. "Or this." Chloe made fast work of the next couple of buttons and pulled his shirt out from his jeans so his entire chest and stomach were exposed. Then she dipped her head, her hair falling over him as she kissed his chest then his abs, tongue darting out to explore each grove of muscle. She'd been wanting to do it ever since she'd seen him strip off his shirt the other day, no matter how much she'd tried to pretend otherwise.

Ryder drew in a sharp breath as she worked her way back up and sucked hard on one of his nipples, grating her teeth gently against the delicate flesh.

"Easy," he muttered, grabbing hold of her hair.

She laughed, fighting to free herself from his grasp. "Or what?"

He yanked her head up, his gaze both deadly serious and playful. "Wouldn't you like to find out."

Chloe was about to push him back and return to her exploration when a loud voice made her jump and grab hold of Ryder's shirt.

"We'll soon be beginning our descent into Las Vegas,

with an estimated arrival time of approximately fifteen minutes."

Chloe sighed as Ryder pushed her hair from her face and back over her shoulder.

"You're jumpy."

She nodded. "I'm kind of a nervous flyer."

His frown made his eyebrows pull together. "You didn't think to mention that earlier?"

"I thought the champagne would take the edge off."

"So how about I distract you some more," Ryder suggested, running a finger from her chin all the way down her chest. "I know exactly how to take your mind off landing."

Chloe looked down at him, the man she had clamped between her thighs, her palms still placed on his firm, golden-brown chest. A moment ago she'd wanted to rip his clothes off and take him right there on the plush leather sofa. Now she was overthinking the whole thing and starting to have regrets. What the hell was she doing? She'd never been this reckless or impulsive before. And what had happened to keeping things strictly professional between them? The moment they'd been alone on the plane her resolve had crumbled.

"Is there anything you need before we land, Mr. King?"

She sighed at the interruption and righted her top before turning her attention to Ryder's buttons. She'd popped one in her hurry to see him bare, but the rest she was able to do up.

"We're fine. Thank you," he muttered, not bothering to look at the attendant, his eyes firmly fixed on Chloe instead.

"We've got a long day ahead of us," Chloe told him.

"Don't give me some bullshit lines," he said, grabbing hold of her wrists and making her stop before she did up the last button.

Chloe didn't fight him, stayed straddling him with his hands holding her still. She stared straight back into his eyes, so unsure of what she wanted. Or maybe she knew what she wanted, she just wasn't sure about the consequences.

"We have as long as we need for you to brush up on your skills," he told her, raising one of her wrists and pressing a slow kiss to the inside of it before letting go. "Tonight I'm taking you out, and you're going to tell me all about your asshole father and how the hell you know how to play poker well enough to bet with the big boys."

Chloe sucked on her bottom lip, biting the soft skin as she watched Ryder. "There's nothing to tell."

"To hell there isn't," he said, drawing her down so her breasts were pressed into his chest, his mouth only inches from hers. "If we're going to play this whole dating thing seriously, I need to know all about you." Ryder kissed her, his lips plucking at hers over and over until she was ready to yield to whatever the hell he wanted from her. "Today I decide what we do. Tomorrow?" He laughed. "Tomorrow I'm yours."

Chloe forced herself to push Ryder away, but not before she cupped his face and kissed him like it was the only chance she'd ever get.

"Fine, you win," she murmured, groaning as she extracted herself from him and wriggled her clothing back into place. He'd had her top pulled down so low her breasts were ready to spill out.

"Darlin', if I were winning, you'd be butt naked and riding me right now."

His deep drawl made it impossible not to smile, the mental picture alone making her want to moan. She might have put a stop to things right now, but that didn't mean she was going to push Ryder away if something happened between them later. Shelly had told her not to be a prude, told her to jump his bones the first chance she had, so maybe she just needed to call her friend for a pep talk when they landed.

"You ever had a cocktail at the Bellagio?"

Ryder adjusted his jeans and sat up straighter, no longer slouching back. "Don't think so. I'm not usually a cocktail kind of guy."

"They're world famous," she told him. "So how about we start with one of those and then go from there?"

Ryder's dimple winked at her, the look in his eyes like that of a wolf about to take down its prey. When she'd called him a devil before, she hadn't been lying. "I say that sounds like a very, very good idea."

Chloe settled herself on the leather seat facing him, turning her attention to the seat belt she was fastening around her waist.

"You know I had no intention of sleeping with you when I agreed to be your fake girlfriend," she told him.

He made a grunting kind of laugh. "And now?"

She shrugged. "Now I'm wondering why I ever thought that abstinence was such a good idea."

As they started their descent, Ryder's laugh was even louder than the engines of the jet.

"You're a hard one to read, Chloe, I'll give you that."

Now it was she who was smiling. "And that's exactly

why I make such a good poker player," she told him. "No one knows what's hit them until my cards flutter to the table."

"And in the bedroom?"

His brazen question took her by surprise, but she wasn't going to back down. Ryder flipped from going easy on her to laying on the sexual charm damn heavy, and she was no featherweight. She'd had to deal with a lot of men with big egos when she played with her dad, and letting Ryder intimidate her because she was attracted to him would be stupid. She just needed to keep reminding herself of the woman she'd been for so many years.

"In the bedroom you'll know exactly what I want, Ryder. Is that what you wanted to hear?"

His smile spread slowly, his mouth turning upward and pleasure heating his gaze. "Yes," he told her. "That was *exactly* what I wanted to hear."

Chapter 7

Ryder waited outside the restroom for Chloe, pulling out his iPhone and scrolling through his emails. His phone vibrated and Chase's name came up on the screen. He was going to send him to voice mail but changed his mind before he pushed the button.

"Hey," he said, leaning back against the wall and scanning the crowd.

"You landed?"

"Yeah, just arrived. We're still at the airport."

Ryder frowned, waiting for Chase to get to the point of his phone call. They only usually dialed when they needed something, and either of his brothers calling him when they thought he was away on a dirty vacation was even more unusual. They didn't exactly call one another to chat for the hell of it.

"I just got back from the feedstore and old Paddy there had a tale and a half to tell me."

Ryder swallowed, his pulse starting to race. Chase sounded too calm to know, but . . .

"What'd that old woman have to say?"

Paddy was more of a gossip than half the ladies in town, and he talked every rancher's ear off when they called in for their feed orders. If anyone was going to tell Chase or Nate, it'd be him.

"He had some bullshit story about you gambling up big-time and that schmuck Parker winning the deed to our ranch." Chase laughed. "I told him to keep his trap shut and stop spreading stupid rumors. Can you believe it?"

Ryder cleared his throat. "Paddy's always been a big talker. Full of shit." He kept his voice level, blatantly lying to his brother and hating himself for doing it. He might have caused his big brothers some gray hairs in his time, but it was never for lying. "Don't tell me you believed him?"

Chase made a snorting noise down the line. "Believed him? Not a chance. Just thought I'd let you know what was being said. Our family's pissed Parker off for years, so it's not exactly news that he hates us and would start a rumor like this."

"Thanks." Ryder waved Chloe over when she appeared. Her mouth hovered into a frown and he realized she was mimicking the look on his face. "Anything else?"

"Nope, just filling you in," Chase said. "Nate would have flipped if he'd heard, but if I see Parker I'll teach him a lesson for you, okay?"

Ryder's heart started pounding again. He'd pressed his balled fist into the wall, ready to slam the hell out of it. "Don't bother. I'd rather do it myself, let him tell me to my face."

"Whatever," Chase replied. "Now go have some fun. I wanna hear all the details when you get back."

Ryder hung up and turned all his attention to Chloe. She looked worried.

"Problem?"

He unclenched his fist and bent to pick up their bags, shoving his phone into his pocket. "Yeah. But there's nothing I can do about it so let's leave it."

Chloe didn't look convinced, but she didn't push the point. "Okay, how about we go find a cab. Unless you have a car waiting for us?"

"Sure do."

He laughed as she made a face. "You do realize I'm not your real girlfriend, right? That means you don't have to try to impress me all the time."

"Darlin', this isn't me trying to impress you," he told her, nodding toward the exit. "I just don't like waiting for cabs."

"Did you live like this when you were riding your way around Texas on your own?"

"No." He glanced at her as they walked. "I slept rough until I won my first belt, which didn't take long, then I just rolled with the punches. Hung out with the other riders. But falling back into this lifestyle hasn't exactly been difficult."

He clenched his jaw at the thought of losing it all for real. He might have wanted to do his own thing for a while, but it wasn't because he didn't appreciate being a King, he'd just wanted to make a name for himself. Now he'd gone and fucked up everything he'd worked so damn hard to prove.

Chloe rolled her eyes and pulled her case behind her.

"You're worried they're going to find out, aren't you? Before we win it back?"

"Chase has already heard something," he told her, waiting for her to walk through the doors and waving to a driver holding a sign with *King* displayed on it. "Even if I stop them from finding out before you win it back, they'll find out one day. It's like trying to stop a train from crashing, and knowing it'll derail on its own anyway."

Chloe's gaze was sympathetic, her brown eyes warm when they fixed on him. She touched his arm as they walked.

"Ryder, they're your family. They'll forgive you."

He doubted it. "Maybe."

"At least you have a family who loves you. Don't take them for granted."

He grunted, not about to argue with her when he knew she'd had it rough with her dad.

"Good afternoon, Mr. King," the driver said, opening the back door for Chloe then loading their bags in the trunk.

"We're headed for the Bellagio," Ryder told him, sliding in beside Chloe.

They sat in silence as the car pulled away, both staring out the window. Soon they were driving through traffic and then they hit the casinos, the tall buildings as extravagant and glitzy during the daytime as they were at night. Ryder glanced at Chloe, watched as she tipped her head sideways and let it rest against the window.

"I haven't been here in a couple of years but nothing changes, does it?"

She raised her head, still looking out. "Me neither. I haven't . . ."

Ryder waited, but she never finished her sentence. "You haven't what?"

She sighed. "Nothing. I, well, let's just say I made a promise to myself that I wasn't ever going to come back here."

"Because of your dad?"

"Yeah. At the time I didn't ever want to see another pack of cards or a casino as long as I lived."

"How about we both make that promise once we're done here," Ryder said. Riding in the car with Chloe, the neon lights seemed tacky, the casinos just a reminder of how stupid he'd been when he'd bet more than he should have the other night. "No more gambling, no more casinos. If we ever come back to Vegas it'll be to see a show or for me to ride rodeo."

"A Britney Spears show, maybe?"

Ryder grinned back at Chloe, pleased to see she was smiling again. Whenever she talked about her dad it was like the lights went out behind her eyes, and it had been those shining chocolate-brown eyes that had drawn him in the first time they'd met.

"How about burlesque?" he asked, covering her knee with his hand. "I prefer naked girls dancing to singing ones."

"I'll make you a bet then," she said, all the spark she'd lost before back on her face. "If you can beat me tonight, I'll go to a girly show with you."

He laughed. Betting against Chloe was something he was sure he'd regret. Although if the stakes weren't that high . . . "And what do you get, if you win?"

"*When* I win, you have to come see Celine Dion with me."

Ryder cringed. "It's not that I don't appreciate good singing, but . . ."

"Kidding," Chloe said. "When I win, I just want to see the look on your face."

The car slowed as it approached their hotel and Ryder unclipped his seat belt as they stopped in front of the hotel's impressive entryway. "How about I take you to a little bar that has a mechanical bull? I can teach you how to ride like a cowgirl as a reward."

He didn't miss the flush in Chloe's cheeks as she held his gaze. "I bet you'd like to teach me that," she said.

Ryder hadn't meant it in a dirty way, but it didn't take his brain a second to switch to bedroom mode. And it wasn't like he hadn't thought about Chloe sitting astride him, naked and grinding.

"Let's just see what the night brings, huh?"

She nodded. "Let's."

They both stepped out of the car and Ryder helped the driver get their bags out before a bellboy rushed over and took them from him. He touched a hand to Chloe's back to guide her through the gold-rimmed doors, the building towering above them as they walked inside. Ryder crossed through the lobby, his boots sounding out on the high-gloss tiles as he walked to one of the front desks to check in. There were plenty of people milling about, the entire place oozing money, but when he turned to glance back at Chloe, there was only one person he was interested in. Even the beautiful concierge wasn't enough to distract him from who he wanted to get back to.

"Mr. King, we have you in the Bellagio Suite. Enjoy

your stay and please don't hesitate to contact me if there's anything you require."

He nodded and took the key cards. "Thanks."

"Please tell me I have my own room?"

Ryder spun around to find Chloe on tiptoe behind him, leaning over to look past his shoulder. When he turned, she ended up peering straight at him instead.

"The bed's a super king. There's plenty of room for both of us."

Chloe stroked a finger down his chest before pushing back and turning. "You better hope so, otherwise you'll end up on the floor."

Ryder watched her go, pausing so she was a few steps ahead of him before he followed. Her jeans were like a second skin, hugging her butt and showing off her long legs. Black heels made her taller than she was, even though she barely reached his shoulder. A leather jacket covered the low-neck tee that he'd been so close to getting off her on the jet. She acted like she didn't know it, and maybe she didn't, but the girl was pure sex on a stick. The only thing better than looking at her rear view would be seeing her bare. Preferably beneath him.

"Ready for a cocktail?" Ryder called out.

Her mouth was tipped up into its delicious smile. "Always ready, cowboy."

Ryder had never found women that hard to read, but Chloe was impossible. One minute she was blowing cool, the next steaming hot.

Chloe listened to the water running and finally relaxed. Being with Ryder was fun, but she felt on high alert all the time, always trying to come back with a quip to match his, flipping between wanting him and wanting to run every other second. She flopped down on the bed and stared at the ceiling, before sitting up and surveying the room properly. It was old-school luxury—gilded frames, luxurious fabrics, and extravagant furniture. She jumped down and stripped, taking off her jeans and T-shirt and rummaging through her case until she found what she was looking for. The dress was simple, black with a plunging neckline, tight to just below her knees when she stepped into it. Something that she knew would make Ryder stop and stare.

She slipped on her heels, four-inch black suede pumps, and then reached for her makeup, carrying it over to the antique table just past the foot of the bed. A huge gold mirror hung above it, and she bent forward to inspect her face. Chloe unzipped the bag and took out her concealer, dabbing it under her eyes and onto her chin, before lightly touching up her foundation. She was distracted only by the view—the suite looked out over the city, and she could imagine how amazing it would look lit up at night. She glanced back at the bed, plump with an oversize comforter and too many pillows— would she be lying in there alone admiring the view come darkness? She smiled to herself and went back to applying her makeup. *Unlikely.*

The sound of running water stopped and she hurried to finish, spritzing some perfume to her neck and into her hair, then adding a quick dab between her breasts.

"Is that for my benefit?"

The husky drawl made her turn, heat flushing her body. Ryder seemed to know exactly what she was thinking, and the way he was staring at her with only a towel tucked loosely around his waist was making her damp between the legs. She was sick of telling herself why she couldn't have him, especially when he looked like that.

"My breasts like it," she told him, setting down the bottle and squaring her shoulders, "and so do I."

He raised an eyebrow, his gaze falling to her breasts, then slowly inspecting the rest of her. His body was immobile, the only movement his eyes.

"Do you like what you see?" she asked, her breathing raspy.

"I do," he replied. "You look amazing."

So do you. She bit back her reply, keeping her mouth clamped shut. It would only take her crossing the room and slipping that towel down to have him naked, and she bet he'd make fast work of her clothes.

"Are you going to put some clothes on or do you want to stay in?"

He shrugged. "Up to you. I hear the room service here is good."

She hadn't been expecting that response. "I'm ready for that cocktail you promised me, actually."

Ryder placed one hand over the edge of his towel as he walked, padding across the thick carpet and stopping less than a foot from her. His big body towered over her, his wet hair dripping onto her when he bent his neck low, too low. Chloe held her breath as his mouth hovered over her cleavage, but it was his nose that touched her skin, gently, so that she could barely feel it. Only she was so hypersensitive when it came to Ryder she'd have felt him breathe on her.

"You smell as gorgeous as you look," he whispered,

raising his head just as slowly and stopping when he got to her lips.

Ryder leaned in, his mouth so close to hers, teasing her, but she refused to move, to invite him in. But just as she was about to push him away, to swallow and stop holding her damn breath, he leaned in and kissed her, as lightly as he'd nudged at her breast. His lips were so soft they were almost painful.

"I don't want to ruin that beautiful lipstick of yours," he whispered, his mouth barely brushing hers as they spoke. "Not yet."

Chloe shut her eyes, inhaled the scent of his just-washed hair, the citrus of his cologne. She wasn't going to beg him, it wasn't her style, but the more he teased her the more she hated herself for wanting him so bad.

"Maybe never," she finally murmured back, but Ryder was gone, backing away then turning.

She was about to tell him that *he* was the goddamn tease, and then he went and dropped his towel, showing off a muscular ass that had her sucking in a breath. Chloe bit her lip and just admired the view. He wanted a reaction from her and he wasn't going to get it—she could punish him later for trying to rile her up. She only wished she'd had a glimpse of the front view as well as the rear.

"Are we going to talk tactics tonight?" he asked, pulling on underwear and then a pair of dark denim jeans.

"Maybe," she said, wriggling her dress down a little farther to show off more of her breasts. Two could play at this game, and just like Ryder, she was used to winning.

"What are we drinking?" he asked, buttoning up a shirt and watching her at the same time.

"Hemingway Daiquiris. And we're going now."

Chloe collected her purse and headed for the door, smiling to herself when she heard Ryder curse, his boots managing to sound out even on the carpet as he hurried after her.

"Ouch!" Chloe spun around when he slapped her on the bum, ready to slap *him*.

Only the look on his face, the cheeky dimple like a naughty wink staring back at her, made her anger turn into a thrill that ran the entire length of her body. Want swirled in her belly, made her desperate to slam him into the door and grind against him. Instead, she put one hand on her hip and glared at him, fighting the smile desperate to take control of her face.

She was staying in control whether she liked it or not.

"You," she admonished, "are a devil. And you're not even trying to disguise it."

He spun her before she knew what he was doing, pinning her arms to her sides, her back hard against the door. His body pressed into hers, hips locked forward, his erection impossible not to notice.

"So they say," he muttered, letting go of one of her hands to run a finger down to her breasts, then dipping between them. "Now stop wiggling that sexy ass at me and let's go get a drink."

"So tell me," Ryder asked, pushing Chloe's cocktail toward her and leaning back. "Why are you so terrified of something happening between us?"

She spluttered on her drink. "I'm not terrified."

"No?" he asked, trying not to take pleasure in how rattled she was. She'd regained her composure now, but she was looking more interested in the bottles lined up behind the bar than she was in him.

"Is it just me or all men?"

Her eyes found his this time, her annoyance obvious. "I don't have a problem with men."

"I'm guessing it's daddy issues," he mused. "I get it, believe me."

She sighed and took a sip of her drink. "I'm not denying I have daddy issues, but I don't have a problem with men."

"So *it is* just me?"

Now she looked ready to punch him. "Is your ego so big that you can't deal with the fact a woman can turn you down?"

"Yeah," he admitted. "It's never happened before." Ryder shrugged. "And don't look so surprised."

"Ugh." She took another sip before pushing her drink away and leveling her gaze on him. "You're so full of yourself it's sickening."

"Come on, just tell me why you're so scared of something happening between us. If it's the gambling, I get it, but it's not that." His smile was infectious. "And I'm only offended that you turned me down because I wanted you so bad."

"How are you so sure?" she asked, but he could tell she was softening, that she was going to open up. "About the fact that I have *issues*."

Ryder moved his hand, his fingers finding hers and closing over them. He didn't just want to bed Chloe. She was the most goddamn intriguing woman he'd ever met, and he wanted to know what made her tick.

"Because one minute you want me and the next

you've got this look in your eyes like you're about to get it on with the Big Bad Wolf."

She laughed. "My dad did kind of screw me up where men are concerned. He always let me down, and the last time he did it I vowed never to let a guy have that kind of power over me again. I guess we both have that in common, huh? Wanting to prove ourselves? But I'm trying to pretend my only family member doesn't exist."

Ryder watched as she slid her fingers away from his. "You're too beautiful to be alone for the rest of your life."

"And you're too charming," she quipped, sipping her drink.

They sat in silence for a moment, Ryder staring at Chloe's face as she stared at the bottles.

"I want to make it myself, Ryder. I love men, but I don't want a relationship. Not with you or any man, so don't take it personally." She looked up. "If you want some fun for the next few weeks, then I say hell yes. But if you want more?" She shrugged. "Then you're out of luck."

It was impossible for him not to smile. "I didn't think you wanted to be my bought-and-paid-for mistress."

Now it was Chloe smiling, her face lighting up as she leaned in toward him. "*Sugar*, I'm not your mistress if I'm the one calling the shots."

Ryder slapped his hand on his thigh. If she was trying to imitate him, she was doing a damn good job with that faux Texas accent.

"Sweetheart, as long as you want to be in my bed, you can call *all* the shots."

"Well now that's settled and you know all about my daddy issues, why don't you tell me about yours?"

Ryder groaned. "Seriously?"

"My dad swindled people out of money all my childhood and he taught me to be a damn good hustler. Only I wasn't good enough to see that I was about to be hustled myself, by the one person I trusted. Whatever your dad was like he can't have been any worse than mine."

Ryder drained the rest of his cocktail before answering. "Your dad sounds like a prick, but so was my old man. Just in a different way."

"Tell me," she asked, moving her bar stool closer to his and leaning in toward him.

"My brothers had it worse than me. I didn't really know what was going on a lot of the time, until the day my grandfather announced that he and Grandma were going to be our legal guardians. He offered my dad money to walk out of our lives and not come back, and my dad took it without a backward glance."

"And you're okay with the fact your grandfather paid him off like that?"

Ryder ran a hand through his hair and waved to the bartender for another cocktail. "He did it because he was the only one who gave a damn about us. Our dad had a choice and the second he was offered the cash he ran and never looked back. My mom had a massive blood clot that went to her heart, about an hour after she gave birth to me, and by the time I was five I didn't have either of my parents. My grandparents took over the role of mom and dad, and they did a damn fine job of it. And when Grandma died when we were teenagers, Granddad stepped up again."

"So I'm taking it he's not your paternal grandfather."

At least opening up to Chloe had gotten her to move closer. After he'd complimented her backside earlier she'd sure as hell made him work for it. Truth was he never talked about this kind of shit with anyone, had never wanted to, until now.

"His parents were long dead, but we were close to my other grandparents because Mom saw them every day. They were pretty tight." He shrugged. "I know from what everyone says that my mom was great, but I just don't get why she married a douchebag like my dad, not when she was so beautiful and had everything she needed. But then maybe that's why she went for the complete opposite of what she'd grown up with, a bad boy from the other side of town."

Chloe raised her glass to his when his second cocktail arrived. "You were right. Your dad is every bit as crappy as mine."

"Add to that a temper that could have heated Texas, and a half-bottle-of-bourbon habit each night, and that's my childhood for you. I was just lucky I had two older brothers to keep an eye out for me, before Granddad took over.

Chloe sighed. "I know you wanted to prove yourself, but why did you really leave home? Was it more than just wanting to show you could go it alone?

"I took off when I was eighteen, became a pro bull rider. They all hated the idea of me riding for a living, but I loved it and it gave me a buzz every time I got up there. And I knew I could make it. Call me stupid, but when I'm told no, it only makes me want something all the more."

Chloe grinned. "It just so happens that I've noticed that particular trait of yours."

"When Granddad became sick I came home. It was about time I showed him I gave a damn instead of causing him more gray hairs, and I'd proven all I needed to prove." He paused, taking a sip of the new daiquiri that had been placed in front of him and deciding he liked it. "So tell me when you started hustling?"

"You make it sound so dirty." Chloe was smiling again and part of Ryder wanted to do anything to make sure her smile stayed fixed there.

She tossed her long blond hair over her shoulder, missing one loose curl that he reached forward to push back for her. His head was full of images of how her hair would look tumbling down her back when she was sitting astride him, but he'd asked her a serious question and he wanted to hear her response.

"I'm pretty sure you made quite an impression on some of the men you played." Ryder could hear the huskiness of his own voice, no longer caring what they were talking about. He had an itch that needed scratching, and he wasn't going to be satisfied until he'd well and truly gotten it out of his system.

"When I was younger I just had to watch and learn, then I was a good distraction for my dad to use." She pushed her shoulders up into a shrug. "He was great at bluffing, so even when he didn't have a decent hand he'd usually clean up. But not always."

Ryder reached for her hair again, twirling a strand around one of his fingers and shuffling his stool a little closer so her legs were arrowed between his open thighs.

"And how about you?" he asked. "Are you lucky or are you good at bluffing?"

Her thick dark lashes hid her eyes so just a glimpse of her chocolate irises were visible when she glanced up, her hair falling forward again. "Why do I get the feeling that we're not talking about poker anymore?"

He grunted. "Because we're not." He'd tried to just talk, but all he could think about was having his hands on Chloe.

Ryder's gaze fell to her mouth, watched as her tongue darted out, her top teeth pressing into her full lower lip. Then her eyes met his and she leaned into him, her breath warm against his mouth as she hesitated then tasted his lips, her mouth hovering, still, before moving again and starting to find a rhythm. Ryder shoved forward so their thighs were jammed together, running one hand down her shoulder, catching in her hair.

He couldn't stifle a groan when her tongue clashed with his, her mouth open wide as she kissed him over and over again.

"I think we need to go back upstairs," he mumbled against her mouth when she gave him a second to breathe.

"No," she murmured straight back. "You're not going anywhere."

He groaned again and took hold of her shoulders, pushing her back just enough to let him breathe. "Seriously, we need to go."

"Why?" she asked, her mouth twisted to the side in a smile so foxy he wanted to wipe it straight off her with his own mouth. "You don't want anyone to see you making out with me?"

Ryder chuckled and stood up, scooping his hands under her butt and removing her from the stool. Her body was hard up against his and he put his arm around her shoulders and spun her around so they were facing. He dropped a kiss into her hair.

"I don't give a damn who sees us, but if anyone gets a look at me they're gonna think I've got a loaded goddamn pistol in my pocket."

Chloe glanced down, then burst out laughing, covering her body with his and tucking her face into his chest.

"Settle down, cowboy. You have been with a woman before, haven't you? Or is that why you're so excited?"

"You might get away with talking smack down here, but once we're up there?" He tugged her closer, his arm locked around her neck in a playful hold. "You're at my mercy then."

Her laugh was wicked. "Or maybe you'll be at mine."

As much as he wanted to throw her over his shoulder and take her upstairs, he didn't. Instead he paused, forced himself to stop, and looked her straight in the eyes.

"I'm not going to hurt you, Chloe. Not all men are assholes."

She smiled at him, gaze trained on his. "I know."

"What makes you so certain I'm not?" he asked as he stroked her face, torn between wanting to be gentle with her on the one hand, and rough as hell with her on the other.

"Same reason you trusted me to win back your ranch."

He smiled. "I doubt that very much. I just wanted an excuse to see you again."

"Liar." Her words were soft, but the heat in her gaze hadn't died.

"All I'm saying is that you don't need to doubt me. I might be a douchebag sometimes, but I'm an honest one." He laughed. "And I really do believe you'll win it. The thing is, me trusting you is a no-brainer. Things can't get any worse for me."

"You'll get your money back, Ryder," she said. "When I give my word, it's binding."

"You're gonna make a damn fine lawyer one day, you know that?"

"Lawyering isn't what I'm interested in right now."

"Oh yeah?"

Chloe licked her lips and made him laugh, but it also made him hard again. The faster he got her back upstairs, the better. He adjusted the front of his jeans and grabbed her hand, pausing only to speak to the concierge as he dragged Chloe toward the elevator.

"Send a bottle of champagne up to our suite," he instructed, before bending down closer to Chloe, his lips over her ear. "You want me to order steaks and fries now?"

She looked confused. "Why?"

"Because after the night I have planned for us, you might get hungry."

Her cheeks turned red but she never looked away. "The champagne will be just fine. For now."

Ryder nodded at the concierge and led Chloe to the elevator. She spun around and faced him while they were waiting, arms slung low around his waist, leaning up to nip his lower lip.

"Maybe we should roll the dice a few times before we go up."

He growled at her, the noise in his throat nothing short of guttural.

"You're a bad influence, Ryder King."

He nipped her lip straight back and made her squeal.

"Don't I know it."

Chapter 8

Ryder's body was like a rock, every inch of him muscled and hard. She surrendered as he pushed her against
the wall outside their room, somehow simultaneously
inserting the key card and kicking open the door. He
dragged her in, mouth hot and wet to hers as he held her
arms above her head and pinned her wrists with one of
his big hands.

"And here I was thinking we were just going to be
friends," he said, lips moving against hers, his voice low.
"Wrong on all counts."

Chloe fought to release her hands but she may as well
have been locked in place with chains. She turned her
head, refusing his kiss. "You don't strike me as the kind
of guy to have friends that are girls."

He took his hand off her waist and cupped her chin,
forcing her to face him again. It was impossible not to
be lost in the web of his gaze, his piercing blue eyes seductive as sin.

"Why do you say that?" he asked, kissing her again,

lips plucking at hers over and over, so soft and then so hard. His tongue tangled with hers, fusing their mouths together and making her moan.

"Because you couldn't be friends with a woman without having sex with her."

His laugh was a throaty rumble. "No, darlin', I just couldn't be friends with you without wanting to have sex."

Ryder let go of her wrists, giving her a three-second reprieve before scooping his hands under her butt. He walked farther into the room, hesitating then moving again. She had her arms locked around his neck, legs wrapped around his waist. There was nothing soft about him, the planes of his shoulders and the ripple of muscle down his back beneath her fingers making her want to dig her nails in. To slice into his skin and make him bleed.

Only she didn't get the chance. Ryder threw her on the bed, looking down at her, his body blocking the light from the window, towering over her as she lay beneath him. Desire thrummed through her, knotting in her belly and rippling across her skin. Ryder's blue eyes were intense, his lazy smile telling her he was about to do something wicked to her. Something that would make her toes curl. He was so damn self-assured he didn't even have to ask if she wanted him back. But he'd told her she could trust him, and she did—if she didn't she wouldn't be lying on his bed right now.

"So, *darling girlfriend*, you like it gentle or rough?" Ryder kicked off his boots and unbuttoned his shirt, dropping it behind him. His abs were perfectly defined, skin taut and tanned, and the arrow of hair that disappeared south into his low-slung jeans . . . it made her want to explore every inch of his delicious body.

Chloe licked her lips, her mouth suddenly dry. She pushed up onto her elbows, unable to drag her eyes away from him. He winked as he peeled off his socks then undid the top button of his jeans, her breath catching as he hesitated on the zipper, then stopped.

She was actually about to do this. She was going to have sex with the man she'd sworn she wouldn't touch, yet from the moment they'd been alone together, there had been no way in hell she'd ever be able to honor the promise she'd made herself. Shelly had been right. He *was* completely irresistible.

"So? You haven't given me an answer," he said, his drawl alone making her wet between the legs. "Or are you having second thoughts?"

Ryder dropped to his knees and put one hand to her shoulder, pushing her back. Her heart started to race, her breath coming in short bursts as he straddled her, his solid thighs locking her in place.

"Chloe?"

He raised an eyebrow, eyes locked on hers, not giving her a second to glance away.

"You'll have to wait and see," she told him, groaning in pleasure as he slipped a hand down the front of her low-cut dress and touched her breasts.

"Let's get rid of these clothes, shall we?"

His question was barely audible, almost impossible to hear with her head tipped back, arching up into him as he removed his hands and pushed her dress up instead and dropped his mouth to her skin. It was hot and wet, the most seductive of touches, and she held her arms above her head to let him remove her dress completely. Ryder was relentless, mouth moving fast, sucking the soft skin of her breast, just above the lace of her bra.

Chloe wiggled, trying to free herself so she could wrap her legs around his waist, but Ryder wasn't budging an inch. He did raise his head though, cupping her face in his hands and tenderly kissing her, sucking on her lower lip before dipping his tongue into her mouth.

"You," he murmured into her ear when he finally pulled away, letting her catch her breath, "are so beautiful."

"Said the lion to the lamb," she whispered into his ear.

Ryder pushed up onto his elbows, his body heavy against hers even though he was supporting most of his own weight. "I've wanted you from the moment you caught my eye at the rodeo," he told her, dropping a slow, sweet kiss to her mouth. "And now I want you naked," he said, pushing himself back up, a determined glint in his eye that sent a fresh wave of desire through her body.

She shook her head when he went to slide her panties off, and he just laughed, kicking his own jeans off instead, one side of his mouth tilting up into a grin, when he caught her eye.

"Too fast?" he asked.

"No," she choked out, her own gaze dropping to his boxers, his erection impossible not to notice. "I just wanted us to be even."

"Good," he said, stripping off the last of his clothing so he was stark naked before her. "Because now it's time to go slow."

She gasped as he pushed her back down, cupping her

breasts, one finger flicking beneath the lace to slide past her nipple. But he was focused on moving down her body, his hands firm on her waist as he dipped his head, making a trail with his tongue from her belly button to the top of her panties, stopping there and licking back and forth. Chloe moaned loudly, not resisting when he slipped his hands beneath her butt to raise it, pulling her panties down. He yanked them down to her ankles and she used her toes to discard them completely, wantonly raising her pelvis when his mouth dipped back down again, her breathing erratic as she waited to feel his warm lips, his wet tongue, against her sex.

Ryder delved deep inside of her with his tongue, licking then sucking, gentle at first, slowly warming her up and then becoming more insistent. One hand cupped her breast, his fingers over her nipple, and she arched her back so she could press herself harder onto his mouth. "Don't stop," she panted.

He tweaked her nipple between his forefinger and thumb, making her moan even harder, but his mouth never stopped. Her body went rigid, the intensity of his mouth so wet against her sending waves of pleasure through every inch of her. Just when she thought she couldn't bear it anymore, she started to ride the steadily building wave of climax, her body humming as she clenched her fingers in Ryder's hair, locking him in place in case he dared try to move.

"Ryder," she whispered, rocking into him one last time as spasms of pleasure sent her slack against the bed, her legs locked around his head as she turned to liquid, riding out the final waves of ecstasy.

Chloe kept her eyes shut, let her arms fall loose by her

sides, but she wasn't allowed even a moment of rest. Ryder had hauled his body up, no longer at the end of the bed. He nudged her thighs back apart, moving in between them, both of his hands seeking out her breasts and caressing them, thumbs insistent on her nipples. She was so sensitive to his touch, her entire body on high alert.

"That was just to get you warmed up," Ryder said, his voice so deep it was almost menacing as he placed his hands on either side of her head. There was a fire in his eyes burning so hot she was scared of being scalded.

Chloe reached for him, arms around his back as she drew him closer, opened her mouth to kiss him, inviting him in with her tongue. Her body still felt like liquid, but there was no part of her that didn't want Ryder inside of her.

"Let me," she said, pushing him back a little, wanting to return the favor.

"No," he ordered. "On your back, now."

She obliged, voluntarily putting her hands above her head after she slipped her bra off. His grin was wicked as he lowered himself, nudging her thigh aside and rubbing his length against her. He was rock hard and she reached for him, sliding her hand up and down, loving the groan she received in response.

"Stop," he growled.

She didn't until he grabbed her wrist and forced her to. "We need protection and if you keep going like that I won't get a chance."

Chloe raised her eyebrows. Lucky one of them was thinking sensibly.

He jumped off the bed and unzipped his bag, and was nestled back between her legs in no time. He tore the edge of the packet and pulled the condom out, but she took it from him, rolling it on and admiring his body at the same time. She'd never been with a guy so . . . She smiled. *Built.* He was muscled all over, abs rock hard and the other part of him that she cared about was even harder.

Chloe looked up at him, laughing when he pushed her back, his elbows falling close to her ears when he dropped down, her body now completely hidden by his. She gasped when he slowly, gently pushed inside of her, their eyes locked, neither looking away. Chloe couldn't help the moan that escaped her lips, and Ryder responded by moving his mouth over hers at the same time that he rocked deeper.

She wrapped her arms around him, nails digging into his shoulders, making sure he couldn't get away. Chloe called out his name, locked her legs around his butt, matching his every move. But he escaped faster than she could stop him, flipping them both so she ended up straddling him.

"I was liking that," she muttered, hands flat to his chest, gasping when he pushed up hard.

"Just liking it?" he asked, one eyebrow raised.

Sweat gleamed across his forehead, his dark hair was pushed back off his face, and his eyes drew her in like magnets. "Okay, so I was *loving* it," she corrected.

"Then you'll love this," he said, running his hands down her chest, cupping her breasts as she tipped forward and adjusted her position.

His hands ran lower and settled on her hips, following her movements as she started to grind against him, back and forth, over and over. She was rocking hard, her head tipped back.

Ryder released one of her hips and yanked at her hair, tipping her farther back at the same time as he partially sat up. His mouth found one of her nipples, sucking hard, making her moan even louder.

"Stop," she murmured.

"No."

"Yes." She hit back, forcing him back down.

"Or what?" he challenged, hand still fisted in her hair.

She laughed, liking being in charge, even if he could flip her and pin her down if he wanted to. *"Or this."*

Chloe pressed one hand to his chest, the other reaching back to touch him, stroking him as she rode faster and faster. He groaned, trying to slow her, but she wasn't going to slow, not now.

"Chloe," he grunted. "Unless you want . . ."

She closed her eyes, the same wave of pleasure she'd experienced earlier building with such intensity she couldn't have stopped even if she'd wanted to. As her body shuddered Ryder went still, his hands clamped down over her hips. He'd been about to force her to slow and instead he'd climaxed with her.

"You," he whispered in her ear when she collapsed on top of him, "are wicked."

"Says the guy who just did something beyond wicked to me?" she countered, gently biting his lower lip.

Ryder turned them both sideways so they could face each other, his arms around her. "You know, I didn't expect this weekend to be so much fun so soon."

"You mean you didn't expect me to be an easy lay?"

she asked, smiling as a look passed over his face that told her he was worried he'd said the wrong thing.

"I just thought you'd insist on this being platonic," he told her, stroking her hair, gentle now where before he'd been rough. "I've wanted you in my bed from the first time I saw you, I just wasn't convinced the feeling was mutual. Thought I'd have to work harder."

Chloe tipped forward, kissing him again, not able to get enough of his plump lips. "If we're going to do this, we might as well have fun. And don't go calling me easy."

"I couldn't agree more," he murmured, tracing his fingers down her arm, then her stomach, dipping down then back to her thigh and settling on her butt. "About the fun part, not the easy part."

"No strings attached," she said, gasping as he moved his fingers again, this time stroking her inner thigh. "Okay?"

"Except for that little rule that while I'm with you I'm not allowed near other women." His tone was teasing, his low drawl alone enough to make her toes curl when he spoke to her.

"Is that going to be a problem?" she asked, pushing him off his elbow so he was lying flat on his back and leaning over him so she could brush her mouth across his.

"With you by my side?" He chuckled. "Honey, I won't be taking my eyes off you."

Chapter 9

"This," Chloe said, stretching her legs out over Ryder and wiggling her toes, "is bliss."

Ryder was alternating between stroking her arm and her thigh—her body was tangled over his as they lay naked on top of the bed. His touch was light, soft enough to almost lull her to sleep.

"That's what all the girls say after a night with me."

She threw a pillow at Ryder's head and received a grin in response.

"I was talking about the view, *actually*," Chloe said with a laugh.

"Sure you were."

Chloe was about to locate another pillow when a knock echoed out.

"And that will be room service," Ryder said, leaning over to kiss her before sliding off the bed.

Chloe pulled the sheet up from where it was bunched down the bed and covered up. She admired the other view as Ryder stretched, then reached for his boxers, his butt firm, shoulders muscular and strong. He wasn't hard to watch, and she could still feel every groove and indent of his beautiful body if she shut her eyes. She wanted to explore him all over again just so she never forgot. She'd been ready to ditch the good-girl persona, just once, and if he was going to be her one indiscretion, then it wasn't exactly a bad one.

Ryder yanked on his jeans and answered the door bare chested—she couldn't see him now because he was in the living room, but she heard him ask for everything to be placed on the table before he tipped the waiter and said good night. When Ryder reappeared he had two silver trays in hand, and a grin on his face that she couldn't help but return. They'd already consumed the first bottle of champagne he'd had delivered.

"Shall we eat in bed?"

She laughed when he waggled his eyebrows at her. "Naked?"

"You know I already like the taste of you, but if you want me to eat you again . . . ?"

Chloe shook her head. "You're not distracting me this time," she told him. "That food smells amazing and I'm starving."

Ryder came closer and carefully set the trays down on the bed. He took the lids off and discarded them, revealing two big juicy steaks and fries.

"We could have ordered something more gourmet, but . . ."

"This is perfect," she interrupted. "And I'm so hungry I could eat a horse."

Ryder left her with the trays and disappeared, returning with two glasses and the second bottle of champagne. She didn't wait for him, propping herself up with the sheet tucked up to her breasts, popping a few fries into her mouth to satisfy her growling stomach.

"Hey," Ryder protested, walking around to her side of the bed and placing a fresh glass on the side table, then pushing down the sheet. It fell to her waist, her breasts bare.

Chloe considered throwing a fry at him but decided not to. "Haven't you seen enough of them for one evening?"

He laughed, bending forward to plant a kiss on her lips. "Never."

She was too hungry to care that he'd so brazenly taken charge, about the fact that he was still wearing jeans when she was as good as sitting naked beside him.

"I was a vegetarian for years," she told him, guiltily cutting into her steak and taking her first mouthful.

"What changed your mind?"

She sighed. "I hate myself for eating meat but"— Chloe shook her head—"it just tastes so damn good."

Ryder considered her, putting down his knife and fork and plucking a few fries instead. "You love animals?"

She nodded. "Yes."

"So what do you think of me riding rodeo?"

"Honestly?" she asked.

Ryder started slicing into his steak and she watched him awhile before answering. She knew she had double standards, that she couldn't judge him for doing something that she'd so blatantly enjoyed watching the other day, but she wanted to be honest.

"I always hated the idea of rodeos, but being there on Friday . . ." She didn't know what to say.

"It was a thrill. That's what you want to say, isn't it?"

Chloe popped another fry in her mouth. "Yeah. It was exciting and loud and fun." She paused. "I loved it, but I hate the thought of those animals being used for our pleasure and forced to buck their hearts out for entertainment."

"I get it, I do," he said. "I've grown up on a ranch and I respect animals, but seriously? The Pro Bull Riders organization has more rules for bull welfare than they do for the riders. There's less than a one percent chance of the bulls being badly injured at any event, they're fed like royalty, and they're worth a small fortune, each and every one of them. I don't know about other countries, but we look after them on home soil, I can tell you that."

"Really?" She didn't doubt him, but she just hadn't realized that they'd actually be that well looked after. "That's not just a sales pitch."

"Really," Ryder said, setting down his fork and reaching for his champagne. "They're never ridden more than once a day, and they're rested on local ranches in between rodeos. Then, when they retire they're put to stud, so they don't have it half-bad if you ask me." He held up his fork. "Better then being fattened for meat I reckon."

"Is that the life you imagine for yourself when you retire? Put out to stud?"

His laugh was wicked. "That's exactly the life I can imagine."

"No playing dad to a brood of kids on the ranch? Pretty little wife walking barefoot alongside you?" She might not peg him for a settling-down type right now, but she bet he wasn't going to be a player all his life.

There was a sensitive side to him that she'd glimpsed earlier, something that told her he wasn't going to roam forever.

"One minute you don't want to get serious, the next we're talking about how many kids you want to have with me?"

She scowled at his joke, knowing he was just trying to avoid answering her.

"So what's our plan tomorrow then?" Chloe asked, slowly sipping her champagne, the bubbles tickling over her tongue before she swallowed. "Are you going to join me gambling all day?"

"Do I have a choice?"

She considered him, watching him eat. "No, actually. You can play with me a bit, then just be my eyes and ears. I've got more chance of running into someone I know at the smaller places than the big casinos, so I might need you as backup. And I want you to start watching for me, see if I miss any obvious tells."

"Are you worried about running into friends or enemies?" he asked.

Chloe grimaced. "*Acquaintances*. Ones that my father pissed off big-time on his last few trips through town."

"Does he owe them anything?"

"Who knows?" She set down her knife and fork, no longer so hungry as a chill ran the length of her spine. "I can't believe I never even thought about running into him. I doubt he'd be back here, but maybe he's back on his feet again. I don't know and I don't want to know."

"Your dad?" Ryder asked.

"Yeah. If I see him, well, let's just say things could get heated."

"How about we cross that bridge if we get to it," Ryder said, taking both their plates and putting them out of the way on the floor. "I have plenty of ideas about what we can do to fill in time before then."

"Oh yeah?" Chloe giggled as he pinned down her arms, grabbing hold of the sheet between his teeth and pulling it down to reveal even more of her naked body.

"Yeah," he growled. "Let's deal with reality tomorrow."

She could live with that. Ryder's mouth fell over hers, caressed her lips, then moved down her neck, his wet mouth making her moan, nails digging into the sheet beneath her as he took one of her nipples gently between his teeth, grating them across the sensitive tip then sucking, first soft then hard.

"Don't stop," she choked out as he moved to her other breast, his tongue moving across her skin then reaching her nipple and starting to suckle.

"Not until you beg me," Ryder murmured, making his way down her body. "I could keep doing this *all* night."

And she could take it all night. Chloe gasped as he let go of her hands and ran his fingers down her thighs, his mouth in hot pursuit. There wasn't a bone in her body that wanted him to stop, not one.

Ryder flicked through the paper, not really reading it. The words were a blur, because all he could think about was why he was here. Chloe was a great distraction, but the reality of the stakes he was playing for now?

Fuck. Every time the phone rang he expected it to be Nate ready to hunt him down and kill him, and he deserved it.

He stood and looked out at the view, the city buzzing even this early in the morning. Right now, knowing Chloe was naked in the bathroom wasn't enough to take his mind off what he'd done, and even if she did win the deeds back as easily as she thought she could, he needed to man up and confess to his brothers. He'd outright lied to Chase the day before. All the things he'd done in his life, the trouble he'd gotten into and the fun he'd had, he'd never lied to Nate or Chase. They'd stolen one another's girls, gotten into fights that'd left them with black eyes and worse, but they'd never lied. He loved his brothers and he'd do anything for them, no questions asked.

The more he thought about it, the more he wanted to just come clean over the phone now, while he wasn't in Texas. And while they didn't have a plane at their disposal so they could come and hunt him down.

"You ready to go?"

Ryder turned to find Chloe, standing with her hands in her pockets and looking sexy as hell, even though she'd made a big deal about dressing down.

"I thought you wanted to slip under the radar."

She looked confused as she glanced down. "What do you mean?"

It was even more amusing that she had no idea what he was talking about. "You might be wearing jeans and a tank, but there's nothing understated about how you look." She had her blond hair loose, tumbling halfway down her back, and that alone would make any man turn to take a second look. "I hope you're not wanting to go unnoticed."

Chloe laughed at him. "You do realize you've already had me in your bed, right? That means you can lay off the flattery."

Ryder crossed the room, stopping a few feet away and looking her up and down. "You're a goddamn knock-out, Chloe."

She didn't move when he ran a hand down her arm, catching her hand and linking their fingers, but she did lean in when he bent to kiss her.

"Ryder . . ."

"Don't argue, just take the compliment," he murmured against her mouth.

She didn't reply so he kissed her again, shoving his body up against hers and wrapping his arms around her waist. Even if he had her in his bed for a week he doubted he'd get enough of her—the closer she was to him the better, and preferably naked.

Chloe eventually pushed him back, hands on his face as she stared into his eyes. "We've had our fun," she muttered. "Now it's time to go play."

"We never did talk about where this was going," Ryder said, rubbing her lower back. "Was it just a one-night thing or can we keep having fun a while longer? Since we're going to be pretend dating and all."

She stood on tiptoe and pressed a kiss to his chin before escaping his hold and heading back to the bathroom. "I'm not done with you yet, Ryder. So yeah," she said, glancing over her shoulder and grinning at him. "We can keep having fun. Until this whole thing is over."

Ryder laughed as he watched her go, then he checked

his phone for the hundredth time. He hadn't missed any more calls from his brothers, and by the end of the day he wasn't going to sweat it out any longer. He owed it to himself to tell them, and after he'd watched Chloe play poker for the day, he needed to seriously consider confessing.

"Let's grab some breakfast on our way down, then we can head to the Orleans. Spend a few hours there then decide if we need to find another room to play in," Chloe called out from the bathroom.

Ryder shrugged on his leather jacket and grabbed his phone and wallet. It was time to see Chloe in action, and he couldn't wait. Being in bed with her was one thing, but seeing her take money from a bunch of guys completely unaware? Now that was something he was dying to see.

Chapter 10

Chloe dug her fingernails into her palms and kept walking. She knew better than anyone what these kinds of places were like, that a shimmer of fear was noticed faster than a drop of blood among swarming sharks, so she kept her shoulders squared. Ryder was at her side and she took his hand. They were supposed to be a couple and after the night they'd had it seemed only natural to touch him. Besides, he might be a devil, but she didn't mind so long as he was *her* devil.

"You ready to play?" he asked.

She smiled at Ryder as they walked. There was no need to tell him to put his game face on—the man was a walking advertisement for a self-assured gambler. No one here would ever guess he'd just lost big-time, and she doubted he'd ever actually had much experience being the loser.

"You bet I am," she muttered. "I've stayed away for so long but now that I'm here I'm itching to feel cards against my fingers." She hated herself for feeling so buzzed, but she couldn't help it.

Ryder laughed and touched a hand to her back, his palm firm. "After you."

They entered the room and she paused to scan the tables. It was just before midday and the place wasn't full, but it was busy enough for her to know she was able to play a few different tables if she wanted to. The whole point of coming here was to get some practice in, make sure she wasn't rusty after a couple of years away.

"Take your pick, darlin'."

She nodded and let go of his hand. "You go get the chips, I'll do a scout, figure out what I want to play."

Ryder grabbed her hand back and pressed a kiss to her cheek. "Thank you."

She turned and looked into his aqua-blue eyes, wishing they were still back in bed, snuggled under the covers instead of standing in a poker room. There was a part of her thrumming with excitement just thinking about betting again, but another part was equally terrified. This kind of lifestyle was addictive, she knew that better than anyone, and she didn't want to get sucked back into playing for a living. When the money was easy it was fun, but she was afraid of when it all turned sour, especially with the types of guys and places she'd used to play. It was an underworld she'd been pleased to be rid of, and she needed to keep reminding herself of exactly that.

"You don't have anything to thank me for yet," she said.

"When you first told me you could do this, I wasn't convinced. Now?" He chuckled as he backed up. "That look in your eyes right now tells me you're gonna kick some serious butt today."

She blew out a breath, listening to Ryder but with her attention focused on the room in front of her. "Here's hoping." It still amazed her that he *had* trusted her, but then again he didn't have much to lose in giving her a shot.

"Here's knowing," he said. "I'll be back soon."

Chloe didn't turn to watch him. Instead she walked slowly across the room, deciding to get a drink so she could choose which table to join first. She'd thought about doing a few lower-limit rounds, then changed her mind. They were only here a short time and the faster she won the ranch back the better. If she couldn't keep up with the big players now she never would—she'd either lost her touch or she hadn't.

"A club soda with lime," she ordered at the bar, smiling her thanks. She turned and took a sip for something to do, the tiny straw resting between her teeth. Ryder was walking back in no time and she waved so he could see her.

"You decide yet?"

She nodded. "Let's hit that table first. You keep an eye out on the others. I want to play the biggest and meanest guys around, okay? If they're winning big I want to play them."

Ryder nodded. "You have any idea how fucking hot you are talking all poker dirty at me?"

She laughed at him. "Wait till I've won a ton of money. Then you can be impressed."

"Good luck, baby," he said, running a hand down her arm and passing her the chips.

"Let's hope I don't need it."

She joined a table playing no-limit Hold 'Em and put her five grand in chips on the table. There were no other women playing and all the men glanced at her, a couple nodding in her direction. The dealer smiled and said hello as she settled herself back into the leather chair. Ryder was still leaning against the bar and looking around, and she was happy to be on her own for now.

As the cards were dealt the familiar old rush of adrenaline was like a shot to her veins, excitement pumping as she flicked the edge of her cards to see her hand. Chloe remembered what her dad had taught her, counted her timings, and kept her breathing calm and even as she surveyed the table. Every man here would have a tell, no matter how subtle, and she needed to pick them apart player by player. Here she was playing Hold 'Em, and when she played Parker she'd probably be playing straight, but it didn't matter what the game was. Her strength was bluffing, and that rusty feeling she'd worried about was long gone now that she was seated, players to her left and right, cards brushing her fingertips.

Chloe had an average two cards but she wasn't going to show it and she sure as hell wasn't going to glance at her cards again, her hand committed to memory. She called when it was her turn, putting up more money, watching as one of the guys folded. The others were all hanging in there.

Eventually the dealer put two cards faceup on the table and Chloe kept her face straight, still counting her breaths, refusing to give anything away. Her focus was always on the other players, and she could tell one of the men was screwed, one of his eyes flickering constantly to his cards. Technically she wasn't in the best position yet either, but there was no way in hell anyone else was going to know that.

Chloe sank deeper into her seat, practicing a self-assured smile, just a hint of a grin to make her look confident. When it was her turn she chuckled and raised the bet, one hand resting over her two cards but still never looking at them, never even toying with the edge of them.

By the time they were in the final round of betting with five community cards faceup on the table, Chloe had them all sussed out. There were only three of them left in the game and she'd half expected to be the last one standing. Her hand was good enough, she had a solid chance of winning, but she was starting to realize that she needed to lay it on more if she wanted to get the men playing here to bail out of the game completely before the final round. She was finding her groove, and it had only taken her one game to do it.

Her blood pumped hard as the player to her left revealed his cards first. Chloe clenched her toes, her only regular tell, which no one could ever see. If that was the best hand at the table right now, then she had it. But it wasn't all skill this time, luck had played a solid part, too.

Chloe nodded to the other two players when she won, not wanting to make a big deal out of it. She liked to be understated, to not draw any more attention to herself than she had to, and she was back playing the table again within minutes.

She fought a smile as she received a few looks from

the other men, hearing a grumble from across the table. The fact that she was a woman winning made her stand out enough, which meant she had to make even more of an effort to stay completely under the radar. She clenched her toes again and gave herself a mental high five. She was back on the horse and it felt damn good.

Ryder sipped his beer. It was the only one he'd had in the entire time he'd been watching Chloe—there was only so long he could be content drinking club sodas. He'd kept his distance but he'd never taken his eyes off of her table, except to scan the room like she'd asked. And now she was heading in his direction, a smug smile on her face.

"How you doin', baby?" he asked, opening his arms and drawing her in.

Her laugh was for his ears only as she slipped her hands around his waist and leaned in for a kiss.

"We're loaded," she murmured. "And I think I've got the bug back."

Ryder stroked her hair and kissed her back. "You're fucking awesome. Playing those guys like that is amazing."

"It was hit and miss with the first game but after that I got my rhythm."

"So you wanna split or play another table?" he asked. Ryder had liked watching her but he was starting to get bored—he either wanted to play himself or take her back to their suite. Not that he wasn't grateful to have Chloe on his side, but still.

"Any tables you think I should hit?" she asked, waving the bartender over and ordering a soda.

"The guys over there," he said, pointing, "have been betting big. The fat guy to the dealer's left is cleaning up. You might want to join for a game or two, and I can go find some old ladies to play somewhere else so I at least have half a chance of winning."

"Play at the next table over. You'll have fun." She downed her drink, touching the corners of her mouth with the back of one finger. "I'm going to the restroom for a second, then when I come back I'll wait for an opening."

Ryder tugged his chair closer to hers and nudged her knees apart so their thighs were pressed tight. "You sure you don't want to go back to bed?"

Chloe laughed but there was heat in her gaze. She was high on winning and he was high on watching her. "Don't forget what I'm practicing for, Ryder."

He sighed, leaning forward to touch foreheads with her, staring into her eyes. "*Never.* You're just so fucking hot right now."

She giggled and jumped down from her chair. "And I'll be even hotter tonight when we're rolling in hundred dollar bills on our bed."

"Don't get too cocky, darlin'."

Chloe pressed a wet, slow kiss to his lips, not talking until she pulled back, her lips still almost brushing his. "I won't."

"If it isn't Chloe *goddamn* Rivers."

Ryder felt Chloe freeze, her fingers digging into his thigh where before they'd been resting softly. Her eyes met his, panic obvious as she stared at him and didn't look away.

Ryder took charge, slipping a hand around her waist and glancing over his shoulder. "Can I help you?" No one was going to intimidate Chloe, not if he had anything to do with it.

He locked eyes with an older man, his greasy hair pulled back into a low ponytail. Ryder stayed seated, not wanting to make a big deal out of someone recognizing her until he had to. It wasn't his style to make a scene.

"I was talking to the lady."

Ryder changed his mind real quick, springing to his feet. "And I was talking to you."

Chloe turned then, leaning back against the bar but staying tight to him. "Long time no see," she said, the terror gone from her gaze and replaced with a steely determination that he recognized from her time at the tables. She sure knew how to put her game face on.

"I could say the same about you, sweetheart."

Ryder bristled but he bunched a fist and kept it at his side. If Chloe could put on a poker face, then so could he. At least until he needed to act.

"You here to pay off some of your daddy's debts?"

She laughed, but it was a fake kind of trill that Ryder hadn't heard before. He instinctively moved even closer to her, staring daggers at the stranger.

"I'm not responsible for my old man's debts now, and I wasn't back then either."

The guy laughed, folding his arms across his chest. He leaned forward and Ryder stood up straighter.

"Not how I remember it, sweetheart," he said. "How about we have a drink and talk about what he owes me, shall we? I'm sure I could find a few more of the old crew who'd like to know you're here, too. There's been a lot of guys keeping an eye out for him."

When he came closer again Ryder moved to stand in front of Chloe. "Back the fuck up," he seethed, blood pumping like liquid fire through his body. "You heard what she said, now you can fuck off."

"Settle down, boyfriend. Chloe knows how things work here."

Ryder laughed, a deep kind of laugh that sounded more like a roar. "No, I know how things work, asshole. Get out of my face and don't come looking for Chloe again. You hear me?"

Chloe moved to stand in front of Ryder, keeping a hand on him. "You heard him, Jim. I don't want to see you or anyone else my dad owes money to. He's dead to me, okay? I haven't seen him in a long time."

Jim sniggered and held up his hands. "Oh, I'll come looking for you, sweetheart. You bailed him out last time and you'll do it again if you know what's good for you. *And for him.*"

Ryder lunged forward, ready to deck the guy to hell with the consequences, but Chloe's hand closed over his.

"Don't," she whispered. "You're better than him."

He clenched her hand and ground his teeth. "No one threatens you and gets away with it," he muttered. "No one."

She shook her head. "Can we just go, Ryder?"

"What about playing the other table?" he asked. "Don't let that idiot scare you, Chloe. He's not going to touch you, no one is. Not while I'm here."

She tucked her body up against his, holding on to him tight. "I just want to go, okay? That was enough of a blast from the past for me. We can go somewhere else tomorrow or later tonight."

Ryder downed the rest of his beer and held her close. "I'll walk you to the restroom, then cash in our chips," he said. "Then I'm taking you out for an early dinner."

The flicker of excitement came back into her eyes, a light there that had so quickly been extinguished only a moment earlier. "That'd be great. I want to forget all about what just happened." She sighed. "But thank you. I'm not used to having someone in my corner like that."

He squeezed her hand, fingers interlinked. "You don't have to thank me. I like you Chloe, a lot, and I look after people I like. Even after all this is over I'll still be in your corner if you ever need me."

The look on her face surprised him, because she looked genuinely dumbfounded. "My instincts are screaming at me right now not to let you come riding in like a knight in shining armor even though I know it's stupid."

He cleared his throat, giving her fingers another squeeze. He didn't know what to say. He did like Chloe a lot, more than just wanting to get her into bed, and it pissed him off to know that she'd never had anyone look after her before.

Ryder waited until she'd disappeared into the restroom and then headed for the cashier. He changed the chips and turned around to find the same guy lined up behind him.

"I thought I told you to fuck off," Ryder snarled.

"Chloe knows how things work when it comes to her

old man," the guy said. "Her dad's debts are her debts. She knew it back then and she knows it now."

Ryder shook his head, glancing over to see Chloe waiting for him outside the restrooms. He turned his attention back to the man standing in front of him.

"It was Jim, right?" he asked.

Jim nodded. "Yeah. You ready to tell her what her old man owes?"

"No," Ryder said, stepping up into the guy's face and fighting the urge to growl at him. "I'm just making sure I have my facts straight. Because if anyone so much as comes near Chloe while we're here and tries to settle your bogus debt, I want to make sure I know who to blame for it. You'll regret it for the rest of your life if you even think about her again. You got me? No one fucks with a King, and that means no one fucks with *me*."

Jim stared at him, clearly not intimidated by threats.

"You so much as mention her old man again and I'll personally make sure you can't make the same mistake twice," Ryder threatened. "I don't want to see your face again, *Jim*, and I don't make idle threats when it comes to my girl."

He didn't wait for Jim to respond, just marched over to Chloe and held her tight to his body as they made for the exit.

"We're out of here," he told her.

"What did he say?" Chloe asked, hurrying to keep up with his longer stride.

Ryder slowed, not meaning to rush her. "Nothing. And he won't be bothering you again so don't waste any time worrying about him."

She nodded and tugged his hand, forcing him to stop when she moved her body slightly in front of his. "Ryder."

He looked down at her, possessiveness rippling through him as he considered her big brown eyes and beautiful face.

"It feels nice to be protected."

Ryder shrugged. "Like I said, it's no big deal."

"Yeah, maybe not for you," she said, grazing her lips across his, "but it does mean a lot to me. Makes me realize you're not just some rich kid asshole."

Ryder could see tears shining in her eyes, knew the whole run-in had shaken her up even though she was trying to joke with him now. "No one will ever get away with threatening you when I'm around, Chloe, and that's a promise I can keep. He so much as looks at you again there will be hell to pay."

She rested her head against his shoulder as they walked, less self-assured gambler and more damsel in distress now, and he knew there was nothing he wouldn't do to keep her safe after seeing that scared deer-in-the-headlights look on her face before. Something about her pulled at heartstrings he didn't even know he had.

"Come on. It's time I taught you how to ride a bull."

Chapter 11

Chloe was starting to get used to Ryder's arm slung low around her hips and being hard up against his body. There was something comforting about having a man as commanding as Ryder by her side—he was big enough to be intimidating to other men and the look in his eyes when he made a threat made it obvious that he'd follow through. She'd had to be tough all her life to get out of certain situations, and it was nice to know that someone actually had her back for once. Although she wasn't sure if it was just because she was the one capable of winning his ranch back for him, or if he really gave a damn. Or maybe that was just the way he was with women, going into alpha protective mode at the drop of a hat. But the way he'd looked at her before . . . She stamped the thought away. She knew better than to get carried away with some fantasy idea of what they had turning into something more.

They stopped outside a bar that had music thumping

loud. Ryder unhooked his arm and took her hand, pausing before they entered.

"You know, this place seemed like a good idea in my head, but now that we're here I'm not so sure."

A woman in teeny-tiny cutoff shorts and a ripped low T-shirt burst out the door and stumbled past them and Chloe watched as Ryder cringed.

"It'll be fine," she said. "So long as we can drink I'll be happy."

Ryder pushed open the door. "When I said this was my favorite dive hangout, I didn't really think it through. I usually come here with my brothers, and we're kind of drunk before we get here half the time."

"So in other words it's not the right place to bring a girlfriend?" she asked with a chuckle. "I don't care, Ryder. Seriously, I'm not going to be offended by a heap of scantily clad girls and cheap drinks."

He grinned and slung his arms across her shoulders, tugging her head closer when he closed his arms into a V and kissed her cheek. "That's my girl." Ryder laughed. "Welcome to Rockhouse Las Vegas."

Chloe tried not to bristle, but it was hard. Having fun with Ryder was one thing, but she didn't want him to get the wrong idea about what was happening between them. She liked him more than she wanted to admit, but she wasn't going to let herself think about this being anything more than fun. Falling for Ryder would end in her heart being splintered into pieces, and the last thing she needed was to be dependent on anyone in this life other than herself. Seeing her dad's old deadbeat gambling buddy had made that crystal clear.

"For all you know I used to come here all the time," Chloe said as she leaned into Ryder on their way to the bar.

He glanced at her, eyebrows raised. "Seriously?"

She laughed. "Not a chance. But hey, you didn't tell me it was Taco Tuesday! This place is looking better by the second."

"Hey, it's the strip's ultra dive bar, what did you expect?"

"So, tacos?" she asked, wiggling out of his grasp and leaning forward on the bar, waving a bartender over to take their orders.

"Damn right I want tacos," Ryder said, pulling out his wallet.

Chloe put her hand over his and shook her head. "This one's on me. After the way you handled Jim back there I owe you."

"It was nothing." Ryder's jaw was set hard again, his eyes stormy when she brought up what had happened. "I told you I'd look after you while we were here and I meant it."

"Still," she said, opening her purse and shaking her head, "it meant a lot to me and I want to at least get the tacos. And the shots."

"Shots?" he asked, one eyebrow raised again, his dimple reminding her of the fun they'd had in the bedroom, the way he'd looked at her when it had been just the two of them. That's what she needed to focus on—it was about *fun* not *love*. She wasn't going to fall for him no matter how sweet he was, and he wasn't going to fall for her.

"Seriously, Ryder, you need to start reading the

blackboards. We'll do shots later, though. Now we're starting with margaritas." She ordered more food than they'd ever eat and two drinks, then perched on a stool and relaxed against the counter. "I guess I should feel lucky that it was an old foe we ran into and not my dad."

Ryder rubbed her back as she slumped forward, and when she didn't sit upright completely he started to massage her shoulders. "What you need is a good ride."

She tipped her head sideways and scowled at him, laughing when he held up his hands in surrender.

"I was talking about the mechanical bull," he said. "Over there."

"Ha-ha, very funny."

She watched as he nodded to the bartender then held up his glass, waiting for her to clink hers against it. "Wait until you've downed a couple of these and you've got a belly full of tacos. Then we can really have some fun over there."

Chloe took a long, slow sip of her margarita and straightened her shoulders. She'd had her slump and now she was going to forget all about who they'd run into. It was Vegas, it would have been impossible not to run into someone her father owed money to.

"You feeling good about how you played today?" Ryder asked.

"Sure," she said, twirling the stem of the cocktail glass between her fingers. "First game was a little rusty, and after that I found my feet pretty quick."

"So you're ready to take Parker for all he's worth?"

She took another sip, moving her glass when their food arrived. "Wow, that was quick." She giggled. "It looks amazing, although I may have gone a little crazy ordering." The tacos were piled high.

"For a buck fifty a pop I don't think we can go wrong."

Ryder picked one up and took a bite. "Man, shrimp and mayo. Life doesn't get any better than this."

Chloe chose a chicken, mayo, and avocado one, nodding her agreement as she polished it off like she'd never eaten before. "Pretty damn good," she managed as she swallowed her last mouthful.

Ryder was reaching forward for another when he caught her eye and leaned in to wipe the corner of her mouth. "You have a little mayo there," he told her.

Her tongue darted out, licking the spot he'd touched, but she ended up connecting with his finger as well as her skin. He seemed to forget all about his taco, replacing his finger with his mouth, kissing her instead. Chloe smiled against his lips, kissing him back.

"Yours tastes good," she said. "Maybe it's time for me to try one."

Ryder pulled back and pushed one in her direction. "Glad I could give you a complimentary pretasting."

They both laughed. "So tell me," Chloe said, toying with her second taco, glancing down at it but not taking a bite straightaway. "What's the deal with your family and Parker's anyway? You mentioned some long-standing feud."

He finished his mouthful and reached for a napkin, wiping his mouth and waving the bartender over for another drink. "I'm switching to beer. You?"

She shook her head, watching as he took a long pull of the Budweiser that was passed to him.

"Parker's family has always been crooks. I'm all for

capitalism, but they're like vultures, sniffing around one man's misfortune and trying to cash in. Let's just say that none of us appreciate the way they intimidate land-owners into selling out."

"And this has been going on for how long?" she asked, no longer hungry and sipping her drink instead.

"Decades," Ryder told her. "But the reason his family hates mine has to do with my dad."

She waited, watching as he took another sip of beer, worrying the label on the bottle with his thumb.

"The story has it that my old man had an affair with Parker's mom. My mother was still alive then, so it was before I was even born, but they reckon it was my dad who had something to do with her leaving town and never coming back."

"And what do you think?"

Ryder sniggered. "That if she was truly involved with my dad she did the best thing by getting the hell away from him."

Chloe nodded. She got that he was bitter about his father, but she also knew how bad that kind of hate could eat away at a person. "So the bad blood started then?"

"That was a big part of it, but my granddad had al-ready made us enemies with them. Whenever he caught wind of what they were doing, he'd get some sort of pro-tection in place for any man being intimidated, and see if he could work out a way to loan the man money to keep his head above water. Obviously it didn't happen all the time, and Parker's family still took a lot from other people, but when Granddad heard about it first, he al-ways stepped in."

She was surprised. "So your granddad's not just some hard-nosed businessman, then?"

Ryder grinned. "Oh no, he is. If they didn't pay their loans back then he'd have to foreclose on their ranches eventually, but he liked to give them a chance to work it off, to do what he could. He firmly believes in giving everyone a second chance."

"And that kind of thing is still going on?" Chloe asked.

"Not so much," Ryder told her. "Parker's old man is long gone, and Parker himself is more interested in roughing women up. There've been too many girlfriends of his with black eyes for me not to hate the bastard."

"So basically, he's just your average nice guy, huh?" Chloe said, shaking her head and downing the rest of her cocktail.

"Enough about douchebags like Parker," Ryder announced. "Finish that taco and we're getting you up on that bull."

Chloe held up her hands. "No way."

Ryder leaned over the bar. "Two tequila shots," he ordered.

"Heaven help me," she muttered, digging into her taco. If she was going to drink shots, she needed a full stomach to cushion the liquor.

"The night's still young, darlin'." Ryder slid his stool closer and collected both shots, holding hers out to her and giving her one of his goddamn sexy winks. "You can teach me poker again tomorrow. Tonight I'm gonna teach you how to ride rodeo."

A shiver ran down Chloe's spine as she threw back her shot and slammed the glass back down on the bar. Ryder was wicked, everything about him screamed trouble, but no matter how much she wanted to stay immune to his charm, she was like a bee to honey. Locked in his gaze, thighs rammed hard against hers, she wanted him bad and she had no intention of denying herself. Not yet.

"I'll be riding that thing like a pro in no time, just you wait and see."

"Oh my god, I'm going to be sick!"

Ryder tried not to laugh and failed epically. He doubled over, struggling to talk. He'd had a bit to drink, but that had little to do with why he was finding the situation so damn funny. Chloe looked like she'd seen a ghost, clinging on for her life, eyes wide.

"You're going to be fine," he choked out.

"Stop laughing at me and get me off this freaking thing!"

Ryder snorted and forced himself to stand up straight. The music was thumping around them and there was a decent crowd, but he didn't notice anything other than the beautiful blonde attempting to ride the mechanical bull in front of him.

"You're still going slow, just imagine you're on a real bull and hold one hand up. I know you can do it."

"If I fall off . . ." she cautioned.

He grimaced. Chloe's eyebrows shot up, eyes wide as she hung on tight.

"Ryder!"

"Come on baby, I know you can do it," he cheered, taking a swig of beer and guessing she couldn't hang on much longer.

Ryder increased the speed, sending the bull into a fast

spin and buck at the same time, which sent Chloe flying off, hitting the cushioned pads—fast.

"You okay, darlin'?" he asked, rushing over to her and trying hard not to crack up, hoping she didn't realize he'd cranked up the difficulty level on her.

The look she gave him was pure rage—she might be drunk but she sure as hell knew who to blame.

"You're dead," she fumed, standing up and tugging her top back into place, giving him an eyeful of her breasts. "If I have so much as one bruise . . ."

"Chloe." He took her hand and pulled her forward, putting a shot in her other hand. "It was just a little tumble."

"Little tumble my ass," she muttered, knocking back her shot and glaring at him.

Ryder clinked his glass to her empty one and followed her lead. "If it's your ass you're worried about then I'll happily inspect it for you." He chuckled. "Maybe we could head back for a butt massage right now?"

She gave him a stern look that quickly turned into a laugh. Ryder looked around at the bar, which was starting to get more crowded, music blaring since the DJ had started.

"Come on, let's get out of here."

Chloe didn't move, her grip on his arm tight. "I actually think I could be sick," she moaned. "That fucking bull has made me all dizzy."

Ryder raised his eyebrows. "Man, we are getting to know each other now. You just unleashed an f-bomb on me."

She clamped her hand over her mouth and laughed. "Did I just ruin my good-girl image?" she teased.

"No, you just made me think you were even fucking hotter, and I think I took your mind off hurling."

"You were right, let's get out of here. I've had enough shots to last me a lifetime."

Ryder hugged her to his body, slipping his hand into the back pocket of her jeans as they walked. Usually he became less interested in a woman after he slept with her—once the chase was over it was over. But Chloe? *Damn.* He doubted it would matter how many times he had her in his bed. He wanted her now even more than he'd wanted her before.

"Do you think we'll pass a street vendor selling hot dogs?" she asked, leaning sideways and looking up at him.

Ryder dropped a kiss into her hair and held her close as they headed out the door onto the street. "You must be drunk if you're wanting greasy food already."

"Or maybe I'm just happy."

He knew she was drunk, but the look on her face right now told him she was right about being happy, because so was he. He might have fucked up at home, but right here, right now, he was just damn pleased to be hanging out with a woman like Chloe. *Dangerously* happy to be with her.

"I'll make you a deal," he said. "If we don't pass one on our way back, I'll tip the concierge an insane amount of money to go find one for you."

"Deal," she said, grabbing his hand and shaking it, tugging him so they had to stop.

The tequila had sent a buzz through his body, too, and when she yanked him close enough to kiss, he had no hope of behaving any way other than badly. Ryder opened his palms against her waist, holding her firm, kissing her rough when she rubbed her body hard against his. She was digging her fingers into his shoulders one minute and worrying the top button of his shirt the next. Ryder groaned, grabbing hold of her hands and forcing her to stop.

"I think we need to get a room," he grumbled into her ear. "As much as I'm all for public displays of affection, I don't want to be arrested for public indecency."

Chloe tipped her head back and laughed, still clutching his shirt. If she hadn't hustled a table full of experienced poker players a few hours earlier, he'd have taken her for a naive young woman who'd had too much to drink in Vegas and needed to be looked after. Only he knew that she was more experienced in this city than half the men who visited regularly. Hell, maybe even more than him.

"Come on. It won't take long."

"You know, being with you is kind of like having a burly bodyguard on duty," she told him, her thumb hooked into his belt as they walked side by side, bodies fused together.

"Is that a compliment?" he asked, not sure what she was getting at.

"For the first time in my life I feel like someone's looking out for me," she told him, her voice low as she dropped her shoulder half against his chest. "No one's ever really given a damn about me before, so it's kinda nice."

Ryder's chest tightened, his hold on her even fiercer. "Where I come from, all women deserve to be looked after." His voice was raspy; he could hear how dark it sounded.

"If only I lived in your world."

Ryder steeled his jaw, hating that her words hit him with the force of a truck slamming into concrete. There was no part of him that wanted a real relationship—he had to get his own shit together—and there was no room in his life for anyone else, not even Chloe. He glanced at her, admiring how damn touchable and silky her blond hair was, her side profile all pouty lips and long lashes framing her dark eyes. And underneath those clothes? He fought not to stop her from walking and scoop her up, remembering what it was like to have those long legs wrapped tight around his waist. Ryder ground his teeth instead, staying in control.

If he'd ever met a woman who could tempt him into something more, it was Chloe, although maybe it was the combination of her being goddamn beautiful *and* capable of winning his ranch back that was making him want her so bad. Once it was all over, maybe the thrill of wanting her would disappear. He groaned when she leaned up and grazed a kiss across his jaw. Or maybe he was a fucking liar.

Chapter 12

The room was dark when they stepped in. Ryder flicked on a light in the living room and then made his way into the bedroom to do the same to the bedside ones. Chloe disappeared into the bathroom and he poured himself a glass of water, drinking it slowly as he stared out at the myriad of bright neon lights shining below. Vegas was sure lit up tonight, but instead of itching to be out partying, all he wanted was to be holed up in the hotel room with Chloe.

He checked his phone, flicking through a couple of missed calls. Tonight was supposed to be confession time, only he'd conveniently forgotten about his promise to himself and become entirely distracted with the woman who was still behind a closed door in the bathroom.

"Can I come in?" he called out.

"Just a sec," she called back. Her voice was no longer slurry and he finished his water and went to lean against the entrance to the bedroom.

When the door opened and Chloe appeared he was glad he'd already put down his glass. "Damn," he muttered, giving her a wolf whistle as she did a little twirl before crossing the room.

She was wearing tiny boy shorts that showed off a heap of ass and an even smaller tank tight over bare breasts.

"I didn't expect anyone to be seeing me," she muttered, stopping in front of him and rising on her tiptoes, nibbling his jaw and then the side of his mouth, slowly moving across to his lips, her teeth grazing the soft skin there before she placed her mouth fully across his. "Otherwise I'd have brought a big T-shirt for bed."

"Hell no," he grunted when she sliced her nails down his back, sharp even through his shirt. "I fucking love it. And I like it even more that this is what you usually wear. It's sexy as hell."

She dropped back down to her flat feet and grabbed the front of his shirt, walking backward and tugging him with her.

"Give me two seconds in the bathroom and I'll be right back," he told her, catching her chin to hold her in place and kissing her, wanting her tongue against his and to rip her clothes off so he could see her bare instead. "The getup is cute, but it'll be even cuter *off*."

Chloe just laughed and headed for the bed, falling down onto it, her golden hair like a waterfall of silk across the pillow. Ryder stopped to look at her again, shaking his head as he considered every inch of her body.

"Don't be long," she whispered, stretching out, toes pointed as she flexed her legs.

Ryder blew out a breath and went into the bathroom,

cleaning the tequila taste from his mouth and then relieving himself fast. He pushed open the door and burst back into the room, ready to strip Chloe and let her have a second chance at riding cowgirl for the night.

"Chlo—" Her name died on his lips. Ryder stared at the beautiful woman lying on the oversize hotel bed. She was on her side, still facing the bathroom, but instead of the wicked smile he'd been anticipating, her lips were slightly parted, eyes shut as she made the faintest snoring sound. *"Damn,"* he muttered under his breath, padding silently over to her and pulling up the sheets. Ryder ran his eyes slowly up her body as he covered her.

He unbuttoned his shirt and jeans, discarded them along with his underwear, and flicked off the lamps, sliding into bed beside Chloe. Ryder spooned his body against hers, burying his face into her hair and shutting his eyes. His sexy gambling and drinking buddy had crashed on him, but he didn't give a damn. Come morning he wouldn't let her off so easy, but there was something different about Chloe. For the first time in his life, he was in bed with a woman without any chance of instant gratification, and he was just happy to fall asleep with her in his arms. She made a groaning noise in her sleep and pushed back into him. It was time to admit that he liked her. A lot. More than he'd ever liked a girl before. And it scared the hell out of him that he was happy to just hold her.

Damn. Unless she kept wiggling that pert little butt into him all night. Then they'd have a problem.

Chloe stretched out and wriggled back, eyes popping open when she realized there was a hard body behind her, with something even harder pressed into her lower back. The body moved, a hand running gently through her hair and down her back. It was Ryder and he was awake.

"Mornin', cowboy."

A low, deep chuckle echoed in her ear as Ryder's lips brushed her skin. "You know how cute you sound when you snore?"

Chloe could have died. "Oh my god, I fell asleep on you last night, didn't I?" She laughed, the memories flooding back. "I was waiting for you on the bed and . . ."

"I was gone two minutes and you were comatose by the time I came back."

She still hadn't turned around, liking the feel of Ryder's arms around her, backed tight against him. He kept stroking her, his fingers like heaven on her body. Ryder's mouth was wet against her shoulder, his kisses reminding her of all the places she liked to feel his mouth, his erection rock hard when she started wriggling back and forth.

"You're asking for trouble," Ryder whispered, his fingers digging into her hip just firmly enough to lock her in place.

Chloe backed in harder to him, moaning when he slid a hand into her shorts and started to pleasure her. At the same time he pressed into her and she didn't hold back, let him move inside her, so slowly she let out a low, guttural noise of desire.

Ryder's hand was as insistent as his cock and she pushed harder, clenching tight, not letting him pull out when he tried to.

"Damn it, Chloe," he muttered. "I don't have any protection on yet."

"Do you ever do it without? I'm on the pill."

"Never," he growled. "But with you . . ."

"I don't either. Not before."

She smiled to herself and moved harder and faster, loving that he was struggling to stay in control, that he was enjoying it as much as she was, that he couldn't stop even if he wanted to. Ryder was trying to get her top off now, and she wriggled to let him push it all the way up so she could struggle out of it, still with him buried inside of her. Then he rolled her onto her stomach, her face pushed into the pillow as he settled himself behind her.

"You asked for it." His whisper was husky, like it was being dragged over gravel.

Chloe matched him with every thrust, biting the pillow to stop from moaning. Only it didn't work. Ryder's fingers were on her again, caressing her as she arched back into him, her climax building fast.

"Ryder," she moaned, "I'm . . ." She didn't get a chance to finish her sentence, the words dying in her throat as a wave of pleasure took over all her senses, her body tensing with the intensity of it before slowly loosening and going slack again. Ryder pumped into her one last time as she collapsed back down onto the pillows, his body heavy against hers when he lay on top of her.

"Now that was a nice way to wake up," she murmured, turning her head sideways so he could hear her.

Ryder chuckled. "That more than makes up for you crashing on me last night."

He kissed her shoulder, stroking her hair aside so he could do the same to her neck. Chloe shut her eyes as his lips moved gently across her skin, the tenderness of his touch surprising her. Something had changed between them, something she couldn't put her finger on yet, but what she was doing with Ryder wasn't just about sex any longer.

She had feelings for Ryder, and they scared the crap out of her.

He pulled out and spooned her again but she turned in his arms so she was facing him. Chloe kissed him, opening her mouth and sighing as he brushed his lips back and forth, his tongue so soft when he touched it to hers.

"So what's our plan for today?" he asked, cradling her against him so her head was to his chest. She'd wriggled down the bed so she could lie in his arms.

"Breakfast, then more poker, she said. "I think we'll just stay here today, though."

"You sure?" he asked.

"Yeah. I'd rather just play the smaller tables, but if we gamble here I won't run into anyone I know. It'll just cost you more money for me to play the big game room. You should have a flutter, too, put into play what I've taught you."

"Your wish is my command," he said against her hair, his lips soft. "But I might stick to some low-level slot machines. I'd rather give my money to charity than come up against you or any of the pros."

"Then how about you order me up some pain killers and a bacon and egg breakfast while I have a long, hot shower." She pushed back and gazed up at him, wriggling so she could press one last kiss to his lips. "Extra bacon and a strong coffee. Maybe some orange juice, too."

"You starting to regret the tequila and tacos?" he asked with a grin.

"Ugh." She sat up and swung her legs off the bed. "I don't think I can ever stomach either of those things again. Just the thought of them makes me want to hurl."

She glanced at Ryder, saw he'd kicked the sheets off completely as he stretched out, naked. If she wasn't so desperate for a shower she'd have run straight back to bed and snuggled up against him again, but the lure of hot water made her keep walking. She could have Ryder to herself again tonight, and she was going to make the most of every second in bed with him.

"I'll order up room service now," he called out. "I need you firing on all cylinders."

"I thought I was," she teased back as she turned on the faucet, peeking out the door before shutting it.

"You are, darlin'," Ryder drawled. "Believe me, you are."

She stepped under the water and didn't move, letting it soak her hair and her skin. There wasn't a doubt in her mind that she could win back Ryder's ranch—Parker was a small fish compared to the serious guys playing at the big tables here, and if she could bluff her way to winning against them she'd be fine back in Dallas. Her only concern was walking away from Ryder when it was all over. She could do it, but she already knew it was gonna hurt like hell.

"Like a Band-Aid," she muttered to herself. When it

was time for it to all be over, she was just going to have
to rip the Band-Aid off and not look back.

"Maybe we should have stayed at the Bellagio."

Ryder's mutter made her laugh. "Hey, just because
you wanted to play against me."

"My mistake. I'm moving over right now."

They both laughed and Ryder dropped a kiss to her
head before moving on, leaving her to play again. She'd
decided it was stupid to worry—the Bellagio wasn't
where she wanted to play—and she was really starting
to hit her stride. It was the smaller places where she really got to play a good variety of solid players.

She glanced up as another player joined the table, a
cap pulled down low, his face impossible to see. She
didn't care anyway, just stared at the table, waited for
the dealer.

Chloe stretched and turned her neck from side to
side, feeling stiff. They only had a few hours left before
they were going to head back to the Bellagio for a dinner reservation—their last day in Vegas was all mapped
out—so she didn't mind putting up with a sore neck for
a little longer. She smiled to herself. Maybe Ryder could
massage her later.

The cards were dealt and she started playing, on a
roll, until there were just three of them left in the game.
She curled up her toes as she took another glance at her
cards, looking at the other two men. The one farthest
away from her, the older guy with the cap, finally looked
up, tipping his hat back, cards facedown on the table.

Chloe gasped as familiar hazel-brown eyes met hers.
She clenched her cards, fighting the urge to get up and

run or call out for Ryder. She glanced over her shoulder to check that he was close, and saw that he was playing only a few tables over.

"You sure been having a good run today."

The gravelly voice sent a shiver through her body, leaving her cold, her skin like ice. It was him. It was her . . . She took a big, shaky breath as he took off his hat and ran his fingers through hair long enough to need a ponytail. *Her father.* It had been a while, but it wouldn't matter how many years passed—she'd always know him.

Chloe stared at her cards, refused to acknowledge him. The other player was staring at her now and when he raised the bet she fumbled, also raising, but giving too much away with her body language, her confidence lost. She didn't want to get up and walk away; she wanted to win, and didn't want her father to be the reason she lost her winning streak, but . . .

Damn. Within five minutes she'd lost, her cards thrown on the table, the money gone. She stood up and pushed back her seat, grabbing her purse and hurrying toward Ryder, but fingers caught tight around her wrist before she could get away, digging in hard.

"Is that any way to treat your daddy?"

She bristled, snatching her arm from his grip even though it hurt like hell. Chloe spun around to face him, knew from looking at him that things weren't going his way right now. When things were rough, he didn't bother to shave, let his hair grow out. If he was worth any kind of money he'd be wearing a nice shirt, showing off a fancy wristwatch with his sleeves pushed up, hair neatly combed.

"I said—"

"You're not my *daddy* anymore," she said, fists clenched as she glared at him, heat rising in her cheeks from anger.

"You got any money, love?" His voice was softer now, his eyes pleading. *Like an addict begging for a fix.* "I just need a bit to tide me over, see me out of a bit of trouble."

"I need you to leave me alone," she told him, not backing down, staring him straight in the eye. "In case you've forgotten, you've already stolen everything I had."

"You're throwing 'round a bit of cash today. I've been watching you, Chloe."

"Everything okay here?"

Chloe had to bite down hard on her bottom lip to stop from crying, the relief she felt at hearing Ryder's deep, commanding voice hitting her with a power punch.

"Ryder, this is my father," she muttered.

"Ah, so you got yourself a rich man, did you? Maybe he can pay up for the privilege. Or is a little bitch like you not worth a dowry?"

"You bastard," she swore, keeping close to Ryder when his hands landed on her shoulders, her back pressed against him.

"Seems like you have a few debts to settle, and I'm not talking about what you owe your daughter," Ryder said, eyeballing her father over her head.

He received a laugh in response. "Yeah? Well, Chloe was always pretty good at getting her old man out of trouble. Never liked the idea of me getting roughed up too much."

The fury that built within Chloe was like an out-of-control storm, swirling inside her head until she couldn't stand it any longer. Before she had time to think she was less than a foot away from the man she hated with every fiber in her body, her hand raised as she slapped him hard across the face.

Ryder grabbed her, his hand closing over hers as he drew her back, his hold firm yet gentle, guiding her away.

"I hate you," she sobbed. "I hope they come looking for you. I hope they find you and make you pay, because I'm never settling your debts again. *Never.*"

She turned to Ryder, letting him hold her, her face to his chest. She never lost control, never cried, but seeing her father, having to deal with the man who should have loved her more than anyone else in the world treating her like that . . . She sucked back her tears and took a deep breath. It broke her heart.

"You don't contact Chloe again, you hear me?" Ryder said, the no-bullshit tone of his voice only making her hold on to him tighter. "She ever wants to see you, she'll find you, but you so much as ask her for a dollar again and it'll be my fist you're facing. Got that?"

Ryder took her hand, walking her away from her father and out the door.

"You're okay," he soothed, keeping hold of her hand even when they stopped. "He's not going to hurt you."

"But he already did," she admitted, wiping her eyes, hoping she didn't look like a panda after bursting into tears. "I lost."

"What? One game?"

She nodded.

"Sweetheart, he's your dad. He's always going to be able to rattle you." Ryder stroked his fingers down her cheek, leaning in for a kiss, his lips soft against hers. "You might be an incredible poker player, but you're only human."

She put her arms around him, inhaled the now-familiar scent of him, sighed as his arms closed around her. Chloe turned so her cheek was pressed to his chest so she could talk to him.

"You do realize that's twice you've saved my ass here."

He kissed the top of her head. "Hey, you're saving mine big-time, so I figure I still owe you."

"Sorry I cried."

He squeezed her tighter against him. "Chlo, you're staunch in there with the guys at the tables, but I'm not going to think you're weak because your asshole father can hurt you. Hell, my dad would probably make *me* cry, so you don't have anything to apologize for."

"Nothing would make you cry," she mumbled, finally letting him go and stepping back.

"You'd be surprised."

She looked up at him, into eyes that seemed to show her all the way to his soul. It was like he was opening himself to her, not shutting any part of him away, and she reached for him again, holding both his hands.

"You wanna call it a day?" she asked.

"I think we need ice cream," he said, holding up her hand and kissing the back of it.

She laughed. "*Chocolate* ice cream?"

Ryder tugged her under his arm and she slipped her arm around his waist, walking alongside him.

"I can't believe I hit my father."

"He had it coming."

"Still."

She sighed as he kissed the top of her head again, something he'd taken to doing that made her feel . . . *loved*. Being with Ryder wasn't just about the sex or the fun, it was about the way he looked at her, the brightness in his gaze when he spoke to her, his laugh when it was just the two of them. Only she had no way of knowing if he felt anything more than lust for her, and she sure as hell wasn't about to ask him.

Chapter 13

"Goodbye, Vegas," Chloe said, stretching her legs out and shutting her eyes.

Ryder passed her a bottle of water and stared out at the view as the jet lifted higher into the air. It had been a fun few days, and he was starting to wish they could hide from reality for longer and stay. Or maybe go somewhere else so Chloe wouldn't have to fear running into her father again.

"Does that mean you won't be coming to watch me ride at the National Finals next month?"

Her eyes popped back open, searching him out. "But by then we'll . . ."

He held up his hands. "I know, I know. Our fake relationship will be over and you'll have moved on." Ryder shrugged. The words came easy, but the idea of what they had between them being over by then was really starting to piss him off. "I just thought you might like to come be my little good-luck charm one last time."

Her smile was hesitant at first. "Well . . ."

Ryder pulled a sad puppy-dog face and jumped over to her sofa, landing on the cushions upside down and dropping his head into her lap. "I know you want to. Besides, after that atrocious turn on the bull at Rockhouse, you really ought to have another go."

"Get up and stop reminding me what a colossal failure I was on the tin bull."

He grinned. "Does that mean yes?"

"It means I'll think about it."

He sat up and grabbed her, pulling her onto his lap. "We're really calling this off once the deed is done?" Ryder still wasn't convinced she was going to walk her talk, but then she hadn't exactly bluffed and not followed through with anything else. Or maybe it was just the fact that he wanted her to stay rather than have to admit how he felt about her and be the one begging her to hang around.

Her expression was solemn again, mouth set in a firm line with no hint of a smile. "No strings, Ryder. Don't push me."

Ryder stroked her long hair, wrapping it around his hand and tugging her head back. He brushed his lips across hers. "Whatever you say, darlin'. Whatever you say." He could talk his way into anything, which meant he was intending to pull out all the stops to keep her from walking once the card game was over. He hadn't had nearly enough skin time with Chloe yet. He'd always been the one making it clear to women he was only interested in short-term flings, and now here he was starting to realize what it felt like from the other side.

"So this next rodeo's a big deal?" she asked, unscrewing the top of her water.

"Yeah, you could say that," Ryder told her, staring at her hand as he stroked the inside of her palm. "It's the biggest competition in the country for all rodeo riders, so it's the one not to miss."

She frowned and fiddled with the plastic bottle top she was holding. "Your brothers seem pretty sure that you need to retire. Any reason why?"

"They have this absurd idea that it's too dangerous for me." Ryder chuckled. "But don't you worry that pretty little head of yours. It hasn't killed me yet and it ain't going to."

"They just care about you." She sighed. "Don't take it for granted that they give a damn."

He stopped stroking and held up her hand to press a kiss against her knuckles. "I won't. And you can stop thinking that no one gives a damn about you, because it's bullshit."

She raised her eyes, stared into his like she was willing him not to say it, not to go too far.

"I give a damn about you, Chloe," he murmured, finding it hard to say the words. "And don't you forget it."

Tears shone in her eyes and she quickly blinked them back. "I give a damn about you, too," she whispered back.

Ryder kept hold of her hand as she looked away, staring out the window at the clouds now that they were cruising higher. When she finally glanced back at him she pulled her hand away to worry the label on her water bottle.

"I have my first shift back tomorrow night," she told him, clearing her throat and turning to face him. "I'll find out when they're likely to play again, get everything set in motion."

Ryder nodded, deciding to keep his trap shut. Something was happening between them that neither one of them wanted to admit to, but like it or not, parting ways had to be done and it wasn't going to be easy. Not for her. And sure as hell not for him.

"How long do you plan on staying at my place?" Ryder asked, watching as Chloe flicked through a magazine. She stopped and looked up when he spoke. "Are you still going to crash with me or are you going back to your friend's place?"

"Maybe only a couple of weeks tops if I end up playing him sooner than later."

Ryder nodded. So there went his months of having her in his bed.

"We'll swing past your place on our way home, grab some of your things."

"Thanks. I've been crashing on Shelly's sofa so she'll be happy to know I'll be gone for longer."

"And I can officially thank her for giving me your number the other day."

Chloe's mouth tilted up into a smile. "I still haven't officially kicked her butt for that. Although after I pretended I was just going to stay with you a couple days, she'll kill me when I tell her where we've been."

"Don't be too hard on her. I'll be eternally grateful."

"She would have told me not to go to Vegas. She knows about my dad."

"What will she say when she knows you've been with me?"

Chloe didn't answer for a moment. "She'll be happy that I've finally let someone get close to me."

She looked up under hooded lashes, not saying anything, but her gaze told it all. The fire between them had only just been ignited, and it was going to take more than a few short weeks in bed together to put out the blaze.

"Are we?" he asked, needing to know how she felt. "Close?"

Chloe met his gaze. "Yeah. I think we are."

Ryder looked around the apartment and she watched him cringe. "How long have you been crashing here?"

Chloe shrugged. "A while."

She finished packing her bag and nudged it in his direction.

"She said she'd be back before . . ." A thump signaled Shelly was back and Chloe grinned. "Speak of the devil."

"You're calling me the devil?" Shelly burst into the room, larger than life as usual, throwing her arms around Chloe in a big hug. "You're the one running off with a boy and not answering your phone."

Chloe grinned. "We were kind of in Vegas."

"Oh my god, don't tell me you guys got hitched?"

"I'll wait outside for you," Ryder said, holding up his palms and edging toward the door.

Chloe smiled at him but kept her attention on her friend. "We're not married. Ryder whisked me away on his plane, and we had a few fun days." She wasn't keeping things from Shelly, she just didn't have time to explain everything right now. "Long story, but I was helping him with his poker game."

Shelly scoffed. "I bet you were helping him with a whole lot more than his *poker*."

"You could say that."

They both burst out laughing.

"I'd say I've missed you but it's kinda nice having my sofa back."

"And your wardrobe," Chloe told her. "I've taken most of my stuff. He wants me to stay for a few weeks, at least until I save enough to head back to law school."

"You really like him, don't you?" Shelly's voice was softer now, all joking aside.

"Maybe." Chloe was lying. She liked Ryder a lot, only she didn't want to admit it.

"Just be careful," her friend cautioned. "Have fun with him, but don't let him break your heart."

"I won't." She hugged Shelly and kissed her cheek. "But it's you I'll come crying to if he does. You should never have given him my number."

"Hey, I haven't seen you like this with a guy . . . ever. So just enjoy him. And save all the details for me."

"I will." Chloe waved as she walked out the door. "I'll see you tomorrow at work."

"All done," Chloe said as she got in beside Rider. "Kind of feels like I'm running away from home."

Ryder started the engine and they drove back to his house in silence, the radio blaring country music as darkness fell around them. He reached for her hand and held it, squeezing her fingers lightly as they pulled into his driveway. They passed Chase's place, then the main home, stopping when they reached the guesthouse, and he knew he'd be lying if he said he didn't like the idea of keeping Chloe to himself for a bit longer. After being with her 24/7 in Vegas, he wasn't ready to give her up yet.

"Welcome back," he said, raising her hand to kiss the back of it before letting go. "It's open so let yourself in. I'll bring your stuff inside."

Ryder opened the rear passenger door and grabbed her bags. Chloe had gone on ahead of him and he followed, smiling as the lights went on down the hall and in his bedroom. He'd only ever lived in this place with Nate, and his brother had never been one for turning lamps on and making the place feel welcoming.

"I gotta say it's kind of nice to have a woman in the house."

She glanced over her shoulder and smiled at him. "It's nice to actually be staying in a house instead of cramped in an apartment."

He grimaced, not wanting to offend her but wondering how the hell she'd bunked on her friend's sofa for so long. "It must have been kind of tight."

"Let's just say it's lucky Shelly and I are such good friends," Chloe said with a laugh. "Otherwise we probably would have killed each other."

"You want me to go get takeout?" Ryder asked, dropping her bags in his room then following her out and wrapping his arms around her from behind. She pressed back into him, her head falling to rest against his chest.

"How about I cook?"

He groaned. "A home-cooked meal sounds incredible. You've got no idea how long it's been."

She twisted in his embrace, her hands linked behind his back. "What do you have in the fridge?"

He frowned. "Beer?"

"The pantry?"

Ryder grazed his lips across hers and chuckled. "I think we need to go back to the takeout option."

She walked her fingers up his back, tugging him forward by his hair and making him kiss her again. Their lips met, tongues fused together as she stood on tiptoe and he leaned down. He could have kissed her all night if he wasn't so damn hungry.

Ryder walked her backward, pushing her down onto the sofa and bending over so he was hovering above her. "How about you relax here and I'll go get us something to eat?"

She looked around and laughed. "Do you have anything other than *Maxim* magazines to read?"

He made a face. "Sorry. They're Nate's."

Chloe punched his arm and yanked him down by his ears to force him into another kiss. "Yeah, sure they are."

"Ouch!"

"Stop complaining and just kiss me," she ordered.

Ryder did as he was told, only the growling of his stomach made both of them laugh. "I think I just ruined the moment."

"Uh-huh," she confirmed. "How about you go get food and I'll unpack. I'm up for a night of comfort food and snuggling up in front of the TV if you are."

Ryder stood up and grinned down at Chloe. "Anyone ever tell you you're the perfect woman?"

"No, but feed me and pour me a glass of wine and I'll tell you all night that you're the perfect man."

"Deal," he said, grabbing her bottom when she jumped up, making her squeal. "I'll be back soon. Any preferences?"

Her eyebrows shot up and she made a face. "Anything but tacos."

They both laughed. He'd never be able to eat tacos again without thinking about Chloe knocking back shots and eating as much as he had. *And riding that bull with a look on her face that screamed bloody murder.*

"Make yourself at home, Chlo," he said, grabbing his keys and giving her a quick kiss on the lips. "I'll be back soon with burgers and fries."

He left to the sound of the television being turned on and Chloe humming a song he didn't recognize. She might be staying with him in exchange for saving his ass, but right now it felt like something a whole lot more real than just a deal to get them both what they needed.

Chapter 14

"I've never asked how long you've been riding rodeo," Chloe said to Ryder. "I'll bet you started horseback riding when you were a kid."

It had been a week since they'd gotten back from Vegas and he'd finally talked Chloe onto a horse. She'd ridden a few times as a kid so she wasn't nervous, but she wasn't exactly confident, either. He spent his days training, working with young horses that he'd reared himself, so being on horseback was second nature to him.

"I've been riding since before you were walking," Ryder said, watching as Chloe sat straighter in the saddle. "I started riding in front of my granddad when I was still in diapers."

"Bullshit," she said with a laugh, stroking her horse's neck just like he'd shown her to do without letting go of the reins.

"My brothers were older and off riding, and Grand-dad said it was either put me up front on the saddle or let them go off on their own." Ryder grinned. "I think he had it easy raising a daughter here, then he was hit with three risk-taking grandsons to deal with. When I was about ten I started barrel racing on my pony, entering a few local rodeo days, and before anyone knew what I had planned I was all grown up and traveling around the state competing anywhere and everywhere I could."

They rode side by side, Ryder holding his reins on the buckle with one hand, Chloe gripping hers a little tighter.

"Do you enjoy riding for pleasure like this?" Chloe asked. "I mean, it must seem pretty tame compared to bucking broncs."

Ryder shook his head, patting his horse's rump. "I just love being in the saddle. Rodeo's a thrill, an addiction that I've never been able to walk away from, but riding like this?" He shrugged. "I'll never tire of just riding out over the ranch. I train horses for ranch work and rodeo, so, to be honest, as long as I'm on horseback or working with them I'm happy."

"I can see the appeal," she replied. "Of this, not the rodeo stuff."

He laughed. "Yeah, somehow I can't see you jumping on a bull any day soon."

"Hey, if I wasn't so drunk I'd have been fine on that mechanical one." Her smile lit her face. "In fact, if I recall correctly, you told me I was a great cowgirl the next morning."

They both laughed. There were memories of Chloe being a cowgirl in Vegas that he'd never forget.

"You do realize that you kicked ass in Vegas, don't you? I mean"—Ryder blew out a breath—"I love that you whipped all those guys. I've never seen a woman play like that."

"I got used to guys I dated hating that I could always beat them. They liked it to start with, then they resented that I was the better player."

Ryder reached out and placed his hand on her thigh. "Darlin', I think it's hot. Don't ever let me beat you, because if I ever manage it, I want to know that I deserved it."

"You'll regret saying that. Guys always do." She shrugged. "Besides, I ruined my winning streak that last day anyway."

He winked, ignoring her reference to her dad. "Not me. I like a challenge, and the harder I have to work for it the better."

She flushed, her cheeks burning a delicious shade of pink. "Talking about cards, have you thought any more about our plan?"

"I have full confidence in you," he told her. And he did, only the fact that his ranch was on the line made him damn nervous. "But card games are unpredictable. I know that better than anyone."

"Yeah, but you have a tell, just like everyone," she told him.

"You've already made it clear what a crap card player I am," he said, giving her a pretend shove. "You can stop insulting my masculinity anytime now."

She made a face, her smile hovering into a frown. "Sorry. Brutal but true."

"Seriously, though," he said, reining back and watching her do the same. Or more like the well-trained old horse she was riding stopped when his did. "Whatever you tell me to do, I'll do it. You say the word and I'll follow your lead."

She winked and lifted her hat. "We're gonna win back every penny," she drawled. "But I'd be lying if I said that losing that last game in Vegas hadn't knocked me a bit."

He scowled. "If that was supposed to sound like me . . ."

Chloe's smile made it impossible for him not to return it. Since he'd been around her it was like she'd scrambled his hard wiring, made him soft when before he'd been tough as nails. It wasn't that he didn't like it, but he damn well found it amusing that the same woman who was blackmailing him was managing to turn him to putty in her hands.

"Come on, I need to get back for my shift."

Ryder groaned. "Do you have to keep working there?"

This time the withering look she threw him wasn't humorous. "No, how stupid of me. I could just write a check from my trust fund to pay my tuition and rent. Duh!" She slapped herself in the face. "Why didn't I think of that?"

"I was implying that we were having too much fun for you to have to go work a long shift."

She kicked her horse in the sides and surprised him by bouncing off into a trot. The look on her face was anything but comfortable, but he knew how damn determined she was and he doubted she'd rein back to a walk. That's why her losing one game hadn't rattled him—she was still going to win, of that he had no doubt.

"Some of us have to work for a living. Fact of life," she called over her shoulder.

"Some of us could hustle and play cards every other night and make a fortune," he shot back, nudging his horse into a canter to catch up with her. "Now wouldn't that be fun."

"Don't bait me, Ryder." She slowed when he did, her breath coming out in short pants. "And how the hell do you make that look so damn easy?"

Ryder tried not to laugh at the pissed-off look on her face. "Sorry."

"I don't tell anyone about my past, Ryder. What I told you stays between us, okay? I don't want to go back there. I want to leave assholes like Jim and my father in my past forever."

Her tone was somber and it wiped the smile clean off his face. "I was just playing with you, Chlo. And for the record, I don't go around telling people about my dad. So what was said in Vegas stays in Vegas, okay?" He wished he could make it clearer to her that he cared about her way too much to ruin anything between them. "I would never hurt you," he finally said.

She glanced at him, squeezing his hand back when he reached over and clasped her palm. "Sorry. I didn't mean to jump down your throat."

"So you're off to work now?" he asked.

"Yeah. I'll see you later. Maybe in the morning if you're already asleep when I get in."

Ryder let his reins slip through his fingers until he was just holding the buckle again. He tipped his head back to look up at the blue sky, the sun shining just enough, the heat bearable. When he'd been away he'd missed everything about Texas—no matter how hard he'd tried to make a life elsewhere, the pull back to the

King ranch had been impossible to resist. And now that he was here, the thought of having to leave again was like contemplating a limb being ripped off. Just like the idea of Chloe leaving him was causing him some serious goddamn pain.

"I can't keep it a secret any longer," he muttered, the shock on Chloe's face telling him he'd actually said the words out loud instead of keeping them inside of his own head.

"You're going to tell your brothers?" she asked. "When there's only a couple of nights tops until the next game?"

He shook his head. "Hell no, I've thought that one through and I can't do it. But I have to tell Granddad. I can't lie to him."

Chloe's gaze was sad. "You do what you have to do. But I'll win it back, that's a promise."

"I know you will," he told her, dismounting when they reached the barn. "But I owe him the truth. I spent years away from here wanting to find my own way in the world and prove myself, and I've never had much of a conscience, but when it comes to my granddad . . ." He took off his hat and ran his fingers through his hair. "He gifted me a third of his estate, and I want him to know that I fucked up. All I ever wanted was to show him I was as capable as Chase and Nate, and now look at me."

"You want to tell him regardless of the consequences?" she asked, letting him guide her down, hands on her hips. Chloe spun in his arms, palm to his cheek as she stared up at him. "Sometimes what we don't know won't kill us."

He pushed his hands into her jean pockets, shoving

her forward so her body hit his. "When did you get so wise?"

She tipped back and he kept hold of her, not letting her get away. Ryder kept his hips slammed into hers, not letting her say another word, mouth covering hers.

"I'm going to be late," she whispered, clutching his shirt and yanking him close so his lips couldn't escape.

"You sure you need to be on time for your shift?" His confession could wait if it meant more sinning with Chloe.

She groaned, grinding her body against his, tugging at his shirt so it came loose and rubbing her hands over his abs, her nails gliding across his skin. "Goodbye, Ryder." Chloe nipped at his chin and he slapped her on the ass as she turned.

"Goodbye Chloe," he murmured.

He adjusted his jeans, hard as a rock after the little stunt she'd pulled, rubbing her body up against him like that. He could play with his fake girlfriend all day and never tire, but it was time to man up to what he'd done.

His phone buzzed in his pocket and he quickly tied the horses up before answering it, knowing it was Chase.

"Hey."

"Hey. You busy?" Chase asked.

"Not now. Whadda ya want?" Ryder flicked his phone to speaker and put it down on a railing, taking the saddles off.

"I need a hand. Can you spare the rest of the afternoon? I'm down a couple of guys and I need to round up some cattle from the other side of the ranch. It'll take a few hours at least."

Ryder patted his horse and threw the saddle back up. "Count me in. I'm at the barn saddling up now."

He rubbed down the horse Chloe had been riding and walked him out to the field, disappearing into the feed shed and returning with some carrots. "Sorry, big guy, just when you thought your work for the day was over, huh?"

Tomorrow he'd tell his granddad. Today he was going to ride out over the land and talk shit with his brother. He lived to work on the ranch, so he wasn't going to say no if his brother needed him.

Chapter 15

Ryder couldn't recall the last time he'd been so nervous. He wiped his palms on his jeans and took a deep breath before knocking, waiting a second before pushing open the door.

"Hello, son."

"Granddad," Ryder said, smiling when he saw his grandfather sitting on the bed, dressed rather than in his pajamas. "It's good to have you back home." It'd been a while since he'd been in residence at the main house. His doctor had kept him in the hospital for the best part of two months now.

His granddad might be almost ninety, but he still had a thick head of silver hair, his body more frail than it had ever been but still impressive at well over six foot tall. Ryder doubted he'd lose that commanding edge until the day he died—just one boom of his voice and he always seemed to make people stop in their tracks to listen.

"What's wrong?"

Ryder felt his eyebrows shoot up. How the hell did he know something was wrong? "Ah, well . . ."

"Come and sit," his granddad said, leaning back into the pillows on the bed and gesturing toward the big armchair beside it. "You look like you need to get something off your chest."

Ryder crossed the room and sat down, looking his granddad in the eye before dropping his head into his palms. He couldn't do this. He was about to confess to the man he respected more than any other human being in the world, and the words just wouldn't come.

"Tell me, son. You know you can talk to me about anything."

"You're never going to forgive me," Ryder managed. "I wanted you to know first, before Nate and Chase find out, but . . ."

"Ryder, go over to the bookcase and pull out that black album."

He hesitated, knowing he needed to just get it off his chest, but he did as he was told, returning with the album and placing it on his grandfather's lap. Ryder sat back down again.

"You broke my heart the day you left here, Ryder," the old man said, voice still as strong and commanding as it had always been. "I might have a heart of stone when it comes to business, but you boys are the most important things in my life. Always have been, always will be."

Ryder balled his fists as he met his grandfather's stare, refusing to give in to his emotions. Tears burned the backs of his eyes, but he refused to let one spill.

"I'm back now," Ryder said, because it was all he

could think to say. "And I'm not going anywhere." He'd been gone too long, the better part of four years, but the time he'd spent with his granddad since he'd been home had told him he should have come back a long time ago. He'd missed out on too much time, time that he could never get back.

"You were young and you needed to find your way. But I want you to know how proud I was of you, even when you were gone." His granddad opened the album, took his time looking at the first page, then nudged it toward him. "You might have been away, but you weren't ever forgotten. Not for a second."

Ryder reached out and took the book, staring at the first page, then the second, hardly able to believe what he was looking at.

"You have clippings from all my rodeo results?"

Clay King nodded. "If you were mentioned, I have it," he said. "I've got every write-up, results draw, photo, you name it."

Ryder flicked through a few more pages before putting the book down on his lap and staring at his grandfather. "Why?"

"Because I'm proud of you." Clay laughed, never breaking eye contact for a second. "You made a name for yourself doing what you loved. What's not to be proud of?"

He'd had no idea. Ryder had left, been one hell of a rebellious teenager, and when he'd finally returned it had been to his brothers telling him to get his act together. Clay had never said anything other than to welcome him home, tell him how happy he was to have all three grandsons back together, but Ryder had always thought deep down than his grandfather had been disappointed in him.

"I never thought you approved," Ryder said.

"Son, you made your own money when other kids were living off trust funds. I've always been proud of you."

Ryder moved to the edge of his chair and put the book on the side table, reaching for his granddad's hand. Their dad might have starved them of affection, but Clay had always made them feel loved. He was formidable to almost everyone except his grandsons. But Ryder had never known quite how much his granddad thought of him.

"I've made a huge mistake," Ryder admitted, finding what he was about to say almost impossible. "What I've done, you'll never forgive me."

His granddad shook his head, patting his hand. "There's nothing you could do that's unforgivable. Tell me what you've done and we'll figure it out together."

Ryder pulled back, leaned into the chair, and blew out a big breath. It was now or never. "I was playing cards with Parker. I'd been winning all night and I bet my third of the ranch."

Clay didn't say a word, just stared back at him before looking away, his gaze now through the window and into the distance.

"I thought it was a sure thing, that I'd win the deeds to his ranch. I hate the bastard and I wanted to teach him a lesson."

Ryder felt like a boy about to be reprimanded, waiting for his punishment to be dealt out. His grandfather had never been rattled, never showed his anger, just used that deep voice and commanded everybody around him. One look had been enough to tell them all when they'd gone too far, one stare had been all they needed to stop and behave. But this wasn't Ryder acting out in his boyhood, this was him fucking up when he should have known better.

"You're aware that our family has been feuding with Parker's on and off for the past three decades?"

Ryder nodded. "Yes."

"And are you asking for my help, or do you have the situation under control?"

This time Ryder met his grandfather's gaze, squaring his shoulders as he stared back at the man he admired most in the world. "Yes, sir. I will do anything I have to do to make this right. I'm dealing with it."

"That's all I need to know then."

Ryder swallowed, waiting to be told what an idiot he was, to be yelled at just like he deserved. He didn't want to be let off, he needed to be told off.

"You're not angry with me?"

"Oh, I'm plenty angry," Clay said, "but you're not a child anymore, Ryder, and if you tell me you've got something under control then I have to believe you."

Ryder stood. "I won't let you down, Granddad. I promise."

"Are you going to tell your brothers?"

"Do you think I should?"

"Son, only you can make that decision," Clay said. "Now how about you pour me a whiskey and tell me all about the gorgeous girl you've been romancing."

Ryder chuckled. "You make it sound like a formal

courtship. And I think you're supposed to be drinking tea, not liquor."

His granddad grumbled. "The doc's told me I'll be lucky to make it another year. If I can't drink whiskey now, then when?"

"Fair point," Ryder said, disappearing into the other room and reappearing with two short glasses.

"So I hear she's blond and good at keeping you on your toes."

Ryder paused before taking a small sip of his drink. "How about I bring her over to meet you once this whole thing with Parker is sorted out?"

"I'd like that." Clay sipped his drink, staring at the golden-brown liquid for a while before looking up. "You know, you boys are great, but it's about time we had a woman around the place. Aside from the housekeeper, if you get my drift."

"What, you want us all married off all of a sudden?"

"No, I'd just like some women around the place. To know that you boys are being looked after." He chuckled then stifled a cough. "Hell, I'd like a woman around to look after me. It's been five years since your grandma died and I miss her like hell every day."

Ryder was about to tell him that Chloe was more than capable of looking after him, but he clamped his jaw shut and swirled the whiskey around the bottom of his glass instead. Chloe was going to be gone soon. As soon as the ranch was his again, as soon as she had what she wanted from him, she'd be gone and he'd most likely never see her again. She wasn't his real girlfriend and he needed to remember it.

"You tell her not to be a stranger. That I'd like to meet her."

He nodded. "Sure thing." Ryder hated that he wanted to introduce her to his family, that he was starting to think of her as way more than just a good time. "I've got some things to do, Granddad. I'll come by and see you again tonight."

"Be a good boy and get me another, would you?"

Ryder took one look at the empty glass in his grandfather's outstretched hand and shook his head. "Your doctor would have my head on a plate. I'll tell your nurse to get you a coffee."

Clay laughed and Ryder paused to press a kiss to his forehead. "Love you, Granddad."

"I love you, too, son."

Ryder walked out the door, keeping his big shoulders squared when all he wanted was to collapse and fall against the wall. He hadn't deserved that, to be treated with so much respect when he'd been such an idiot, and the fact that Clay had a record of all his wins, all his rides? *Unbelievable.*

"Where're you sneaking off to?"

Ryder spun around to find Nate standing behind him. He cleared his throat. "I was just in seeing Granddad."

Nate kept walking and Ryder walked alongside him toward the front door.

"He okay?"

"Asking for whiskey, so yeah, I guess he's fine."

Ryder stopped at the front door, pulling it open, then leaning against it to listen to Nate.

"You sure *you're* okay?"

"Fine," Ryder asked. "You off to work?"

"Yeah. I'll catch you later. How about we grab a beer tonight, the three of us?"

"Sure thing."

Ryder headed for his truck and jumped behind the wheel, heading down the drive even though he had nowhere he needed to be. What he needed was to get his ranch back, secure his stake in his family's land before it was too late, before he had to admit what he'd done to Nate. His grandfather believed in him, and he believed in Chloe.

She was expecting Parker to be there the night after next, which meant it was almost over. All she had to do was kick ass like she had in Vegas and it wouldn't be a problem. If only it was that easy.

Chapter 16

Ryder grinned at Chloe as she put three shots of tequila in front of them. Her blond hair was pulled up into a ponytail and he was itching to reach across the bar and yank the tie out so he could see it tumbling over her shoulders. It wasn't that she didn't look hot with it up, but when it was down it reminded him of how she looked in his bed.

"Bottoms up, boys." She laughed. "And I don't envy you one bit."

Nate slapped Ryder on the back but he was busy grinning at Chloe. He knew she'd never throw back tequila again.

"This one's a keeper," Nate said with a laugh. "She actually wants us to drink shots. Perfect woman in my books."

Ryder bristled. When Nate decided he wanted a woman, he stopped at nothing until he got what he wanted, but there was no way he was touching Chloe. Not now and certainly not when their arrangement ended. He was still trying to figure out himself how to keep her in his bed.

"You do realize how big your tips are, right?" Ryder asked. "She's a bartender and you're a big drinker. Of course she's gonna keep pouring."

Nate chuckled, clearly not giving a shit what Ryder said about him. And then Ryder saw a pretty brunette tossing her hair over her shoulder, saw the way she glanced at Nate from across the bar. *Bingo.* If there was ever a way to get Nate all twisted in knots it was seeing the one woman he refused to talk about, or look at.

"Hey, isn't that Sam's little sister?" Ryder asked, giving Chase a nudge as he spoke. "She's all grown up now, ain't she? Think we should go say hi, see if it's her or not? I reckon she looks just like your type."

Nate spun around to look, his face like thunder when he turned back to Ryder. "Back off," he demanded.

"Hey, I'm just looking. It's Chase you need to worry about."

Nate turned his glare on Chase, who just held his hands up in the air. Chase's wink in Ryder's direction didn't help the situation, and both he and Ryder howled with laughter at how easy their brother was to rattle. Ryder had no idea what had gone down with Nate and Sam's sister, or maybe it was what *hadn't* happened, but Nate went into serious protective mode just talking about her.

"So you don't want her, but you don't want anyone else to have her either?" Ryder asked. "Sound about right?"

Nate made a noise that sounded like a growl. "Back off. Just back the fuck off, okay? I don't want you guys near her. Don't push me on this, just leave her the hell alone."

Chase shrugged and Ryder laughed again. He'd missed this when he'd lived away, the hours spent hanging out with his brothers and talking shit. He reached for the shot he'd forgotten about and raised the tiny glass in the air. Nate might be fun to tease, but Ryder had no intention of riling him up any more—he had his hands full just trying to figure out what the hell was going on between him and Chloe, without worrying about an itch that Nate hadn't been able to scratch.

"To chasing different women," he toasted.

Nate knocked their glasses, waiting for Chase to lift his and banging theirs together a little too hard. "Too fucking right."

"Hey, how did Sam get on with that colt?" Chase asked. "I saw him working him in the round pen the other day. He looked good."

Nate's big shoulders relaxed, happy to talk about his best friend so long as it didn't involve that friend's little sister.

Ryder tuned out the conversation around them when Chloe caught his eye, although he did see Nate disappear through the crowd.

"What time do you get off tonight?"

He frowned when the big smile she'd been flashing him wiped from her face. Ryder went to reach for her, then froze when she shook her head, eyes wide. He slowly looked over his shoulder and saw what she'd seen. Parker was standing at a table near the entrance. *Fuck.* They hadn't expected him to show until Saturday.

Chloe came closer and leaned over the bar toward him, her hand on his shoulder. "You need to go."

Ryder stared into her eyes, wished to hell things weren't so damn complicated.

"If he says something things are gonna turn nasty," he muttered. "For me and for him."

"Just tell them," she murmured in his ear so only he could hear. "Get the hell out of here and tell them before he does. He's gonna be pissed you haven't already handed over the place."

"You think he's here to play tonight? That something changed?" Ryder asked.

She shrugged as she pulled back. "Don't know. But if he is, then tonight's the night. I'm prepped either way so we can pull it off whenever we need to. Shelly can cover my shift, I've told her what's going on."

Ryder nodded, knowing he could count on her. She'd planned everything, what she was going to say and how she was going to join the game once they started playing, and it was just a matter of setting the ball in motion. Their plan was as simple as her teasing them, making them think she didn't know what she was doing, then winning the lot out from under an unsuspecting Parker. "If I come crawling back in here on my hands and knees after telling them, will you still want me?"

Chloe leaned forward again and placed her hand on his cheek. "Even if you're black and blue, I'll still want you." She kissed him, her mouth warm as it covered his. There was something familiar about her touch now and he was starting to crave it, liking the fact that he knew the feel of her lips against his, the softness of her palm across his skin. "I'll win it back, just keep reminding yourself of that. It'll all be over soon."

"Boys, how about we get out of here," Ryder suggested, pulling away from Chloe and facing his brothers now that Nate was back. "Time to move this party, huh?" He didn't want to have this particular conversation with anyone in earshot.

"You okay with this, Chloe?" Chase asked with a wink.

"Just make sure he's a good boy. I can trust you guys with that, right?"

Ryder slipped on his jacket and winked at Chloe as his brothers laughed, keeping his head down as he headed for the door. He knew it was impossible for him to blend in, especially with his brothers flanking him—they were all six-four and it wasn't exactly easy to go incognito. All he needed was to get past Parker. The table he was at was off to the left, not in the direct line to the door, but still . . .

"Hey, King!"

Ryder cringed, recognizing Parker's drunken slur. He kept walking, hoping his brothers either hadn't heard or didn't care enough to stop.

"I'm talking to you, King boy. Come over here, you lying bastard."

"What the fuck did he say?" Nate asked, stopping and staring in Parker's direction.

Ryder slapped a hand on Nate's shoulder. "Let's just go. We don't need this shit."

"No one speaks to you like that and gets away with it. What the hell's he on about?"

Chase came closer. "That scumbag's the one spreading the bullshit rumors about you. Time we ended this feud once and for all, huh?"

Ryder stood his ground, not taking his eyes off Parker for a second. Everything was about to turn to shit and there was nothing he could do about it.

"What bullshit?" Nate asked.

"Let's go, come on," Ryder said, giving them both a shove forward. It didn't work—he might as well have tried to push solid marble through the bar on his own. "It's not worth it."

"To hell it isn't," Chase said, stalking toward Parker before Ryder could do anything about it.

Damn. Ryder had been ready for his brothers to beat the shit out of him when he told them, but he hadn't anticipated them doing the same to Parker first. Which meant he either had to tell them damn fast before it came to that, or just ride out the shit storm and hope for the best.

Fuck. He knew what he had to do.

"Nate, stop," Ryder said, closing his hand over Nate's shoulder just as Chase swung a punch at Parker.

"You fucking asshole," Chase yelled as his fist connected with Parker's cheek.

Fuck! Parker stumbled backward, but before he was down his two goons came in swinging. Ryder ran forward and shoved Nate out of the way, one of the heavy's fists grazing the side of his face as he ducked too slow before he managed to slam his bunched fist into the guy's stomach.

"Don't tell me your brothers forgave you already," Parker called out, his laugh grating as he sat back and watched the show.

Parker's two men were down. Nate and Chase were panting beside Ryder, blood smeared across both their shirts.

"Leave it, Parker. Just fucking leave it," Ryder muttered.

"Leave it? What, don't tell me they don't know the truth about our little bet?" Parker lit up a cigarette, his cheek red. "And I'm still waiting for the keys and the deed. Haven't seen them arrive yet and I'm just dying to let myself in."

"What the fuck's he talking about, Ryder?" Nate asked.

"Let's go," Ryder said, his voice low. He glanced back toward the bar and saw Chloe. She was shaking her head, her mouth fixed in a grim line. She didn't have to say anything for him to know what she was trying to tell him—she wanted him out of there, to get the hell away from Parker and deal with his brothers on his own.

"Ryder?" Chase asked.

"Look . . ." he started.

"He hasn't told you that he bet his third of the ranch and lost it?" Parker asked, his smile sickening. "And here I was thinking you boys were tight."

Nate turned slowly and glared at Ryder, his gaze unforgiving. He didn't utter a word, just stalked past him toward the door. Chase's stare was just as deadly, only he didn't walk out. He gestured with his head instead, waiting for Ryder to go first.

"Guess I'll be seeing a lot of you boys soon, huh?"

Ryder left the bar with Parker's high-pitched laugh ringing in his ears, drowning out the country music and loud voices. This was it. It was time to confess to his brothers and it wasn't gonna be pretty. He glanced at Chloe over his shoulder, forgot everything else when he saw the heartbroken expression on her face. And then he was walking through the door and toward Nate in the parking lot.

"I'm gonna ask you again, Ryder, and I want a straight answer. What the fuck was Parker talking about?" Nate's voice had the same commanding, deep edge as their grandfather's, only Ryder knew that unlike their grand-dad, Nate was capable of talking with his fists if he didn't get the answer he wanted.

Chase moved around to stand beside Nate, his arms folded across his chest. Both Ryder's brothers were staring at him, unblinking, waiting for an explanation.

"It was the night after the rodeo," Ryder said, shoving his hands in his pockets. "I'd been gambling all night, playing poker, and I screwed up."

"When you say screwed up, what exactly do you mean?" Chase asked.

Ryder glanced at Nate, saw the grim set of his mouth. "Parker upped the stakes, I had all aces, and I bet my third of the ranch." He blew out a breath. "I thought I was gonna burgle his ranch out from under him. Instead I lost mine."

"You lied to me," Chase ground out. "You fucking lied to me when I told you what I'd heard."

Ryder hung his head. "Yeah, I did. I wanted to get it sorted before you guys had to find out."

Nate stalked the few feet between them until his big frame was almost touching Ryder's. Nate had a slight height advantage as he locked eyes on his, his anger almost tangible.

"You thought you had the right to gamble our land away?" His voice was a low, menacing rasp.

Ryder met his brother's stare. "I've done a lot of stupid shit in my life, Nate, but I'll never forgive myself for this."

"Damn fucking right you won't."

The punch connected with the side of his face before Ryder even saw it coming. One second Nate was staring at him, the next his fist was flying through the air. The blow sent Ryder reeling, stumbling backward with the force of it, head pounding as he covered his face in case Nate came at him again.

"What the hell are we going to tell Granddad?" Ryder heard Chase say. He tried to focus on his brothers. From where he was staggering it looked like there were six of them standing there.

"He knows," Ryder muttered, spitting to see if he was bleeding.

"What did you say?" Nate asked, coming closer again.

Ryder straightened and held up his hands, not wanting to get into a fight. He was prepared this time, wasn't going to let Nate too close, or miss one of his fists again, but he wasn't going to say anything.

"He knows. When you saw me in there with him this morning, I was telling him everything."

"Fuck, Ryder! He's got cancer. Have you missed the part about us trying not to cause him any stress?"

"This is low, even for you," Chase muttered.

"Don't you fucking dare," Ryder hissed. "Yeah, I've screwed up big-time, but don't you make out like I've always been some kind of royal fuckup."

Chase looked as imposing as Nate now, standing way too close and glaring at Ryder like he was ready to draw blood. But Ryder had had enough.

"Do you have any idea what it must have been like for Granddad worrying about you all those years? When you went off to have fun and we never heard from you?" Nate asked.

"You heard from me plenty," Ryder said. "And I'll have you know that Granddad was damn proud of me."

"Don't—"

"No," Ryder said, interrupting Nate. "You're the golden boy primed to take over the family business. Chase, you've wanted to run the ranch all your life. Where did that leave me?"

"Don't play the poor-me card," Chase said, unfolding his arms. "We've all been lucky and we know it."

"I'm not saying I haven't been lucky. But you guys knew your place in the world and I didn't. So for all the shit you give me about what I do, it's my choice. I've fucked up big-time here, but I'm gonna make it right. Just you wait."

"That what you told Granddad?" Nate asked, his fists still bunched.

"I told him everything. And I also told him that I wasn't telling you two."

Ryder could see why other people found them intimidating when they were out in a crowd. Having Nate and Chase gang up on him in a parking lot wasn't exactly something he was enjoying.

"How are you going to get it back?" Chase asked, glancing at Nate as he spoke. "There's no way Parker's just gonna let you buy it back. He hates us as much as we hate him."

Ryder wished Chloe was with him right now, because he wasn't convinced his brothers were going to like the idea of him using her to get it back. They were rightfully angry with him, and the whole winning-it-back concept probably wasn't what they'd been expecting.

"You know how I went to Vegas with Chloe?"

They both just grunted and stared at him like a pair of heavies.

"It just so happens that Chloe's a damn fine poker player."

"Don't tell me you're using that sweet girl just to win the ranch back?" Nate asked.

"That *sweet girl* is going to win the deed to my third of the ranch back in exchange for some money for her tuition fees," Ryder confessed, not seeing any point in lying now. "The game's going down soon, maybe tonight, and it'll be like this never happened."

"And you're sure she can do this?" Nate asked. "'Cause we can do this plenty of other ways."

"Like what?" Ryder asked. "Beating the shit out of him? Paying a fortune to try to buy it back? Believe me, I've thought of everything and this is the only way."

"So let me get this straight," Chase said, eyebrows pulled together like he was seriously confused. "You lost the ranch being a dickhead in a poker game, and you've managed to meet a woman who's capable of winning it back? You might have been shit out of luck when you lost it, but damn, talk about lucky finding her. You trust her?"

"I've got no reason not to. I can't sink any lower and she's got nothing to lose and a whole lot to gain."

Nate still looked like he wanted to kill him, but Ryder could see that Chase had softened. Maybe his brother liked that he was going to have his ass saved by a girl.

"You want us there when it goes down?" Nate asked.

"No." Ryder shook his head. "We've got the whole thing planned. Chloe wants it to be real low-key, take him by surprise and lose a bit of money before turning the tables on him."

Nate took a few steps closer again. "So this could happen tonight?"

"Yeah. Now that he's here, he'll be wanting a table to play out back."

"Then we better not mess up that pretty face of yours too bad, huh?"

Ryder froze, knew from the dark expression on Nate's face that he hadn't calmed down even a little. His brother flexed his fists and gave him an evil grin. Chase just laughed.

The punch came swift and fast, a sucker punch to the stomach that left Ryder doubled over and groaning, every bit of air knocked from his body.

"Don't you dare lose tonight, Ryder, you fucking hear me? There's one thing that's not happening in Grand-dad's lifetime, and that's even an inch of King land not being owned by our family."

Ryder stayed doubled over, still trying to catch his breath. It was Chase's hand on his shoulder as Nate walked away that made him rise, sucking back air that just never seemed to fill his lungs.

"You'll get it back. You always get what you want be-cause you're one stubborn motherfucker," Chase said in a low voice. "Don't let this be the exception."

Ryder watched him go, saw both his brothers drive off in Nate's SUV. That was when he stumbled back a few steps and dropped, catching his breath properly and running his fingers gently across what he was sure would be a massive bruise on the side of his face. Given what he'd done, he'd gotten off pretty lightly. He'd been able to hit them with his exit strategy, which had probably helped them to digest the whole thing.

"Ryder?"

He looked up and back toward the bar, locking eyes with Chloe. She stopped, took one look at him, and ran toward him.

"I'm fine," he said, hauling himself up as she stopped in front of him, tears in her eyes as she raised her hand, hovering like she was torn between touching him and not wanting to hurt him.

"What did they do to you?"

Ryder laughed. "A couple of punches aren't going to kill me, sweetheart." But her concern was nice. The more time they spent together, the harder it was to re-member they were faking it—he was starting to get used to Chloe's touch, to looking into those beautiful brown eyes when she was concerned, or even better, when they were all wild when she was het up over something.

She reached out for him, slung one hand around his waist, and touched the other to his chest. He wanted to draw her close, inhale the sweet smell of her perfume, and tell her how damn much she meant to him. But he didn't.

"Ouch!" Ryder grimaced as she slid her hand down to his stomach, retracting it the second he reacted.

"What the hell did they do to you?" she repeated, grabbing the hem of his T-shirt and tugging it up. *Damn.*

Ryder looked down and saw the angry red mark that was fast turning ugly. If his stomach looked that bad he hated to think what his face looked like.

"Are we on?" he asked.

Chloe blew out a breath, sending hair that had escaped from her ponytail flying off her face. He reached out and pushed it back, but she shook her head and tugged out the band that was holding her ponytail in place, letting her hair fall loose around her shoulders.

"I've swapped shifts with Shelly. Parker's already gone into the back room to play and I want to get changed before we head in together."

Ryder's heart started pounding, the all-too-familiar rush of adrenaline powering through him at the thought of what they were about to do. "You realize this is going to come completely out of left field, right? I mean, they're not gonna believe what's about to go down in there."

Chloe's smile was slow. She twisted her mouth like she was trying to stop from grinning, but within a few seconds she was having to bite her lip to stop from smiling hard. "I want to pretend like I'm not insanely excited about taking this guy for all he's got."

Ryder stepped into her space, circled his arms around her waist, and drew her close, grimacing when she bumped into him a little too hard. "Baby, I love the fact that you're hyped about doing this. And believe me when I say I'll make it up to you all night if you pull this off."

She scowled, leaning back in his arms. "*When* I pull this off, you mean."

"Exactly," he said, leaning down and kissing her. He was sure going to miss that beautiful mouth of hers once this was over.

"So what's the plan?" he asked. "We still heading in together, or do you want me to go in first."

"Not a chance." Chloe stood on tiptoes to press another kiss to his lips before backing away. "After what went down with your brothers before, you need me in there right from the start as a distraction." Ryder followed her as she walked slowly back to the bar. "Tell them I want to play a little that you're good for any bets I make and you're pissed with your brothers, and then let me take it from there, just like our original plan."

Ryder reached out and touched Chloe's arm, his fingers pressing just hard enough to indicate that he wanted her to stop. "Thank you," he said. "I know we've both been having fun, but I won't ever forget what you've done for me, Chloe."

She laughed, shrugging off his hold and trying to act like it was no big deal. "You would have figured out a way to get it back with or without my help."

"Maybe," he said. "But I would have lost a lot in the process. And I wouldn't have met you."

She stared at him, unblinking. "Just promise that you won't forget me when this is over." Chloe's voice was low, her words barely a murmur.

"Forget you?" Ryder chuckled and reached out to stroke her face, cupping his palm against her cheek and smiling when she leaned into his touch. "I meet a crazy sexy woman at a rodeo and she ends up being an ace poker player and saving my ass. Not to mention she's amazing in bed. Do you really think I could forget any of that?" He could have kept going, but he still didn't want to admit quite how much she meant to him, how much he craved her.

Her expression was hard to read—Chloe's smile was fading as she pulled away again.

"I'll meet you at the bar in ten," she told him.

Ryder stood and stared after her, checked out her butt like he always did, admired her long hair that was so fun to wrap around his fist when they were in bed. But for the first time in his life, he knew that if she walked out of his life right now, she wouldn't be easy to replace. Before it had always been about having fun. Now he was starting to realize that there was only one person he wanted to keep having fun with, and that scared the shit out of him. His time with Chloe was coming to an end— the minute she had what she wanted she'd be gone.

So why the hell was his brain going into overdrive trying to think up ways to convince her to stay?

Chapter 17

Chloe wriggled her black dress down lower and checked out her cleavage in the mirror. Thank god she'd already had the dress packed in her car. She might be doing the gambling tonight instead of just being bait to distract the men, but she still wanted to try to put them off their game if she could. Her push-up bra was doing its job, and she squirted a little perfume between her breasts— that was for Ryder's benefit when he was up close and personal with her later on. Chloe ran her fingers through her hair one last time and applied some more lip gloss before stuffing her things back in her bag.

Her heart was racing, mind and body wired over what she was about to do. She'd tried so hard to leave this life behind, told herself she'd never play again no matter what the stakes, and yet just the thought of what she was about to do was enough to ignite her pulse. All she wanted was a life far removed from gambling, a clean lifestyle where she worked hard and was respected for what she did. Not to mention a husband one day and a family. And yet here she was playing poker again. Chloe laughed. Not all roads led to Oz though, and to get to where she needed to be, she had to use the one skill she knew wouldn't let her down.

She took one last look at herself in the mirror and headed for the door, entering the bar and making her way toward Ryder. She spotted him straightaway, his big frame perched on a barstool. He was holding a beer bottle to the side of his face.

"How you feeling?" she asked, talking directly into his ear and loving the smile she received in response. He dropped the beer to the counter and turned.

"Holy hell." Ryder let out a low wolf whistle and took her hand, turning her so she did a twirl on the spot. "Damn, you look good."

It was the dress she pulled out when she wanted to impress, so she loved that Ryder had noticed. He was so tall she was able to wear five-inch heels and not even come close to meeting his height, and when he stood he looped her arm through his and leaned in close.

"Parker's not going to know what hit him tonight."

Ryder retrieved his arm and took hold of her hand instead, nodding to the guy standing outside the room they were about to walk into. It wasn't like they needed an invite to go in, but someone had obviously made it clear they didn't want just anyone wandering on in, not with the kind of money they bet in there on any given night.

"Let's do this," she muttered as they headed for the table, hating the way all the men ogled her the second they saw her. But she'd dressed this way for a reason and she needed to ignore them, just focus on what she was here to do. The only man she liked checking her out so openly was Ryder.

"Well, if it ain't pretty boy come back for another hiding." Parker laughed furiously at his own joke. Chloe glanced at Ryder, knew he'd love nothing more than to punch the guy's lights out, but she admired the way he kept his cool. They had a plan and she doubted he'd let anything rattle him, not with the stakes she was going to be playing for.

"Settle down fellas, I'm just here to let my girl have a flutter." Ryder nodded at Parker. "I haven't forgotten what I owe."

All the men had a chuckle at that, but one of the older guys stood up and pulled a chair over, making space for Chloe.

"Come and sit next to me, love. I won't bite."

Ryder's hand was steady against the small of her back, the tiny amount of pressure he was applying telling her he was there for her. But it was all up to her now. Ryder would be in the room, but otherwise she was on her own.

"You supplying the ready cash?" Parker asked. "Don't take offense, sweetheart, but you ain't exactly gonna have enough money from tending the bar to play here."

Chloe forced a giggle and leaned back to press a kiss to Ryder's jaw, lazily wiping away the lipstick she'd left. "He's a real darlin', this one. Said I could bet all I wanted just to learn the game."

"Hey, so long as he hasn't forgotten about our last bet, I don't have no problem taking more of this asshole's money."

Chloe watched as Ryder's jaw tightened, his actions giving away how he really felt about Parker.

"So can she play or not?" Ryder asked.

"You joining us?"

Ryder shrugged and glanced at Chloe. He'd planned on just getting a drink and watching, but he didn't want to draw attention to himself. "Yeah, why not."

He pulled up a chair from another table as Chloe made her way around the other side, sitting between two of the other guys. Ryder waved for a couple of drinks.

"Y'all have to go easy on me, boys," she said with a giggle. "I've only played a few times in Vegas."

"Watch and learn," Parker said, opening a fresh pack of cards. "I'll never say no to cleavage like that joining the table."

Ryder's temper flared but he just took the drink placed in front of him and enjoyed a long, slow sip. He could pummel the guy's face in later; tonight was about following Chloe's plan.

"Any of you fellas keen to tell me how much money we're playing for?" Chloe asked.

It was almost impossible not to smile at her doe eyes and glinting smile. Chloe was making the perfect impression of a dumb woman wanting a flutter with cards, and he couldn't wait to sit back and watch. He owed her so much if she won, more than he could ever repay, and he intended on making his appreciation well known as soon as he got the chance.

"You actually played this game before?" Parker asked. "We ain't got no time to teach you."

Ryder pulled his chair in closer to the table, looked the other men in the eye. He didn't need this turning sour before they even got started. "I'm good for whatever she bets. She's got cash in her purse to get her started and she knows an ace from a queen."

There were a few sniggers, but even Parker looked more relaxed.

"You got me those keys?" Parker asked, raising an eyebrow as he dealt out the cards. "And we're playing straight poker here darlin', not Texas Hold 'Em."

Ryder took a slow sip of his drink, keeping his gaze firmly trained on the enemy. "Just getting a few things in order first."

He was desperate to clench his fists and slam them into something, but instead he glanced at Chloe, returning her smile.

"Come on, let's play poker," Ryder said. "It's time I showed this lady how to win a card game."

Ryder was prepped to lose. Chloe had told him what to do if he ended up having to play, to distract the table by losing an amount that'd make most people cringe.

The cards were dealt and Ryder took a peek. Nothing remarkable. He thumbed the edge of his stack of five, watching the others as they took a look at theirs. Chloe was grinning, glancing down at hers more often than any seasoned gambler would.

Parker looked to his right. "I'll bet a grand to get things started."

Ryder nodded. "Yep." He pushed a wad of cash into the center of the table.

One of the guys folded and Chloe looked up, wide-eyed. "Um, me too. One thousand."

Parker sniggered, then discarded two cards and dealt himself two. They did the rounds until they were back at Chloe again and she shook her head.

"Sweetheart, if you're not happy with your hand, you remember what to do, right?" Ryder asked.

She laughed. "I might be blond but I'm not slow."

The betting got to five thousand before Ryder folded, losing his money. Chloe folded and dropped her cards faceup so everyone could see them. A classic mistake and one she'd made deliberately.

Ryder groaned loudly, shaking his head. "Chloe, that was an okay hand."

"You're lucky she's got money," one of the guys grumbled. "This ain't some learners table, King."

Ryder waved to the waitress for another two drinks. "Sorry, boys. She'll get the hang of it this time around."

Ryder winked at Chloe as she bent forward, her full breasts almost spilling from the low-cut dress she was wearing. A necklace dipped dangerously low into her cleavage, as good as swallowed up, and Ryder glanced at Parker and saw he wasn't the only one who'd noticed.

"You wanna stop checking out my girl?" Ryder asked, slamming his hands down on the tabletop.

"Hey, you brought her here. There's the door."

Parker's smarmy smile cut straight through Ryder, who knew exactly what Parker had in mind for Chloe, or would have had in mind if he had it his way. There were plenty of women who regretted getting into bed with the town's local asshole, which was one of the reasons Ryder had wanted to knock him down a peg the last time he'd come up against him. Ryder might like bedding women, but he also loved the fairer sex—he'd never raise his fist to a woman, and he'd never take pleasure in sharing every intimate detail of what happened between him and any woman, either. He still remembered the last time he'd seen Parker humiliate a girl at a bar, and it made him sick.

Chloe's dress was starting to stick to her, perspiration beading lightly across every inch of her skin. She wasn't nervous, but the buzz of being back at the table and playing for big stakes was a thrill she couldn't deny. It didn't help that the men were a bunch of idiots, most of them drunker than they should have been to bet so much cash, but it was Parker she had her sights set on.

Her hand was good, and it killed her to act like she didn't have half a brain. The men she'd played against in the past had known who they were up against, whose daughter she was and that she wasn't a featherweight, but these men had no idea. And it was working to her advantage. Only now was she starting to play like normal, not giving anything away.

"I'll raise to ten."

Parker sniggered. "Dollars?"

"Grand," she quipped straight back. Ryder was looking at her but she ignored him, slipping dangerously away from the persona she'd been playing and wishing she could take her words back. She cleared her throat. "Is that too much?"

"For me? Don't fuck with me, little lady."

Parker matched her bet and Ryder bowed out. He'd lost close to twenty thousand for the night, and she was sure he'd be sweating it by now. She'd lost her fair share too, but it was time to turn the game around.

She held her three queens. It wasn't unbeatable by any means, but she'd been studying Parker long enough to be fairly confident that he was about to lose. Ryder had gotten cocky when he'd played him, had been drinking too much and only looking at the obvious signs, but she'd watched the man like a hawk, as well as the others. When he had a good hand he stared a little too long, and with this one he'd barely glanced at it. There was no change in his face regardless of what hand he had, except the smack he talked when he was trying to make out like he was about to win, but she knew what she'd seen and he definitely had a tell.

The rest of the table had folded; it was just the two of them now. Chloe waited, watched him, nauseous just acknowledging the way he looked at her, the way he licked his lips and glanced at her cleavage almost every few minutes.

"It's show-and-tell time," he said, his voice way too loud despite the noise in the room.

She dropped her cards and fanned them out in front of her, waiting for him to do the same. Parker's face was dark as he turned his cards over, not even close to beating her.

"Lucky," he sniggered, looking at Ryder. "Maybe you should let the little lady do all your betting for you."

Ryder leveled Parker with his gaze and she couldn't take her own eyes off him. His shoulders were squared, jaw like it was carved from stone as he considered Parker. "You saying you want to bet big again?"

Parker laughed. "What, put your ranch on the table again?"

Ryder shrugged, as if it was completely inconsequential to him. She admired the role he was playing, knew how hard it must be for him, and inside she wanted to scream. Parker had played right into their hands, suggesting the ranch before they had to try to bring it up.

"We both know you'd be too chickenshit to do that, Parker," Ryder said in a loud voice, glancing around the table as he did so. "You've been wanting to get your hands on King land for longer than you probably even remember."

"Who the fuck are you calling chickenshit?" asked Parker.

Chloe cleared her throat and reached across the table, dropping her hand over Parker's. She purposely angled her body away from Ryder, looked Parker straight in the eye.

"I'm starting to really get the hang of this. Can we just play again?"

Parker sniggered and Ryder took it as his cue, slamming his glass down on the table so hard it threatened to break. "Fuck this. I'm outta here."

He didn't go far, just to the bar, and she glanced over her shoulder and shrugged.

"Hey, are you sure you haven't played before?" one of the men asked as she was dealt her hand.

"If you mean in college, then yeah," she said, her cards on the table facedown. "Strip poker was a real favorite at the frat houses."

She received a few laughs for that. The betting started and she matched what was on offer, making sure her breathing stayed even as she considered her cards, counted out the six seconds she was allowed to look at what she had before putting them down again. Everything she did when she was playing was practiced, consistent. She had no tell, nothing that anyone could read when they played against her. She counted out the seconds every time so she never took any longer looking at her hand, whether it was good or not.

"So tell me, Parker. Was Ryder right? Are you too scared to bet his ranch against, say, me?"

There were four of them playing now, but she could see the other two guys shifting in their seats. The last thing they wanted was to bet up that big.

"Why would I bet a ranch when you've got jackshit to bet against it?"

"You have a hundred grand on you?"

He laughed and looked at the other guys. "You hearing this?"

"I'm deadly serious. I want to bet a hundred, and if you don't have the cash to join me, why not bet the ranch?" She laughed. "Unless you're about to fold, or you're too scared to bet against a girl?"

This time his laugh lacked confidence. "You're good for a hundred?"

Chloe made a show of squaring her five cards into a perfect little pile before bending to retrieve her purse and pulling out a wad of thousand-dollar bills. "Yes." She pushed them into the center of the table.

"I ain't fucking folding and you're bluffing," he said, knocking back the rest of his whiskey. "I'd love to take that hundred K off you, so yeah, go for it. The ranch is up for grabs."

Chloe wished she could see the look on Ryder's face, but she pushed all thoughts of him from her mind.

She watched as Parker only discarded two cards. Her hand wasn't terrible, but it wasn't great either. But she knew what she had to do. The other two players had folded, so now it was only her and Parker, just like it had been when Ryder had lost to him. But now the ranch was already on the table, whereas last time Ryder had bet it right at the end. If she was playing to win with her hand she would have discarded a couple of cards, but she knew better than anyone that all she had to do was make him think she was holding the perfect hand already.

Chloe smiled at Parker, knowing there was little chance of charming him with a seductive gaze and flash of her cleavage any longer. If he hadn't already, he was about to figure out that he'd been played by a seasoned pro. She put her cards down, glancing at them on purpose, and grinned as she reached into her bag and pulled out some more cash. She slid the smaller pile onto the table, pushing it forward.

"Here's another twenty, just to make this fun," she purred. "What do you say?"

"I say you fucking lied when you said you hadn't played before," Parker growled out.

"Who, me?" she asked, drumming her nails on the table. "Now what do you say? Are you up for it, or don't you have that kind of cash to play with?"

Chloe was acting a role, and it was one she loved as much as she despised it. The truth was, doing this kind of thing was a thrill, especially with someone else's money.

"Would you rather it be thirty?" she asked, not breaking eye contact with him for a second, smiling to herself when he glanced down at his cards in a panic. He never turned them over, he wouldn't have needed to, but she'd fast learned that his tell was the glance down.

"You little bitch," he sneered, slamming his fist onto the table and standing, leaning forward in an obvious attempt to intimidate her.

"It's just a card game, isn't that right, fellas?" she said with a giggle.

No one laughed. Parker's anger was tangible in the room. Out of the corner of her eye, she saw Ryder move away from the bar and come toward her. She was still staring at Parker but her heart was starting to pound—there was nothing harmless about the man she'd just swindled. To him, she doubted it'd be losing the ranch that was the problem, it was being humiliated and beaten by a woman in front of his gambling buddies.

"Fuck you," he yelled, throwing his cards down before his hands moved fast, cupping the table and hurling it over.

Chloe jumped up but she didn't move fast enough, stumbling back on her heels as glasses came flying in her direction, smashing around her, the table hitting her leg as she went sailing across the floor. She fell back, arms flailing out to break her fall, anticipating the thud of her head, but her fall was broken by someone else. Ryder was on his knees, big arms catching her as fast as she'd gone down.

"Chloe?"

She leaned back into Ryder, sighed as he peered down at her like she was broken. The room was spinning a little but she was fine—thank god she hadn't had more than one drink otherwise she'd really be tripping.

"It's no big deal," she muttered, tugging at her dress

to make sure she wasn't showing off more than she'd intended on.

"He's dead," Ryder snarled, setting her on her feet and running a hand down her back.

"Leave him," Chloe murmured, slipping an arm around Ryder's waist to pull him closer. "We did it, I won the game, so let's just go. The ranch is yours."

In the seconds between the table being flipped and Ryder coming to her rescue, she'd forgotten about the hothead who'd sent her flying, but now he was coming at them like a furious bull about to charge.

"You watch your back," Parker snarled. "No one makes a fool of me and gets away with it."

Chloe grasped Ryder's hand, as much to settle him as to hold him back.

"Get out of my face, Parker. She beat you fair and square; her hand was better than yours. You knew what you were playing for."

She relaxed at the tone of Ryder's voice. She'd expected him to be all fists blazing, but he was staying calm.

"Come on, baby, let's go," Chloe said, bending down to gather up their money while Ryder and Parker squared off, neither moving an inch. She stuffed it all in her purse, wanting to get out as fast as she could.

Once she'd finished, Chloe stood and looped her hand through Ryder's arm, playing the part of dumb blonde one last time as she winked at Parker.

"Thanks for the game," she said, her tone as sweet as pie. "Now why don't y'all hurry off home and stop making empty threats."

Her leg hurt from the fall, but she squared her shoulders and walked on her heels as effortlessly as she could, not wanting him to take any satisfaction in what he'd done. She'd beaten him, it was over, she'd bluffed and he'd folded. Now she just wanted to get the hell out of dodge.

"I don't make empty threats, darlin'."

Chloe paused when Ryder did, but she didn't bother looking back. She let him do the talking—she'd won his ranch back, the rest was up to him.

"Oh, they're empty," Ryder said, his voice low and menacing. "Because if you even think about hurting this girl? It'll be the last thing you ever think. *Or do.*"

Ryder didn't waste time hanging around. He tugged Chloe tight to his body and they walked out of the room, through the bar, and out into the parking lot. Once they were finally outside, the cool night air shocked her back to reality.

"We did it," she whispered, spinning in Ryder's arms and looping hers around his neck. "We actually did it. I was so worried I'd ruined my winning streak in Vegas, but we did it."

He shook his head, dipped down to press a slow, lingering kiss to her lips. "No, Chloe, you did it," he murmured against her mouth.

"And I never doubted you for a second."

She sighed as he kissed her again, arching her body so she was pressed tight to him all the way from her pelvis to her breasts. For once she didn't have to stand on tiptoe, her heels making up most of their height difference.

"I'm so pleased you have your ranch back," Chloe told him. To start with she'd thought he was an idiot, a guy with too much trust fund money to appreciate what he had. Now she realized that he'd just made a stupid mistake, and she doubted he'd ever do anything so reckless again.

"You've got no idea," he muttered. "I don't think I'll ever be able to thank you enough."

Chloe stepped back and held her purse out to him. "Here's your money," she said.

Ryder let out a low laugh. "It's yours."

"No," she protested. "It's too much. We had a deal and . . ."

"It's yours. You saved my ranch, Chloe. You deserve every goddamn penny."

A vehicle approaching too fast made her turn, taking Ryder's hand and tugging him back toward the entrance of the bar. It slowed just in time, but it took her a moment to recognize that it was Nate's truck, the lights blinding in the dark. The driver's door opened and Nate's eyes locked on hers.

"You're smiling. Does that mean you won the game?"

Chloe nodded and Ryder hugged her protectively to his side. "You're a bit late to be backup crew. Parker already lost it in there."

"I bet he did." Nate's scowl was replaced a smile now. She knew he'd been pissed at his brother, but angry didn't suit him anywhere near as well as happy did.

"Will you get a ride home with your brothers?" she asked, taking a step away from Ryder, wanting to put some distance between them.

"Ah, no," he muttered, sliding his arm back around her and trying to tug her back in again. When she resisted he moved in front of her so she had to stare at him. "Aren't we heading out to celebrate?"

She shook her head, forcing herself to look at him. "It's over now, Ryder. We always said it was only until we both got what we needed, right?" Her voice was softer than usual, her uncertainty audible.

"Fuck that." He took her hand and linked his fingers with hers. "You're not going anywhere yet. Come on."

"You lovebirds coming or not?" Nate called out. "We're just heading home for a few quiet beers."

"Chloe?"

She wanted to say no, knew she *should* be saying no. They'd made a deal and she'd made it because she didn't want to get hurt. Because she didn't need a man right now, needed to stay focused on her goals and building a future for herself with no complications. But she did want Ryder, no matter what she tried to tell herself.

"We can talk about this tomorrow," he said, running one hand gently down her face and pulling her forward with his other hand at the same time. "Let's just pretend like our expiration date isn't until then, huh?"

Chloe nodded, squeezing his hand. What harm was there in one more day?

Chapter 18

Ryder poured Chloe a glass of wine and carried it over to the sofa. She'd kicked off her shoes and had her feet curled up, leaning into a cushion and chatting with his brothers like it was completely normal for her to be holding court with the pair of them. He chuckled as he joined her—trust Chloe to be able to charm his brothers so quickly.

"I take it you've given them the blow-by-blow account?" he asked.

Chloe shook her head, her long blond hair falling over her shoulders and resting on her breasts. Ryder shot Nate a dirty look—his brother's eyes had dropped instantly to her chest. The smile he received in return made him scowl, but it was over fast, with Nate focused on Chloe again, only this time it was her eyes he was looking at.

"I was waiting for you before we gave them the lowdown."

Ryder had to give his brothers credit—they had

every right to still want to throttle him, but they'd treated Chloe like a long-lost friend and they'd given him a break, too. He went to scratch his face, then cringed. Maybe it was the bruise around his eye that was reminding them to go easy on him.

"I hope it was me you were waiting on."

Ryder and his brothers all turned at the deep voice and saw their grandfather standing in the open doorway that led from the living room to the hall. He was dressed in a wool sweater and slacks, despite being told to stay in his pajamas in bed, his silver hair brushed and his eyes bright. They were hoping he'd stay at home longer this time, but Ryder guessed it would be a few weeks at best before he ended up back in the hospital.

"Granddad, what are you doing out of bed?" Chase asked, the first of them to jump up and go over to him.

Clay shrugged off Chase's hand and slapped his grandson on the back instead. "I heard a lady's voice and I thought, what in god's name am I doing stuck in here when there's a woman to meet." His chuckle made them all smile. "If I don't have long then what's the point wasting it on my back?"

Ryder smiled when Chloe uncurled her feet and stood up, holding out her hand when Clay came near. She stepped forward and clasped his hand, laughing as he pulled her in to plant a kiss on her cheek.

"You must be Clay. I've heard so much about you."

Clay let go of her hand and sat down in the armchair Chase had vacated. "It's nice to meet you, Chloe," he said. "Now tell me if you had a successful night? Are you celebrating already or have you not played this Parker fellow yet?"

Chloe sat back down, closer to Ryder this time, their thighs pressed together. "I won the ranch back and I fleeced him out of his cash, too."

Clay laughed like Ryder hadn't heard in a long time, his shoulders shaking first from laughter and then from the cough that took over. They all waited, knowing he wouldn't want a fuss. Ryder glanced up and saw Clay's live-in nurse hovering in the hallway—help was on hand if they needed it.

"Your lovely grandsons invited me back for a few drinks to celebrate," Chloe continued, ignoring the fact that Clay was so obviously sick, her smile and eye contact with him unwavering. "I was just about to tell them how I did it."

"Did you have a winning hand?" Clay asked. "Or did you bluff and make him sweat?"

Chloe grinned. "Sounds like I'm talking to a poker aficionado."

"Takes one to know one," he replied.

Ryder raised his eyebrows when he realized Chase was staring at him, his brother as surprised as he was that Clay was up to chatting with Chloe so late at night. It was like having her around had brought the old man back to life.

They were watching Chloe, all eyes fixed on her. And then it hit him—how the hell was this his last night with her? All this time, hanging out with her and having fun, knowing that it was only short term, and now . . . *no*. He wasn't letting her walk away without a goddamn fight, that was for sure.

"He probably had a better hand than me," she confessed, taking a sip of her wine and glancing up under ooded lashes. "But I kept my cards, made him think I lready had the winning hand from the start, and he fell or it hook, line, and sinker. I bluffed and he folded."

"Bullshit," Nate said good-naturedly. "Parker's legndary at the card table."

Chloe's low laugh made Ryder smile straight back at er. "Is it about now that I confess to playing poker since was big enough to walk?"

They all laughed and Ryder jumped up to get Clay a lrink when he started coughing. "Water?" he asked.

Clay frowned. "Whiskey, son. How many times do I ave to tell you boys that I drink whiskey, not goddamn vater?"

They all exchanged glances, but it was Chloe who poke.

"Well, get the man a whiskey, someone," she drawled, naking them laugh all over again.

"My grandson tells me you were studying law?"

"She'll be back in law school soon, Granddad. Now hat her bet paid off."

He watched as Clay looked at Chloe. "Is that right? You blackmailed my grandson into some sort of deal to ay your tuition fees?"

Chloe looked guilty. "Yes," she admitted. "Although lackmail isn't the exact word I'd use. More like we ame to a mutually beneficial agreement."

Nate went and got a few more beers, grinning while e walked. "Darlin', that's blackmail through and hrough, no matter how you try to sell it."

"And it's damn fine blackmail," Clay continued. "Ryler deserved every penny he lost to you and then ome."

Ryder held up his hands, knowing he should be of fended but liking the fact that Chloe was holding cour with his family. A roomful of King men was intimidat ing at the best of times, let alone during the grillin they'd been giving Chloe. And besides, he knew it wasn' blackmail—they'd helped each other and it had al worked out great.

Chloe laughed. "I'll be heading back to law schoc as soon as I can," she told his granddad. "I had to finis partway through the year due to some, ah, financia hardship, but the university was very understanding. had good grades, but if you can't pay your tuition it turn out all the brains in the world can't help a girl."

"I think we need to drink to Chloe," Ryder said, grin ning at her. "For saving my ass," he toasted.

Chloe held up her glass and took a sip, curling he long legs back up beneath her. "It's time I put my card playing alter ego back in her box."

"Why?" Nate asked. "Seems like you did a damn fin job out there tonight."

"Been there, done that," she told him. "It's a danger ous game to get used to."

"Yeah," Chase said with a laugh, stretching his foc out to kick Ryder. "Let's hope this idiot's learned his les son, too."

"I'm sorry," Ryder said, eyes trained on his grand father. "It's all turned out for the best, but I want yo all to know how sorry I am."

Nate grunted and Chase held up his drink, but it wa Clay he was waiting for, his acceptance what he needec

"All's right in the world," Clay said. "And with tha I'm heading back to bed." He swallowed the rest of hi whiskey down and stood, waving Ryder away when he jumped up to help him. "It was a pleasure to meet you, Chloe. Don't be a stranger. These boys need a woman like you around to straighten them out."

Chloe smiled up at Clay and they all said goodnight. Once he'd gone, it was Nate who spoke up first.

"So speaking about having you around," he started, "are you leaving now you've won, or has Prince Charming here convinced you to stay?"

Ryder could have killed him. This wasn't a conversation he wanted to start with his two brothers listening.

"Nate, tell me about the gorgeous brunette you were talking to earlier," Chloe asked, catching her bottom lip between her teeth for a moment while she stared at Nate. Ryder exchanged an amused glance with Chase. "You got pretty worked up when you saw her at the bar."

Nate wasn't laughing anymore, his expression serious. "She was no one. Just a girl I know."

Chloe raised her eyebrows, her smile teasing. "Sure. Whatever you say."

Nate grunted and tipped back his beer bottle, draining half of it in one long pull. "I get it. You don't ask me about her, I won't ask you about this douchebag over here." His laugh was husky. "You don't need to prove anything to me, I already believe you could cut me off at the knees if I played cards against you."

"And with that, I think it's time for me to call it a night, too," Chloe said, stretching her legs out and twirling her hair between her fingers. "Thanks for making me so welcome."

"Stay," Ryder blurted out, not caring that his brothers were listening. "Don't even think about packing up and heading back to Shelly's. It's late and you've been drinking."

He couldn't read Chloe's gaze, but he sure as hell hoped she wasn't about to walk out that door before he had the chance to thank her properly for what she'd done tonight. And try to convince her that she didn't need to flee Dallas quite so quickly just because she had money burning a hole in her back pocket.

"Well . . ." She glanced at his brothers, then looked back at him again. "I guess you're right."

Ryder didn't need any more encouragement to be convinced. "Damn right I am. We're off, boys."

Nate grinned. "You can stay here, you don't have to go running off to the guest house."

Ryder had no intention of answering his brother—they could tease him all they liked and not get a rise out of him right now. "Thanks for the offer, but we're outta here. I just won the place back, I think it deserves me staying there a night, right?"

The room seemed cooler than usual when they entered and Chloe went and sat on the bed. She listened to Ryder's boots echo out on the wooden floor in the kitchen, before the door was nudged open and he appeared in the room. She wrapped her arms around herself, wondering if maybe it was just her feeling the cold. Goose bumps ran the length of her body, her heart thudding when Ryder came and sat beside her, his thigh pressed hard to hers.

"Something's already changed between us, hasn't it?" he asked, angling his body so he was facing her, reaching out to wrap his fingers around her chin and tilt her face toward his.

"Yeah," she managed, suddenly finding it hard to look into his eyes when she usually loved gazing back at him.

"You don't have to go," he said.

Chloe's smile was sad. "Yes, Ryder, I do. I can't stay now."

"Because you're scared of Parker?"

No, because I'm scared of you. That's what she should have said because it was the truth, but she didn't.

"We had a deal. You didn't want this to be anything serious and neither did I," she said. "What happened to you wanting me just as your mistress?"

Ryder stroked her face, his touch so soft that it was impossible not to lean into it. "You've done something to me, Chloe. Screwed up my brain or something. And you were *never* just my mistress."

"How? Why?" she murmured, knowing as she asked that she should have stayed silent.

He shook his head and leaned in to kiss her. Chloe had every intention of turning her face away so they couldn't connect, and instead she was reaching out for him, cupping Ryder's skull to lock him in place. Her lips moved in time with his, drinking in the taste of him, committing to memory what it was like to have Ryder's arms around her, to be on his bed.

She didn't need him, or any man, but it wasn't about needing right now. It was about wanting something she already had and not wanting to let it go, no matter what she told herself. So much for putting her Band-Aid theory into practice.

"We can't do this," she whispered, trying to convince herself and failing.

"I want you, you want me," Ryder replied, gently pushing her back onto the bed, her head falling down into the feather-filled pillows. "Nothing's changed."

"Everything's changed," she managed. "After I won back the ranch—"

"Stop talking," he commanded, catching her wrists and pinning them above her head.

Chloe wanted to argue with him, but even more she wanted to feel his lips on every stretch of her bare skin, to have him inside of her. She could think of plenty of reasons why she should have said no, yet here she was lying beneath Ryder, her moans of pleasure impossible to swallow.

Chloe wriggled to let Ryder push up her dress, gasped as his mouth closed over her stomach, his kisses erotic as he plucked at her skin with his wet mouth.

"You can't bribe me with sex," she muttered, back arching as she shoved her dress down lower and his tongue darted inside her bra.

Ryder's head popped up and his grin was wicked. "No, but it's a damn good way to say thank you."

His mouth closed over the top of her breast and she relaxed back into the bed. He was right—this was the perfect way for him to say thank you. In the morning she could go and never come back, figure out how to tell him, *and herself*, that what they had was over. Tonight she could just enjoy being a woman in bed with a man, one who knew exactly how to touch her to send her over the edge again and again.

"If you make this good," Chloe gasped, locking her legs around Ryder when he dropped his body over hers, "I'll stay the night."

"Sweetheart, I'm gonna make this so good you'll never want to leave my bed."

"Cocky bastard," she grumbled.

She didn't need a man and she never had, but Ryder? *Damn.* For the first time in her life she could have settled down, could have finally let someone in close enough to give a shit about her, and yet here she was spending one last night in Ryder's arms. She had to protect herself, and the last thing she needed was to fool herself into thinking this was more than just a fling. One with lots of sex and plenty of hanging out together. Because even if she did let herself fall for him, stayed in this fantasy bubble, one day it would end. It always did, she knew that.

"Stop thinking," Ryder demanded, pulling back to look her in the eye. "There's nothing to think about, not while I'm at the helm."

And that's what scared her, letting Ryder take control even a little bit. It wasn't something she was used to doing and it made her feel helpless. She let him slip her dress off completely, yanking her panties, too. Then he stripped fast, discarding his boots, jeans, and T-shirt in record time, then covering her body with his.

Ryder locked eyes with her, gazing at her with a tenderness she'd never experienced before. It was like he

was reaching out to her, telling her he felt the same way
she did, although she doubted he'd have any idea of the
emotions running through her mind right now.

She wrapped her arms around Ryder, her legs around
his waist as he entered her. There was nothing rough this
time, none of their usual desperation. This time he
was gentle with her, treating her like it was her first
time, his strokes long and his gaze never wavering from
her as he moved back and forth.

"You are so beautiful," he murmured. "So damn
beautiful you take my breath away."

Ryder kissed her, his lips soft as he started to rock
harder and faster into her. She ran her hands over his
shoulders, down the strong planes of his back, and looked
up into his dark eyes. If this was their last night together,
she wanted to commit every part of him to memory so
she didn't forget a thing.

Chapter 19

Ryder's arm was going numb but he didn't move it. Chloe had fallen asleep, her shallow breathing only just audible, and he was still lying awake in the half light with her cradled in one arm, head tucked to his chest. They'd left the curtains open, letting moonlight drizzle inside, and because of it he could make out the features of Chloe's face, see her full lips slightly parted, her long dark lashes just touching the top of her cheekbones.

He'd fallen. No matter how hard he tried to convince himself he wanted Chloe because she was great in bed, or because she was fun to hang out with, it was way more than that and he knew it. Reality had come crashing in when she'd made it clear she was leaving, that their stupid agreement was real, and he didn't want her to go.

Ryder slowly inched his arm out from beneath her, pausing when she stirred. He dropped his legs over the edge of the bed, reached for his boxers and pulled them on, then walked barefoot from the room. On second thought he went back and got his jeans, headed for the kitchen to pour a nip of whiskey and grab his phone, then went and sat on the step outside the house.

He took a sip, then dialed Chase. He doubted either of his brothers would be asleep yet; they'd be drinking and talking shit still.

"Hey," Chase answered.

"Hey."

"Everything okay over there?"

Ryder put down his drink and leaned forward, elbows resting on his knees. "Where are you?"

"Just walked out the door, heading for my place."

"Want to swing past this way first instead?"

"Sure thing. See you soon."

Ryder finished his drink and hauled his body up to go get another. He paused in the bedroom doorway first, checked to see that Chloe was still sleeping, before grabbing another glass and the bottle of Wild Turkey. Then he headed back out to wait for his brother. The air outside was cool against his bare torso but he didn't bother going back in for a sweater; he just leaned against the wooden railing on the porch and stared into the dark looking for Chase.

"My phone usually only rings after midnight if it's a booty call." Chase laughed as he appeared out of the darkness, making his way up the steps and reaching for the glass Ryder was holding out.

"So what are we drinking for? Don't you have a gorgeous blonde in there keeping your bed warm?"

Ryder grunted. "Yeah." He poured them a nip each and joined Chase on the front step. "She's asleep."

"I don't mean to state the obvious, but what the hell

are you doing shooting the breeze with me out here when you could be asleep next to Chloe?"

"She's leaving in the morning." Ryder ground out the words, furious that she was getting to him so bad. "Tomorrow she walks away and it's over."

"You know you've been with her a few weeks now."

Ryder locked eyes with his brother, watched as he sipped his drink. "And?"

"And it means that you've been with her longer than you've been with any other woman before," Chase said. "You like her."

Ryder scowled. "Of course I like her."

"Then why are you sitting out here with me?"

He poured himself another nip and downed it, cringing as the straight liquor burned a fiery path down his throat and all the way to his gut. "Because I fucking love her," Ryder muttered.

Chase didn't say anything, just stared straight ahead out into the dark. He swirled his drink around in his glass before turning to face him. "You're serious."

Ryder nodded.

"Then do something about it."

He ground his teeth together, hated that he was even having this conversation with his brother. They didn't talk about feelings or any of that crap. They worked hard and played harder, enjoyed beautiful women but didn't stay with any one woman for long. And now here he was talking about . . . *fuck it*. He didn't even want to admit it to himself. He'd traveled all around the country, met beautiful women in so many different states, but he'd never fallen before. Never.

"She wants to go."

"Then make her stay," Chase replied.

"I shouldn't have told you," Ryder muttered, standing up and pacing down the porch. "Just forget I said anything."

Chase stood too, finishing his drink and leaving the glass on the railing. "Have you ever heard me say that about a girl before? Or Nate?"

Ryder shook his head. Of course not—they didn't fall in love, they had fun. Which was what he was supposed to have done with Chloe. The best part of what they had going on was that they'd both known it was a short-term thing, no strings.

"What's your point?" Ryder asked.

"You honestly feel that way about her, you have to tell her. Don't be a douchebag and let a woman like that slip away just because you're too scared to man up and be honest."

Ryder was listening, but he didn't answer. His brother was right, of course he was, but talking to him about it and actually telling Chloe were two entirely different things.

"Thanks for coming over."

Chase chuckled. "So that's it? I'm dismissed?"

"Yeah, and don't go telling Nate. The last thing I need is him giving me shit."

Chase walked up the step and came closer, giving him a one-armed hug and slapping him on the back. "We'd give you shit about a lot of things, but if you're serious about this girl? No fucking way."

Ryder watched him go, called out before he disappeared from sight completely. "Thanks, Chase."

His brother raised one hand in the air as he walked away. "Anytime."

Chase might have had a lot to drink, his swagger made that obvious, but his words had been real. If Ryder didn't stop Chloe from walking away now, didn't man up and tell her the truth? Then he might regret losing her for the rest of his life, and he wasn't prepared to take that chance.

He collected both glasses and left them on the counter before heading back into the bedroom. Ryder stripped and pulled the covers down, sliding into bed beside Chloe and scooping her into him. She stirred, snuggling in closer when he put his arms around her.

He loved her. He fucking loved her, and now he'd admitted it to himself and his brother.

Ryder dropped a kiss into Chloe's hair and held her tight. In the morning he'd tell her how he felt. Right now he needed to get some sleep.

Chapter 20

The room was still dark when Chloe woke. She turned carefully, not wanting to disturb Ryder as she slid out from underneath his arm. Before she'd fallen asleep everything had seemed perfect and now uncertainty was clawing at her mind, all her doubts creeping back in like they'd never left.

She had to go.

Chloe sat on the edge of the bed, glanced back at Ryder one last time. She'd started out being attracted to him because of the way he looked, then everything had changed until it was back to physical attraction again. And now? Now she didn't know how she felt, but she did know that the only way to walk away from him was to do it now. She needed to do it quick and fast.

She leaned over and kissed his cheek, pulling away as tears welled in her eyes, catching in her lashes as she stood up and gathered her things. Chloe dressed quickly and zipped her suitcase, grabbing her other still-packed bags, too, and walked out of the room, refusing to look back. If she did, she could so easily end up back in his arms, curled up beside him in bed again, when what she needed to do was stay focused on her future. On her plan.

She needed to finish her law degree. She needed to build a future for herself that didn't involved relying on a man. *She needed to walk away* now matter how bad she had it for him.

Chloe put down her luggage and grabbed her purse from the living room, pushing aside a sweatshirt of Ryder's to get it. She turned, then changed her mind, bending back down and grabbing the sweatshirt, tugging it over her head and wrapping herself in the familiar smell that was him. Just because she had to go didn't mean she hadn't loved every second of being with Ryder. The memories of being with him were enough to last a lifetime. Chloe checked her purse, divided the cash in half, and left the balance on the table. He'd promised to pay her tuition, then last night told her to take the money she'd won. She'd just take her portion of the cash and call them even—this was more than enough to see her through to graduation.

She walked as quickly as she could down the hall and slipped out the door, shutting it behind her and heading down the drive. Chloe dialed a cab without slowing down, hoping like hell she'd be able to get past the main house lugging all her things without one of Ryder's brothers seeing her. She couldn't explain what she was doing to anyone yet, because she still didn't know herself. All she knew was that she had to leave now, before she lost her nerve.

Tears pricked her eyes again and this time she let them fall. *It hurt.* It hurt so damn bad walking away, it was like a stake through her heart. Ryder had shown her what it was like to be with a real man, a man who called it like it was, who wasn't afraid of saying what he wanted and wasn't intimated by a woman who did the same. He'd treated her with respect and made her feel . . . Chloe hugged her arms around herself, inhaling the scent of Ryder on his sweatshirt, wishing his arms were still around her. He'd made her feel loved, and no matter how much she told herself it didn't matter to her, it damn well did.

The sunlight falling across his face woke Ryder. He reached out, hand feeling around the bed for Chloe, anticipating the warmth of her bare skin. Instead he connected with a cold sheet. Ryder groaned and sat up, the covers falling away as he rubbed his eyes and looked around the room. Chloe was gone, her clothes no longer in a rumpled heap on the floor. Damn it. He'd been looking forward to waking up to her body, warm and soft from sleep, and instead he was either going to have to wait for her to come back to bed, or ignore his hard-on and get dressed.

He waited a couple of minutes, then decided to go looking for her. The house was silent as he walked toward the kitchen, doing up his jeans as he moved.

"Chloe?" he called. "You out here?"

Ryder stopped when he realized she wasn't in the kitchen or living room. Hmmm. She must have taken his truck and gone on a coffee run. If it meant keeping her in bed for longer in the morning, he was definitely going to have to invest in a coffee machine. He wandered to the side window and cast a glance outside. *What the hell?* His truck was still parked where he'd left it. There were no other vehicles at the guest house, and unless she'd gone for a walk . . .

He scanned the living room, then went back into the bedroom to see if she'd left a note anywhere. Nothing. Then he checked his phone. Ryder's heart was starting to pound too fast for his liking—this was looking less and less like a coffee run and more like . . .

She'd gone.

Ryder dialed Chase and got his voice mail. Damn it. He was probably out doing the rounds on the ranch already. He went to throw his phone down, then changed his mind and called Nate. His brother picked up on the second ring.

"Mornin'," Nate said.

"Hey. Have you seen Chloe?"

Nate made a noncommittal noise.

"Nate. You seen her or not?" Ryder demanded.

"I saw a cab pulling away about an hour ago. I didn't think anything of it at the time but . . ."

"Fuck." Ryder threw his phone down on the bed and stormed toward the door, marching outside and then turning on his heel and walking straight back in again. What the hell was he doing? She'd left. Chloe was gone. They'd talked about it being their last night and he'd just presumed he'd be able to talk her around in the morning, that she wouldn't really go when they were having so much fun together.

He'd been wrong.

Ryder sat down on the bed, head in his hands. Maybe

it was karma. He'd finally met a woman he could fall for and she'd up and left him like the time they'd spent together meant nothing.

His phone rang and he reached for it, seeing Chase's name appear. He wasn't going to answer, then changed his mind.

"Hey."

"What's happening?" Chase asked.

"You need a hand this morning?"

"What about—"

Ryder clenched his right fist, wishing he could smash it into something. "Don't ask. Just put me to work and don't mention her name. I told you I was going to work alongside you now that I'm back, and I wasn't lying."

There was silence on the other end for a moment. "Meet me at the barn. I've got cattle to move and some fences to check. I was going to get the guys to do it, but how about we head out just the two of us?"

Ryder unclenched his fist. His brothers might give him shit a lot of the time, but when it came to something like this, he knew he could count on them not to be assholes.

"Thanks. I'll see you in ten."

Ryder left his phone on the bed and pulled on socks and a shirt. He went into the bathroom, brushed his teeth, and headed for the back door, tugging on his boots. *To hell with Chloe.* He'd make Chase work him till he dropped, and do his best to forget all about her. Although he knew damn well there was no way in hell he'd be able to get her out of his head.

"Ryder!"

He looked over his shoulder, seeing Nate jogging in

his direction. His oldest brother was dressed in worn-out jeans and a checked shirt with the sleeves rolled up—nothing like his usual weekday attire.

"What are you doing?" Ryder asked, making an effort to wipe the scowl from his face. It wasn't Nate's fault Chloe had walked out on him.

"Chase said you're working on the ranch with him today," Nate said, catching up and falling into step beside him. "I decided it was about time I did the same."

Ryder chuckled. "You're sounding more and more like Granddad every day."

"You can't run an empire without getting your hands dirty on the land every once in a while," Nate said, perfectly imitating their granddad's commanding voice.

"Damn right," Ryder muttered.

They walked in silence for a while as they headed for the barn. Ryder rolled up his sleeves and glanced at the sky, the day already heating up even though it was early.

"So are we talking about Chloe today or not?" Nate asked.

Ryder didn't look up, just kept walking. He shook his head. "Not a chance."

Nate slapped him on the back and kept his hand on his shoulder until Chase appeared and he waved to him. "Sure thing. Let's find some cattle to round up then, huh?"

Ryder stopped and watched his brothers, wishing he wasn't feeling so pissed off with the world. Hanging out with them both for the day should be fun, and instead all he wanted to do was kill something, take his frustration out on someone with his fists.

"Hey, when's your next bull ride?" Chase asked as he

joined them, throwing Ryder a halter and lead rope. They all walked side by side to the corrals to catch their horses, collecting their saddles on the way. Ryder slung his over his arm.

"I've got the National Finals in a month. Nothing till then." He grunted. Damn it. The last thing he needed was to think about heading to Vegas again after the time he'd had there with Chloe. "And don't even think about giving me shit about riding, not today."

Nate nodded. "Fair call. You get a twenty-four-hour pass."

Ryder haltered his horse and gave him a quick brush down, following every indent and groove. There was something therapeutic about brushing down an animal—he could have done it for hours.

"You want us to come watch this year?" Chase asked.

"Of course we're going," Nate said with a chuckle. "We can take the jet, make the most of going to see our little brother in Vegas, meet some gorgeous women . . . Do you need any more reasons to go?"

Chase laughed. "Hell no. We're definitely going there."

"Sounds like a plan." Ryder tried not to grumble and found it impossible. He was pissed off and he wanted to get going, to do something to take his mind off Chloe and every other thought running through his head like a steam train. He quickly finished saddling and bridling his horse and led him from the corral, checking the girth one last time and hauling himself up. "I'm gonna go ride off some steam. I'll catch up with you guys soon."

Ryder didn't wait around to hear what they had to say. He nudged his horse into a walk and fought the urge to kick him straight into a canter as they headed north. The only thing that stopped him was not wanting to injure a good horse, and not wanting to be a complete asshole. As soon as the horse was limbered up he'd go for a good gallop before meeting up with his brothers, and if that didn't help then nothing would. Except for maybe whiskey. If all else failed, he'd have to resort to drinking himself stupid.

Chapter 21

"So let me get this straight."

Chloe curled up on the sofa beside Shelly, her spoon lodged in a tub of ice cream as she pulled the blanket over herself. When she retrieved it she slowly licked the chocolate off, taking her time to avoid having to look at her friend.

"You have an amazing time with Ryder, your words not mine," Shelly said, waving her spoon as she spoke. "He whisks you away on his jet, you have crazy good sex, and he's fun and rich. *And then you just walk away*, never to be heard from again."

Chloe pulled a face. "You make me sound like a real bitch."

Shelly patted her hand and frowned. "Sweetheart, you *were* a real bitch to him. I'm sorry, but you were."

"We had an arrangement," Chloe told her. "I got his ranch back, we had some fun, and then it had to end."

"Did you sign a contract with an end date? You know

the kind with a penalty clause if you don't follow through?"

Chloe dipped her spoon back into the ice cream and rolled her eyes. "I know what you're getting at but it just wasn't that simple."

"No, it was that simple, you're just scared."

Chloe glared at Shelly. "I'm not scared. You have no idea."

"Bull," Shelly insisted. "You're scared you were falling for him and you couldn't stand not being in control. I know you better than you know yourself sometimes, Chlo, and you had it bad for that guy. Just admit it."

"Fine, I like him. A lot. But it was better to end now than . . ."

"Than what?" Shelly asked. "Seriously, are you that scared of giving a relationship a chance? *Any relationship?* Could it be any worse than how you feel walking away from him now if it didn't work out in a month or a year?"

"It wasn't a relationship," Chloe snapped. "We were having fun and now it's over. End of story. It wasn't real to begin with."

Shelly put her ice cream down on the coffee table and reached for the remote, hitting play on the DVD. "You know you can deny it all you want, but you're not fooling anyone but yourself."

Chloe didn't answer. Shelly was right, of course she was. But what could she do about it now? She'd walked out on Ryder without even saying goodbye. There was no chance he'd forgive her now, and part of her knew that's why she'd done it, so he couldn't talk her out of it and so she couldn't just change her mind and go back to him.

Shelly paused the DVD and reached for Chloe's hand, holding tight and squeezing. "Can you just tell me why you're so scared of something happening? Why can't you just see what happens with him?"

Chloe took a big breath, swallowing away the choke of emotion that was bubbling hard in her throat. Growing up she'd moved around so much that she'd never had time to make friends, hadn't found it easy to make close girlfriends, which meant that talking about her feelings or decisions didn't come easy to her. If her mom hadn't disappeared and left her, maybe things would have been different, but she hated thinking about *what ifs*.

"I can't," she said. "I just . . ."

Shelly squeezed harder. "You can. What's scaring you, Chloe? You don't have to bottle it all up."

Chloe pushed her ice cream away and curled up under the blanket, tucking her feet up and leaning back into the sofa. She shut her eyes, biting on her lower lip before finally meeting Shelly's concerned gaze.

"Anyone I've ever let close to me has let me down, except you," she said. "I don't want to fall in love with a man and let him hurt me. I don't want to rely on anyone. I don't . . ." Chloe tried to laugh but it sounded more like a cry. "Sorry, you don't need to hear all this."

Shelly leaned forward and put her arms around her, drawing her in for a big hug. "Sweetheart, if not me then who?"

Chloe blinked away tears. "I'm not used to letting anyone in."

"You're in love with him, aren't you?" Shelly asked.

"That's why you ran away from him. Because you love him."

A big sob escaped Chloe's mouth, and the more she tried to fight it the worse it became. Tears ran down her cheeks as she let her friend hold her, wishing to hell she'd never met Ryder in the first place. All these years, all her adult life, she'd refused to let anyone in, never let a man get close enough to hurt her, and yet here she was sobbing over a man she'd chosen to walk away from.

"It'll all work out," Shelly whispered as she stroked Chloe's hair. "Ryder King isn't a man to give up when the going gets tough, you hear me? I'll bet he'll forget all about you leaving him like that if you tell him how you feel."

Chloe shook her head, wiping away her tears with her hand. Shelly was wrong. Ryder would hate her for what she'd done, and besides, he'd only wanted her to stay longer because they'd had so much fun together. She had to get her life back on track, finish her degree, make a future for herself. All she'd ever wanted as a child was stability, and she was going to work damn hard to give it to herself.

"Still feel like watching the movie?" Shelly asked, passing her the tub of ice cream again and holding up the remote.

"Yeah, why not. There's nothing a night with Carrie and Big can't fix, right?"

And there she went making fun of things when inside she felt like her stomach was being shredded by shards of sharp glass. Because Shelly was right. She did love Ryder, only she didn't want to admit it. Her future didn't involve white picket fences around some pretty ranch house—if she went back to Ryder he'd tire of her in a few months, maybe a few years, and then what? She'd be back to having a life screwed up by a man she loved and relied on, and then it would be her childhood repeating itself all over again.

Ryder pushed his thumbs through the loops of his Wranglers and hitched one foot on the rail behind him. He'd just been interviewed by a local news crew and he was posing for his photograph to be taken. Usually he'd bow out of any kind of publicity, but the sponsors expected him to do a few press junkets and he didn't want to let them down. He was defending his title and it was something he took seriously, the highlight of his year.

"Hey, King! Good luck."

He waved to a cowboy he didn't recognize sauntering past, grinning to the photographer and receiving a nod in return. Ryder tipped his hat and wandered off to check the schedule. He had about an hour to kill before his title ride, and he liked to keep himself occupied, not overthink his rides too much. He'd already won the Saddle Bronc Riding title, and his final competition for the event was the bull riding. *His favorite.* He hadn't been training as hard as he had been every day to not win.

"You ready?" Nate's deep voice carried across to him and Ryder turned to see both his brothers waiting for him. Nate passed him a soda.

"Didn't think you'd be hanging around for this one," Ryder said. Nate disliked a lot of Ryder's rodeo work, but he hated the bull rides—Ryder's last two concussions had been in the ring with a bull.

"Hey, someone has to be here to pick up the pieces," Nate grumbled.

Ryder ignored what he was saying. They'd both been taking it easy on him the past few weeks, and they'd had fun flying to Vegas together, drinking too much and talking shit. "You seeing the brunette again tonight?"

"You mean the model I met at the bar?" Nate asked with a shrug.

"No, the other hot brunette you took up to your room." Ryder punched him in the arm good-naturedly. "Of course that one."

"Fuck yeah," Nate said with a laugh. "Want me to ask her if she has any friends?"

The three of them laughed and Ryder knocked back his soda, pausing to listen to the announcer. He didn't like hanging around after they announced the rider before him—the organizers would be pissed if he cut it too close.

"Sounds like I'm up soon," he told them, passing Chase his soda can and stretching out his arms, moving his neck from side to side to limber up. "Wish me luck."

"You got your helmet today?" Nate asked, voice gruff. His disapproval was obvious even if he was trying to be supportive.

"Yes, Dad, I have my helmet." Ryder laughed as he spoke, but the smile fell from his mouth faster than it had appeared. He stared into the crowd, certain his eyes were playing tricks on him.

"What is it?" Chase asked.

"Nothing," Ryder muttered. "I just thought I . . ." *No fucking way.*

He caught sight of the long blond hair that had made him turn in the first place, thrown over familiar shoulders and reaching almost halfway down her back. When she turned, her dark brown eyes met his, her expression changing from impassive to surprised. Then a slow smile broke out across her face, and one hand raised as she waved out to him.

"It's Chloe." He could hardly believe what he was saying. Ryder was still staring at her, but he didn't wave back. After walking out on him a month ago and disappearing, she'd just decided to turn up at a rodeo she knew he was competing in. *In Vegas?*

"You're kidding," Chase said, shielding his eyes from the sun to look. "You sure you're not seeing things?"

Nate folded his arms and nudged both of them. "Stop staring at her."

Ryder had already turned away. "What the . . ." He balled his fists and stared at his brothers. "She's got some damn nerve," he muttered.

Chase's hand closed around Ryder's forearm, and his brother staring him straight in the eye. "Don't be an idiot. She's here, and if she's here to see you don't let your goddamn pride stand in the way."

Nate grunted. "He's right. Go talk to her."

Ryder wanted to ignore her and head straight off to prepare for his ride, but she was heading his way and that meant he had less than a minute to decide what to do.

"Ryder," Chase cautioned. "Don't be a douchebag. It's Chloe, for Pete's sake."

He didn't need to be reminded why he had to act like an adult right now instead of being immature and holding a grudge. "Yeah, I know," he said, watching as she headed in his direction, head down as she navigated her way through the crowd. "You want to give us some space?"

They both nodded and turned, Nate giving him a slap on the back before walking away. "Good luck in the ring. See you from the sidelines."

Chase grinned. "Knock 'em dead."

Ryder wasn't sure if his brother was talking about the ride or Chloe, but he was guessing he meant the former. He didn't have another second to think about it though—suddenly Chloe was standing in front of him, her warm, chocolate-colored eyes shyly meeting his.

"Hey Ryder," she said, pushing her hands into the back pockets of her jeans. She'd done it because she was obviously nervous, and all she'd accomplished was straining the fabric of her T-shirt so he could see the perfect outline of her breasts. He swallowed and looked away, wishing he could pretend that he wasn't interested in her. The truth was he'd missed Chloe like hell and he was desperate to feel her body hard up against his again.

"Chloe," he managed, folding his arms across his chest. "What are you doing here?"

She smiled. "It's not because I've suddenly decided I love hanging out at rodeos."

"No?"

Chloe's grin was infectious, impossible not to return no matter how hard he tried. "I wanted to see you defend the title."

Now that he hadn't expected. After everything, she'd

just decided to show up out of the blue to watch him compete?

"Were you in town?" he asked.

She shook her head, doing her cute bite-down-on-her-lower-lip thing and making him want to kiss those pillowy lips of hers and just forget what had gone down between them.

"I arrived this morning," Chloe told him. "I wanted to see you, then I'll head off again I guess."

Ryder knew how much she hated Vegas—she'd made that beyond clear the time they'd come together. He cleared his throat and glanced at his watch. He only had about a minute to get his ass over to the ring, otherwise he'd be scratched from the program.

"Chloe, what are you doing here? You just disappear and then show up without even a phone call?"

She grimaced. "Can we talk after your ride?"

Ryder wanted to ask her what the fuck had happened to make her run like that, but he also didn't want to push her away. She'd traveled to be here and he bet that hadn't been easy for her to decide to do, not when it was Vegas.

"I have to go," he told her, unfolding his arms and letting them hang at his sides instead. "But yeah, let's talk after. Come by the ring as soon as my ride's over and we'll go somewhere."

"Sure thing," Chloe said, reaching out to touch his arm and standing on tiptoes to press a warm kiss to his cheek. "Good luck out there."

Ryder smiled. He couldn't deny how good her body felt against his, how much he wanted that mouth of hers over his instead of just on his cheek. "You always were my good-luck charm, right?"

Her eyes met his, the familiar flash of her deep brown irises warming a part of him that he'd thought would be permanently cold. Only Chloe had ever made him want to let a woman that close, and right now he wanted to tug her into his arms and make sure she never left again. Screw being angry, he wanted her and he wasn't afraid of admitting it, not now that she was standing in front of him.

"Good luck, Ryder."

He touched his hat and disappeared into the crowd, making his way over to where they'd be waiting for him. Ryder had to jog to make it in time, the announcer already giving him his introduction before he was even ready.

"Next up we have Ryder King defending his Bull Riding World Championship title. King is also our current Saddle Bronc Riding champion, and this year's defender of the World All-Around Rodeo Champion Cowboy title. Last year he was the highest earning cowboy in the National Finals Rodeo, and talk is that he's as unbeatable this year as he was last."

Ryder quickly grabbed his helmet and secured it, shrugging on his back protector. He checked his hat, raised it to the guys waiting for him, and patted some powder into his hands to take any sweat away and let him get a good grip once he was out there in the ring.

"Sorry to keep you waiting, fellas," he said as he climbed up.

"You gonna kick some butt again today, King?"

He grinned at the guys before settling carefully onto the bull. "Damn right." The bull was calm while he was confined, the big animal breathing steadily beneath him. Ryder could feel every exhale the bull made, admired his sleek black coat and the rippling muscles on display across his neck and shoulders.

"And here he is! They don't call this the rodeo Super Bowl for nothing, folks! Please give it up for the *one* and *only* Ryder King!"

"You ready?"

Ryder adjusted his grip, flexed then clenched his fingers, and put one hand high in the air as he listened to the crowd cheer and clap. "Ready!"

The bull leaped out of the crush, heading straight for the center of the ring, his big body twisting and contorting as he bucked like the wild, massive beast that he was. Ryder tuned out everything else—he couldn't hear the crowd, couldn't see anything, all his senses tuned in to the powerful beast beneath him. He rode through every jilt and spin, the bucks as big as any he'd ever felt before. Time was irrelevant right now because he had no idea how many bucks he'd ridden through or how long his hand had been wrapped around the rope he was holding.

His body slammed back and forth, but Ryder kept his shoulders soft, went into his zone of feeling the rhythm of the bull, and didn't fight it. Then one buck was followed by another, too quickly, the beast spinning around so fast that Ryder lost his rhythm and then had to release his hold, not prepared to get his hand stuck. *Fuck.* The bull was mad, continuing to buck and charge even when

Ryder had given up, was fast about to meet the ground, and he knew then it was all turning to shit.

He was struck as he was falling, a kick from the bull's hoof distorting his fall, and all he could see was the ground and then black, the screaming crowd fading as the bull snorted way too close to his head.

No. "No!" Chloe's scream echoed so loud in her head she couldn't hear anything else. It was like glass splintering into shards around her; she had no idea if she was still screaming over and over again or whether it was just in her head.

Ryder was lying on the ground, his body eerily still. The way his head had slammed into the hard-packed dirt was a memory she'd never forget. It seemed like years before a group of guys ran to him and scooped him up, the bull distracted by the clown. She wanted to scream to them not to lift him like that, to be careful of his neck, of his head, but all she could do was watch in silence as they hauled him over the fence away from danger. They didn't have any choice *but* to move him.

When she couldn't see him any longer she ran, pushing blindly through the crowd, desperate to find him, to make sure he was okay. *He had to be okay.* She'd just been talking to him. He'd been standing in front of her, and she'd touched his cheek. *He had to be okay.*

"Chloe."

She ignored her name being called, didn't give a shit who was trying to get her attention.

"Chloe!" This time the call was followed by a firm hand closing over her arm, forcing her to stop.

"Let me go!" she screamed, frantically searching fo Ryder, desperate to see where he was, where he'd bee taken.

"Chloe, stop."

She spun like a wildcat, ready to claw at whoever wa holding her, and then she met Nate's gaze, saw Ryder oldest brother standing before her, his hold softer now that he had her attention.

"Where is he? What—"

"Shhh," he said, wrapping his arms around her an drawing her close, holding her tight to his chest as sh sobbed. "Just stay here with me."

Chloe couldn't hold back, tucked hard against Nate clutching his shirt as her body heaved with sobs. H smelled like Ryder, their cologne the same, and it onl made her pain worse.

"Where is he?" she choked out, pushing back to look up at the man holding her.

"There's nothing we can do but wait," Nate said, hi voice gruff. She looked up into his eyes, looked throug the blur of her tears to see the pain in his own gaze. "I anyone can pull through this, Ryder can."

"But his helmet," she stuttered. "He was wearing helmet, he must be okay. Nate? Please tell me he's go ing to be okay?"

She watched as Nate's big shoulders lifted. H looked away, then back at her, taking her hand in his "His helmet broke open, but maybe it saved him. Chas is riding in the ambulance with him. You can com with me."

Chloe was numb. She held tight to Nate's hand as h walked with her over to the ambulance. All they saw was Chase as he stared out the back window at them, his hand raised in a solitary wave as the ambulance pulled away, lights flashing, siren blaring. She followed Nate fast, keeping up with his long, loping stride, through the parking lot and to his car. Chloe managed to open the door and get in, but it was Nate who leaned across and clicked her seat belt into place. She couldn't think, couldn't focus. All she could see was Ryder's body flying through the air like a rag doll, the bull's hoof connecting with him, the impact as he hit the ground headfirst.

Nate backed out and hit the road, driving fast. She let him take her hand again, squeezing her fingers and bringing her back to reality. This was Ryder's brother, he should be the one in shock, and instead she was.

"How long will it take us?" she asked, not recognizing her own raspy voice.

He let go of her hand. "I need you to work the GPS," Nate said. "I know roughly where I'm going but I want it on the screen."

Chloe leaned forward and took a deep breath. The system was similar to the one in the rental she had, so she quickly found the nearest hospital and programed it in. Then she turned in her seat to face Nate, wiping at her cheeks and under her eyes with the backs of her fingers.

"You're probably wondering why the hell I'm here," she murmured.

Nate shrugged. "None of my business."

"I love him, Nate. I know I walked away from him, but I love him. I came here to tell him that and now . . ."

Nate took his eyes off the wheel for a second and

glared at her, his expression dark. "You'll get to tell him, you hear me? Don't even think like that."

She sucked back a breath. "Okay," she muttered, staring at the road ahead instead of the man seated beside her. They were different in so many ways, but Nate was so similar to Ryder, too—their smiles, the intensity of their gazes, the way they took charge of a situation, calm yet strong.

"So this is why you hate him riding rodeo, right?" Chloe asked.

She saw Nate's knuckles turn white as he gripped the steering wheel. "Damn right. A couple of years back one of the top bull riders fell, we were all there, but his hand was stuck in the rope. He flipped forward and they reckon the bull killed him instantly, then threw him around like a featherweight and stomped all over the poor bastard."

Chloe dug her nails into her palm. Ryder had looked like a rag doll up there today, just for a second, and if he'd . . . She squeezed her eyes shut. It wasn't worth thinking worse-case scenarios, not yet. Just the thought of Ryder's big, strong body being made to look all floppy like that, so powerless, made her sick to her stomach.

"Ryder's had a few bad falls over the years, from bulls and broncs, and his last big knock gave him a pretty bad concussion. He started wearing headgear after that."

It was Chloe reaching for Nate's hand now, linking their fingers and holding on tight.

"You don't think I distracted him by turning up today, do you?"

Nate slowed as the traffic became more dense, his

yes meeting hers for a second, a warm smile spreading across his face. "No, darlin', I don't. He's damn stubborn and he'd hate to admit it, but seeing you there today would have made him all the more determined to win."

Chloe blinked away a fresh wave of tears. "Really?" She didn't want Nate to think he had to talk like that just to make her feel better.

"Really. Now don't you worry that pretty little head of yours about anything other than being there for my brother when he comes around." The phone rang and Nate pulled away from her to answer it. "You need to be there so I can control myself, otherwise I'll give him a damn piece of my mind for having such a stupid job."

She sat back and watched Vegas whizz past as Nate answered the phone. From what she could hear it was his granddad. Nate gave him a quick rundown of what had happened. It didn't surprise her that Nate was the one in charge of running the family business—he was cool as a cucumber in the face of crisis, strong enough to intimidate if he needed to, and he was charming to boot.

"Chloe's here, Granddad."

That made her sit up straighter, glancing over at Nate.

"Yeah, he did see her. And she's on her way to the hospital with me now."

She hoped they didn't all hate her for the way she'd disappeared on Ryder, but she'd had her reasons and she was ready to explain. They might be wealthy and inanely powerful, but they were also just a really nice family that she'd missed like heck. It wasn't just Ryder.

She'd loved the time she'd spent with all of them, and i
he'd give her a chance, it was a family she wanted to b
a part of.

Chloe checked the GPS. "Next left, Nate, and we'r
there."

He accelerated down the road, took the turn, and the
put his foot down again when the hospital came int
view. Chloe's stomach lurched, bile rising in her throa
just thinking about what they were going to see. If h
didn't make it, she'd never forgive herself for not tellin
Ryder how she felt.

Chapter 22

The disinfectant smell in the hospital was making Chloe nauseous. She sat with her elbows resting on her knees, head hanging as she waited for news. Before she'd had Nate and Chase to sit with, but now they were gone, in with the specialist and then being ushered into Ryder's room, but because she wasn't family she was stuck in the waiting room. Alone.

She'd thought about calling Shelly, but all she'd end up doing was bursting into tears when she was better sitting alone, staying strong. Waiting to hear something.

"Chloe?"

She jumped and turned around, locking eyes with Chase. He crossed the room and held out a hand, helping her to her feet and putting his arm around her shoulders once she was standing. His hug was warm and friendly as she leaned into him. She'd only met Ryder's brothers a couple of times, but they'd treated her like a member of the family all afternoon.

"He's not out of the woods yet, but it looks like he's

starting to come around," Chase told her. "Nate woul rather punish him, but I thought you'd like to be ther when he woke."

Chloe glanced at Chase. "Are you sure? The docto said they had a strict family-only policy."

He laughed. "Are you kidding me? If Ryder woke u and found out we'd left you in the waiting room alone he'd kill us. He'd rather your face be the first he see than one of our ugly mugs."

She took a big breath, then blew it out. "Thanks Chase. You guys have been so nice to me and I don' even deserve it."

Chase kept his arm around her as they walke through a set of double doors, then down a corridor, be fore he stopped outside a room that had *King* displaye in the small window, blocking the view inside.

"You know, we've all been douchebags in the past the three of us I mean," Chase told her. "Ryder has bro ken his fair share of hearts over the last decade, so yo not being in touch for a month isn't the worst you coul have done."

She shook her head. "I shouldn't have left him lik that. We had a deal but . . ."

He held up one finger and touched it to her lips. "Sto talking. Just go in there and let him see your beautifu face when he comes around. He's already forgiven you so stop beating yourself up and forget it."

The smile that hit her lips was impossible to stifle "He told you that?"

"It wouldn't matter if he hadn't," Chase said with laugh. "One look at you when he comes around and he' forgive you all over again."

Chloe squared her shoulders and walked in ahead of Chase, smiling over at Nate stationed on the other side of the bed before dropping her gaze to the man lying on the hospital bed. She gasped, clamping her hand over her mouth at the shock of seeing him there like that. Ryder's chest was bare, the rest of him covered with a sheet and blanket. An IV line was hooked to his arm, a tube in his nose for oxygen, his big body looking so fragile when she was used to it being so strong and tough. His hands were by his side, hands that she so desperately wanted on her again, his touch what she'd fantasized about every night since she'd left him.

"Can I hold his hand?" she asked, looking up at Nate.

He nodded and she watched as Chase moved around to join his brother, sitting on the other side of the bed. Chloe pulled a chair closer and carefully took Ryder's hand, picking it up like it was a baby bird's, wrapping her palm around his and dropping her lips to his skin.

Then she reached out with her other hand to stroke his forehead, keeping her touch light as she stared at his handsome face.

"I don't want to hurt him," she whispered.

"You're not," came a deep voice from behind her. She turned and saw the doctor standing by the door. "Your touch and voice will do more good than harm."

Chloe gazed down at Ryder again, running her fingers down the side of his face this time, watching his eyes for any sign of life. Her heart pounded when she noticed a flicker of one eyelid, then another.

"Did you see that?" she asked, glancing at Nate and Chase.

They nodded and she leaned in closer, tears of joy

falling down her cheeks when his eyes opened for the briefest of seconds, shut, then slowly opened again.

"Ryder, can you hear me?"

The doctor stepped in, watching Ryder's progress as his eyes flickered then stayed open for longer, groaning when a bright light was shone directly into his pupils. He tried to move and was told to stay still, and Chloe sat watching, silent, biting down hard on her lip. Surely this was all a good sign.

"What the hell happened?" Ryder muttered, his words barely discernable. "Where am I?"

"You're at Mountain View Hospital," the doctor said, checking the numbers on the machine beside him and jotting down some notes before sitting on the edge of the bed. "You suffered a serious concussion, and we're still concerned that you could have some bleeding on the brain."

Ryder shut his eyes, either from pain or from the news he'd just received. When he opened them he sat up slightly, cursing and touching his forehead. "I feel like I've been slammed into a concrete wall."

"May as well have been," Nate muttered, moving closer to the bed.

"You guys saw what happened?" Ryder asked. "Did I win the title?"

"Goddamn it, Ryder! You just about killed yourself and . . ."

"He's alive," Chloe said, surprised by how loud her voice was, expecting her words to catch in her throat. "That's all that matters."

Ryder turned, grimacing, until he saw her. Then he went still, eyes fixed on hers. "Chloe?"

She nodded and stepped closer. "I can go if you don't want me here," she offered.

Chase and Nate both laughed at her comment, and the doctor put the chart at the end of the bed and said goodbye. "I'll be back to check you again shortly. Stay in bed and if you feel tired let a nurse know and try to get some sleep. You're very lucky that you don't have any other injuries aside from some big scrapes and bruises, but we have to carefully monitor you in case of any brain injury."

Ryder was still staring at her, unblinking. "I don't want you to go."

"Didn't I tell you that already?" Chase asked Chloe.

"I just . . ."

"You must think I'm a complete idiot," Ryder said, shaking his head then wincing. Chloe sat down so she was closer to him.

"You could have died out there today, Ryder," she told him.

His expression was solemn. "I know."

"And yet you still want to know if you won the title?" Nate fumed.

"A guy needs to know if he's retired on a high or not," Ryder said in a quiet voice, his fingers seeking out Chloe's when she nudged her hand closer to his.

"Bullshit," Nate swore.

"No shit," Ryder said, his eyes still trained on Chloe's. "I've pushed myself to the limit and now it's time to walk away."

"How about we leave these two for a bit, huh?" Chase suggested. "We'll go grab a coffee and something to eat. Want anything?" he asked Chloe.

She shook her head, smiling up at Ryder's brothers. They'd been kind to her when they could have ignored her and just focused on Ryder, and she'd forever be grateful to them. "I'm good. Thanks."

"Ryder?" Nate asked, standing closer to the bed as Chase headed for the door.

"Yeah?" Ryder finally looked away from Chloe, his focus on his brother now.

"I'm proud of you, for knowing when to call it a day. Your helmet smashed down the center, so if you hadn't been wearing it you'd either be a vegetable or ten feet under by now."

Chloe shuddered, goose bumps breaking out across her skin. She saw Ryder's reaction, the expression that crossed his face, and she knew it had rattled him, too. All the years he'd been the fun-loving rodeo rider, and he'd come so close to a grizzly death doing what he enjoyed the most.

"I'm done, Nate. You can tell Granddad I'm ready to settle the hell down."

Nate touched Ryder's shoulder, holding his hand there as he looked down at his brother, before joining Chase and heading out the door. Chloe watched them go, then turned her attention back to Ryder.

"You saw the whole thing?" he asked, squeezing her fingers with his.

Chloe nodded, tears welling in her eyes again. "I didn't think I'd ever see you again. I thought you were dead."

He chuckled, but it wasn't his usual, deep laugh. "First thing I did when I opened my eyes was move my toes, then my legs." He paused. "Until I saw you. You were a pretty good distraction."

"Did you mean what you said? About retiring?" she asked, shuffling her chair even closer.

"Yeah," he grunted. "All this time I've been a selfish shit, not caring what anyone else tried to tell me. But knowing you were watching me today, what I put you through? I'm done, Chloe. I guess I have to be. It's time to hang up my spurs."

She climbed onto the bed beside him, needing to be closer, to feel him against her. Part of her didn't even believe he was alive, that he was lying there talking to her like nothing had happened, the only reminder the fact that they were in a hospital and there were machines bleeping beside him.

"You won," she said. "The title, I mean. I heard them announce that you'd won it."

"No shit?"

She smiled. "No shit. You might have just about killed yourself, but you won."

He reached for her hand, squeezing it gently.

"I'm sorry," she whispered as she carefully tucked her head against his chest, one arm around him, palm pressed just below his shoulder.

"I guess that makes two of us."

Chloe tucked herself tighter against him, tipping her head back to look up at the man she thought she'd lost. "I thought you'd tell me to go," she said, "that you'd be so angry with me for the way I left that morning—" He groaned and she pulled back, realizing she was holding him too tight. "Sorry."

"Just don't go running off on me again, okay?"

"I won't." She sighed.

"Because I'm not running from you, Chloe. Not now, not ever."

She didn't reply, just listened to the steady beat of his heart, let her head rest against his chest. There was so much she wanted to say, so much she'd rehearsed in her head, but right now the words were hard to find. All she wanted to do was be in his arms.

"Huh-hum."

Chloe raised her head to see who was clearing his throat and saw the doctor at the door again. He was frowning, not looking impressed at finding her on the bed with his patient.

"It's time to let Mr. King rest," the doctor said. "Once I've done a full consult and he's slept, I'll let you back in."

Chloe wanted to hold on tight to Ryder and refuse, but she also wanted him to get better and if he needed to sleep, then so be it.

"I'll be out in the waiting room," she told Ryder, gently kissing his lips and slipping off the bed. "I won't leave."

He chuckled and cupped the back of her head, pulling her down for another kiss. "Go," he said. "I don't want you waiting out there all night."

"But . . ."

"No buts." His voice was firm this time, but she could see how fatigued he was. His eyes were crinkled around the sides, lids heavy. He'd just had a major accident and she didn't want to waste time arguing with him when he should be sleeping.

"I'll be back first thing in the morning then," she said, dropping a final kiss to his forehead and grabbing her bag.

"Go find Nate and Chase. They'll look after you."

"They already have," she told him, backing slowly away. "I don't know what I would have done without Nate today."

Ryder's eyes widened, the spark she was used to evident as he bristled at her words. "If he even tries to pull a move on you . . ."

Chloe laughed. "I meant he'd been great in a brotherly kind of way. Don't go worrying over nothing, okay? You're the one I love."

Ryder's expression changed again, his mouth opening to say something then shutting just as fast, eyes never leaving hers. She could have died right there on the spot. She'd just told him she loved him, in front of his doctor, and he was staring at her like she'd just announced she was running for president.

"I'll see you in the morning," she mumbled, raising her hand in a wave and pushing open the door, head down as she hurried away.

"Oomph."

Chloe walked smack into what felt like a brick wall, only this wall threw an arm around her to steady her and stop her from falling straight over backward.

"Nate," she said, pressing a palm to his chest and taking a step back. "Sorry, I . . ."

"Please tell me you're not running again," he joked. "I don't want to be the one to tell Ryder he's lost you for the second time. Or the one to have to chase you since he can't."

Chase laughed and passed her a coffee, standing beside his brother.

"No, um, it was doctor's orders. He wants us gone until morning. No visitors, just rest."

Nate nodded and took a sip of his coffee. "You guys head to the car, I'll go have a quick word with the doctor and meet you out front."

Chloe's hands were starting to burn from being pressed to the takeout coffee cup, but it was preferable to the burning embarrassment inside of her. She had no idea what Ryder was thinking, what he might have said back to her if she hadn't left his room in such a hurry. All she knew was that her timing sucked.

"You okay?" Chase asked. "You seem kind of rattled."

She nodded and fell into step beside him. "It's just been a long day." It wasn't a lie, she was exhausted.

"Where were you staying?"

"Where *was* I staying?" she asked back. "Just some little motel off the main drag."

"We'll go grab your things, then head back to the Bellagio."

The Bellagio? The last thing she needed was to go back to a place so full of memories, the hotel where she'd first been intimate with Ryder. "It's fine. I can just meet you guys here in the morning."

Chase slung his arms across her shoulders as they walked, like it was the most natural thing in the world for him to do. "Not a chance. You're staying with us now and you can argue all you like, but that's a fact. You can take Ryder's suite."

She guessed Ryder's attitude ran in the family. Chase

had no intention of taking no for an answer, and if he was anywhere near as stubborn as Ryder was, there was no point in even starting to protest.

"Why the Bellagio?" she asked. It was a stupid question—the Bellagio was the best hotel in Vegas, and they had a lot of cash to burn.

Chase chuckled, taking his arm away and reaching into his pocket for the car keys as they stopped at the elevator.

"Ryder was already booked in there and we just tagged along. Why?"

"No reason," she lied.

"Bullshit," he said with a laugh, turning to face her. His dark brown eyes were almost impossible to look away from, his stare intense. "We asked him the same question, 'cause he never usually stays anywhere like that when he's riding."

Chloe squirmed on the spot, looking up to see what floor the elevator was on, then checking her wristwatch.

"Chloe?" Chase's grin was infectious and she burst out laughing.

"All right, all right," she muttered, shaking her head and wishing she didn't find the King brothers so impossible to resist. It was Ryder she was in love with, but Chase was so damn charming that she just couldn't blow him off. "It was where we stayed together."

Chase was silent, then a slow smile broke out across his face. "Oh, I get it. He wanted a reminder of your filthy dirty weekend away."

She could feel her cheeks heating up, the burn slowly crawling up her neck and to her face, but she refused to look away. She raised an eyebrow and shrugged. "It was actually a midweek getaway, not a weekend. And it was purely for research purposes."

Chase burst out laughing and gestured for her to step into the elevator ahead of him. "I can see why my brother's so besotted with you."

Now it was Chloe's turn to laugh. "Besotted? Give me a break," she snorted. "He's probably had a different woman in his bed every night since I left."

"No, sweetheart, you're wrong," Chase said, his tone suddenly a whole lot more serious. "And that's why you're staying with us until he's out of here. You're one hell of a girl, and he'd kill us if you weren't safe and pampered while he isn't here to take care of you."

"You make it sound like I'm a child in need of a minder." She was flattered, but the attention made her uncomfortable.

"Look, we'll dote on you for as long as we need to. Your every wish is our command." Chloe laughed at the same time he did. "Okay, so not quite. But seriously, just let us look after you. We can drink, eat, gamble, take in the sights . . ."

"Did you say gamble?" she asked, folding her arms across her chest as she watched Chase.

The elevator dinged and he gestured for her to step out ahead of him.

"Is that a trick question?" Chase asked.

"No, it's my first wish. Let's get my things and go play us some poker."

"I thought you didn't play anymore?" Chase asked as they walked.

Chloe linked her arm through his. If Chase and Nate

wanted to play brotherly protectors to her, then so be it. She was going to enjoy being in the company of Ryder's two gorgeous brothers until she could be back in his arms. Or at least in the same room as him to see what he had to say about her grand statement of love.

"Desperate time, desperate measures," she told him.

"And just like that, we're gonna see the pro play in Vegas."

Hell yeah. If there was ever a time to play poker to take her mind off things, it was now.

"You and Nate play?" she asked.

"A little. We used to have boys' poker nights at home."

"Maybe you should start them up again, and invite me."

"What? So you can fleece us all out of every penny on the table? We'd lose all our card-game buddies pretty damn quick."

She thought about Ryder lying upstairs on the hospital bed as they walked farther away from the building, stopping beside the rental car that she'd traveled in with Nate earlier. Here she was joking, and Ryder was up there being poked and prodded by doctors.

"If Ryder lets me back in the house, I'll host your poker nights. Give you boys some pointers."

Chase jumped behind the wheel and started the engine at the same time she slipped into the back seat, leaving the front for Nate since there was more room.

"Sweetheart, either you have rocks in your head or we've been giving you the wrong impression." He turned in his seat to face her, his left arm resting on the staring wheel. "If you didn't mean a hell of a lot to Ryder, we wouldn't be looking after you like you're our long-lost sister already, okay? Of course he's gonna let you back in the damn house."

Chloe looked away, staring out the window and biting the inside of her mouth to stop from smiling. Maybe today wasn't the worst day of her life after all.

Ryder's head was pounding so badly he was struggling to sit up, desperate to succumb to sleep. But the doctor was still reviewing his charts and about to run through a series of tests again.

"Should I feel this tired?" Ryder asked.

"Like the worst fatigue of your life?"

He nodded at the doctor, then winced. Holding Chloe in his arms, concentrating on what she was saying, and trying to sound upbeat had taken it out of him. "Yeah."

"Mr. King, you suffered a very serious concussion. I'm not going to pretend that you weren't incredibly lucky to make it through a fall like that without suffering a brain bleed or worse."

Ryder grunted and carefully lowered himself back down. He'd wanted to be given the facts straight, and now he was.

"At this stage, you're looking at making a full recovery. But you take a knock to the head again? In rodeo or anything else? You'll likely die or suffer a serious brain injury. That's how serious this is. The fact that you didn't have to go straight in for surgery is nothing short of a miracle."

Ryder let the doctor prod him and check him over,

smiling his thanks at the nurse as she passed him more pain meds and a glass of water in a paper cup.

"So I can go to sleep now?" He stopped short of asking if there was a chance he wouldn't wake up if he did.

"Get as much sleep as you can, and keep doing that for the next month," the doctor said. "And stay away from bulls and horses. That's my advice."

Ryder made himself comfortable and shut his eyes, willing sleep to find him fast but seeing Chloe behind his closed lids instead of blackness. *Chloe.* He could think about her all night. The feel of her soft, warm body against his; the smile in her eyes when she gazed up at him; the press of her lips against his. *Damn.*

And then the words that had tumbled from those pillowy lips as she'd turned to leave. He opened his eyes and groaned. She'd told him she loved him and all he'd done was stare at her. The truth was he'd never been loved by a woman before, and he'd never loved a woman himself. Until Chloe. He loved Chloe so fucking much it hurt.

Ryder was tempted to dial Nate or Chase and check that they were looking after her, only he had no idea where his phone had ended up and there was no chance he could make it to the one across the room. They were probably getting a pizza somewhere, having an early night, or maybe toasting the fact that he was still alive. Either way he'd see her in the morning, which meant he had time to pull his shit together and figure out how the hell to tell her how he felt, before it was too late.

Chapter 23

Ryder slipped his key card into the slot and pushed the door open. He walked in and stopped when he saw a pair of high heels kicked over in the middle of the room. One glance into the bedroom and it was obvious there was someone in his suite. He pulled off his boots so he didn't make any noise and made his way in, taking his wallet and his phone out of his pocket and leaving them on a sideboard. Long blond hair was pooled over one of the pillows, the woman's face obscured, but there was no mistaking who was in his bed. He'd been in the hospital two nights and she'd been keeping his bed warm.

He lowered himself onto the bed, not giving a damn about how sore he was if it meant cradling Chloe in his arms. He pushed the covers down a little, frowning when he saw that she wasn't naked. Only . . . He chuckled. His favorite sweatshirt had been missing for weeks and all the searching in the world hadn't found it. Until now.

Chloe groaned, one arm rising from under the covers, her hand falling over her face. He went to touch her, then hesitated, not wanting to scare the crap out of her.

"Mornin', gorgeous," he murmured in a low voice.

The groaning stopped and she flipped her body, facing him in a second.

"Ryder?"

Her eyes were wide, hair all tangled around her face and mascara smudged under her eyes. She was tousled from bed but still sexy as hell.

"I'm guessing you had a big night?"

She groaned again and fell back into the pillows. "My head feels like it's about to split open. What time is it?"

"Nine thirty," he told her.

"Shit!" She sat up, one hand pressed to her forehead. "I'm so sorry, I promised to come see you first thing and . . ."

"You're forgiven. You know why?" Ryder reached out to brush some tangled locks from her face, resting on one elbow so he could watch her.

"Why?" she mumbled, her gaze hooded as she half shut her eyes when he stroked her face.

"Because I'm guessing my brothers are to blame."

"They're evil," she said, dropping back down and wriggling closer to him, snuggling her face into his chest. "They need to be punished. Severely punished."

He laughed, but it wasn't his brothers he wanted to talk about right now. "They got you drunk?"

"Worse. I beat them at every card game we played, so they decided I needed a handicap." Chloe's groan turned into a moan as he brushed her hair back to reveal her neck, nuzzling her soft skin. He kissed her gently, lips moving softly across her skin, inhaling the scent of her perfume. Even mixed with a hint of alcohol from the night before she smelled good enough to eat.

"Just tell me they didn't talk you into strip poker," he asked, talking straight into her ear before nipping her lobe. "I don't want either of them seeing my girl naked."

Chloe laughed and shook her head. "Don't worry. I still beat them, so even if it had been strip it would have been me seeing them naked, not the other way around."

Ryder watched as she nestled back into the pillows, her eyes on his, flickering to his mouth and back again. He lowered himself half over her, resting on his elbows so she didn't have to take his weight.

"And that's one of the reasons I love you," he told her, the words coming easier than he'd expected.

Her eyes widened at the same time a slow smile spread across her face. "You do?" she asked.

Ryder nodded. "Yeah, I do," he told her. "I love you, Chloe. I was a goddamn fool for not telling you at the hospital, but I'm telling you now." Ryder dropped his lips to hers, caressing her mouth as gently as he could, wanting her to know that he meant every word. "I love you," he whispered as her lips moved against his. *"I love you."*

A knock echoed, followed by an even louder series of thuds on the door as Chloe kissed him back, her arms wrapped around his neck, tugging him down like she was never going to let him go.

"Chloe? You in there?"

"Go away!" Ryder yelled over his shoulder.

The knocking started again and Chloe pushed him

back, one hand to his chest. She was smiling up at him when she shook her head. "Go tell him you're in here."

Ryder grunted. "No. He can piss off."

"Seriously, if the way he ran off a guy who so much as looked at me last night is anything to go by, he'll probably ram the door down to check on me before he just gives up."

"Fine," Ryder mumbled, pushing up and striding across the room and out into the lounge. "But get that sweatshirt off. You stole it and I want to see what's underneath."

He yanked open the door to the sound of Chloe's laughter.

"Hey," he said to Nate as his brother almost tumbled into the room, his fist midpound when the door swung back.

"What the fuck are you doing here?"

Ryder shrugged. "Could say the same to you."

Nate grabbed him and pulled him in for a brotherly hug, slapping his back, then pushing him away to look him up and down.

"When did they release you?"

"It was more a case of me talking the doctor into letting me go this morning."

Nate glanced toward the bedroom and Ryder moved in front of him, not giving him a chance to see Chloe. For all he knew she'd stripped off his sweatshirt already, and he had zero intention of letting his brother see so much as a flash of her body.

"I was just coming to check in on Chloe." Nate blew out a breath. "That girl can keep up with the best of us. Seriously, she knocked back shots like one of the guys and she still managed to take us for every penny we had on the table."

Ryder placed a hand on his brother's shoulder to turn him around. "And that's exactly why it's time for you to go," he told him. "I have some time to make up for."

Nate folded his arms across his chest, his friendly gaze turning into a hard-as-nails stare. "She's something special, Ryder. Don't you go fucking this up."

He scowled, not liking being told what to do. "Or what?"

"Just man the fuck up and tell her you love her," Nate muttered, turning to go. "You let her go this time, you're more of an idiot than I thought."

"This is one thing I'm not gonna fuck up, Nate. Now get the hell out of here and don't come looking for us again." He chuckled as he pushed his brother out the door. "Don't call us, we'll call you."

Ryder locked the door and wasted no time heading back to the bedroom.

"Chloe, you . . ." He paused as he realized she wasn't in the room. "Chloe?"

"I'm in here," she said through the closed bathroom door. "Just taking something for my head."

Ryder stripped off his jeans and shirt and got under the covers. With any luck she'd be coming straight back to bed.

"You must have made quite the impression on my brothers," he called out. "They're not exactly known for falling for women, but I think you're the exception to the rule."

The door clicked open and he pushed up to watch her emerge. She was wearing a pair of pink and black lace panties with a matching bra, her face scrubbed clean and her hair still falling messy around her shoulders. Ryder looked her up and down, spent extra time admiring her breasts pushed together in the sexy bra, her toned stomach and legs golden from the sun. *Damn.*

"They're pretty cool," she said, walking to the bed and sitting down beside him.

"Just promise me you'll never let them see you in your underwear," Ryder begged. *"Please."*

Chloe giggled as he kicked the covers off and grabbed her wrists, pinning her down on her back and straddling her, hard just from seeing her sauntering across the room with her banging body on show.

"Why?" she asked, breathing heavy as he stared down at her.

"Because then I'd have to fight them off, and I don't want to waste any time." He groaned when she wiggled her body, raising her pelvis so she was grinding against him. "I want to spend every second," he swore as she rubbed herself harder against him, "pleasuring you."

He gripped her wrists tighter, grinning when she struggled to break free. He transferred his hold so both her arms were above her head, only one of his hands holding her as he used the other to stroke down her chest, dipping in between her full breasts then inching his way down her stomach. He kissed her when she gasped, tasting her mouth, and exploring lower, his fingers finding their way inside her underwear.

"Did you mean what you said?" she gasped, raising a knee to force his hand away, her eyes on his as she looked up at him.

Ryder knew what she was talking about. The question in her gaze showed her vulnerability, a softness there that he'd only glimpsed before now. She was always so in control, so confident, and now he could see her vulnerabilities.

"That I love you?" he asked, whispering his question against her mouth.

She nodded, eyes shut as she escaped his hold and pressed both palms to his face, fingers gentle as they caressed his skin.

"I love you, Chloe. I've never said those words to another soul," he admitted. "But I can't hide from the truth forever."

He touched his forehead to hers when he saw tears spring into her eyes, wrapping his arms around her and rolling sideways with her pressed tight against him.

"What does it mean? For us?"

"It means that any bullshit agreement we had about our relationship is over," he told her. "No more running, no more pretending like this is just about sex."

"But . . ."

He raised a finger to Chloe's lips, silencing her. "No more questions. We're together and that's the end of it."

Chloe smiled, her eyes shining.

"I fucking love you, Chloe Rivers, and I'm not letting you walk away from me again." He kissed her lips, running a hand down her back, touching her soft skin.

"I'm not giving up my life for you," she whispered. "I can't just . . ."

"Shhh," he murmured, shaking his head. "Do you want to be with anyone else?"

"No!"

"Then that's all I give a damn about. You can do whatever the hell you like, so long as it's my bed and my bed only that you fall into each night."

She kissed him and nipped his lower lip. "That goes both ways, Mr. King."

He growled against her mouth. "Bite me again and you'll regret it."

"Tell me you agree," she countered.

"There's no other woman I want in my bed and you know it."

She cupped the back of his head and pulled him closer. "Then I think we can come to some sort of arrangement."

"Damn right we can," he said against her mouth.

Chloe pulled back. "Are you sure you're allowed to be doing this? I mean, shouldn't you still be in the hospital?"

"Uh-uh," he replied, leaving her mouth and making his way slowly down her neck, then her chest with his lips, sucking the soft spot between her breasts until she moaned. "It just so happens this is exactly what my doctor told me to do."

"Oh yeah?" she managed as she sucked in a sharp breath.

Ryder nudged the lace of her bra aside and closed his mouth over a nipple. "Yeah."

"I was right about you all along, Ryder," Chloe said with a giggle. "You *are* a devil, but at least you're mine."

Chapter 24

"So when are you heading back?" Chloe asked, snuggling against Ryder and running her fingers down his chest. His skin was warm, his muscles taut as she teased across his abs.

"You mean when are *we* heading back," he corrected, grabbing her hand and bringing it swiftly to his mouth to bite her wrist just hard enough to make her squeal.

Chloe shut her eyes when Ryder kissed her, tilting her mouth up to his. "I guess we can't stay holed up in here forever."

He chuckled, tugging at her lower lip as he kissed her slow. "There's nothing wrong with a few days of sex, champagne, and room service."

Chloe giggled. "You do realize your brothers will probably send a search party if we don't emerge today. They haven't heard from us in a while."

Ryder stretched and kicked the covers down farther. They were lying naked, the sunshine streaming in through the bedroom window, plush pillows scattered around them and the sheets tousled from hours spent playing in bed.

"I think it's time we let housekeeping pay a visit."

Chloe sat, too, stretching her arms above her head and surveying the room. It was a mess. Their trays of half-eaten food from the night before were on the floor, along with clothes they'd first stripped off close to three days ago, and there were four champagne bottles she could count empty and tipped over.

"Ryder, don't get me wrong, this has been fun, but . . ."

"No," he said, his gaze piercing when he turned and stared at her. "You don't get to blow me off, Chloe. I'm not listening to some bullshit it's-not-you-it's-me speech, not after all this."

She blinked, keeping her eyes downcast, worrying the edge of the sheet with her thumb. She was suddenly conscious of how bare she was, exposed when before she'd felt so comfortable being naked.

"I just, well." She sighed, looking up at him when he cupped her cheek and forced her head up. "You're not a long-term-relationship kind of guy, Ryder. I knew that from the start and I still know it now."

"You're putting words in my mouth," Ryder said, his voice so low it almost sounded menacing, as deep as a growl. "Have I not made it clear that I'm in love with you? I thought we already had this discussion."

"Ryder," she started, reaching for him, trying to put her arms around his neck.

"Damn it," he swore, getting out of bed and storming toward the bathroom. He flung open the door and she listened to the faucet running. "You want me to prove myself to you, I will," he called out, disappearing from sight when he entered the shower cubicle.

Chloe sighed and got out of bed. She retrieved a thick white bathrobe from the back of the bathroom door, standing for a moment to admire Ryder in the shower. He was pissed, she got that, but they'd lived in a bubble the last few days without talking about the future, about what would happen when they had to come crashing back to reality. She tied the robe tight around her waist to stop it from gaping open and smiled as Ryder aggressively rubbed shampoo into his hair, sliding his fingers back through his hair to rinse it, the suds running down his tanned back and over his buttocks. A lick of desire swept through her but she refused to acknowledge it. Stripping and stepping into the shower behind him, wrapping her arms around his slick wet body and letting him take her in the shower was what she wanted to do. Every beat of her body wanted to join him in there, even though it felt like she'd had him between her legs for more of the past seventy-two hours than not.

He turned, as if he knew she was standing there ogling him. Ryder's gaze was still angry, his eyes flashing as they met hers, a combination of pissed off and sexual heat merged into one delicious bout of fury.

"I'm gonna prove it to you," Ryder said, shaking his head and sending water flying at the same time as he opened the shower door, his muscled body glistening as he stood there naked before her. "Now get the hell in here."

Chloe thought about hesitating, but the decision was taken away from her when Ryder stepped out, water dripping off him as he yanked the knot free at her waist

nd shoved the robe off her shoulders, leaving it to fall
ff her body and pool on the floor. The heat in his stare
vas enough to set her on fire, sexual want licking
hrough her body as he cupped the back of her head and
anked her forward into a searing hot kiss, grunting as
e bent to scoop her up, mouth never leaving hers. Chloe
ocked her legs around his waist as he walked backward,
aking her under the hot water, pushing her back against
he tiled wall of the shower. The water was angled so it
vas falling in between them, splashing up over both
heir chests, dripping into their mouths to make their
isses even wetter, bodies slick as Ryder slid inside
f her.

She moaned as he thrust hard, no foreplay, just hard,
ugged sex. They'd played all night, pleasured each other
or hours, but this was more animal, a raw need inside
f both of them.

"I don't want this to be the last time," she gasped out
s he gripped her waist hard.

"Don't you fucking say that," he ground out, cover-
ng her mouth with his again so all she could do was
noan. "Don't you dare."

Chloe held him tighter, her arms around his neck.
yder was pumping hard into her but she still wanted
im closer, wanted more of him.

"I love you," she whispered against his ear.

Ryder didn't respond, not with words, but he slowed
own, taking a hand off her waist to brush his fingers
cross her face instead. He gently took her down, cra-
ling her weight, looking into her eyes as he lowered
er onto the wet tiles below. The water was still cas-
ading down on them as he slipped inside her again,

supporting his own weight so she could just arch below
him, digging her nails into his back as he rocked gently
back and forth.

Her body starting to hum, she forgot all about how
hard the tiles were, only aware of the feel of Ryder inside of her.

"Ryder," she gasped out, clawing at him, fighting to
breathe as she rode a wave of pleasure.

He grunted, and when she opened her eyes he was
watching her, his lids heavy. She knew he was close, too,
and as she shut her eyes and gave in to her climax, tears
spilled down her cheeks. She hoped Ryder hadn't noticed, didn't want him to see how much it hurt her just
being with him right now.

She didn't want to lose him. The thought of not having him in her life was like a knife through her heart.

Ryder's lips brought her back, his mouth soft against
hers, plucking so gently, caressing her. When she finally
opened her eyes the tears were long gone, washed away
by the steady stream of water still sheeting down over
them.

He dipped his head so his mouth was against her ear,
and she went still, his words so low she could only just
hear him.

"I'm going to prove myself to you, Chloe. Just you
wait."

Chloe let Ryder pull her back up to her feet, and raised
her mouth so he could kiss her before he stepped out
of the shower and dried himself off. She watched him
wrap the towel around his waist, then rinsed her body,
lathering shampoo through her hair as Ryder brushed
his teeth then walked out of the bathroom. They'd just

ad crazy good shower sex. She should have felt fantastic and known that he felt the same. Instead she had a dull ache inside of her, a feeling that the bubble had burst, that nothing was ever going to be the same again.

When she turned the shower off and reached for a towel the bang of a door made her jump. Ryder was gone. He'd just left without saying goodbye. Chloe was numb as she dried herself, wrapping her hair in a towel and walking naked into the bedroom to find clean underwear and something to wear.

She slipped on a G-string and bra, pulled a T-shirt over her head, and then grabbed her jeans. Her stomach was dancing, nerves all over the place, but there was nothing she could do but wait.

Chloe looked around the room and wondered how much longer she'd be staying here, if today might be their last day in Vegas. She spied the room service menu and decided the best way to settle her stomach was with something delicious to eat.

She opened it and glanced down the breakfast list, picking up the phone and waiting for the operator.

"Can I order an orange juice, croissants with jam, a latte and . . ." She paused, trying to make her mind up. "Actually, forget the croissants. I'll have the bacon and eggs, with hash browns and mushrooms."

She was starving and it wasn't like she hadn't been working out since she'd locked herself away in the Bellagio Suite with Ryder.

Chapter 25

"She's the most infuriating fucking woman I've eve[r] met."

Ryder tipped his glass and swallowed down the en[-]tire shot, wincing as the liquor burned a fiery path dow[n] his throat and deep into his stomach.

"Which is why you're drinking whiskey before lunch time," Nate said with a laugh. Chase cracked up, too[,] and Ryder turned to glare at them. He'd half expected them to have been long gone, but they'd been having too much fun partying to leave and Nate had decided to take a few extra days off.

"Since when do you two let me drink on my own?" Ryder muttered.

"Uh, since you started drinking before eleven a.m.," Chase replied.

"Oh, I know, maybe it's because you ditched us fo[r] the woman you're talking about three days ago and jus[t] about ripped my head off last time I dared knock o[n] your door."

Ryder leveled his gaze on Nate and then shrugged. "Fair point."

"So are you pissed off because you're still too chicknshit to tell her that you love her, or is it something lse?" Nate asked.

"How the hell do you . . . ?"

"You don't need to pretend like you're not head over eels for this girl," Nate interrupted. "Hell, if you weren't vith her I'd be knocking down her door."

Ryder glared at his big brother. "Easy," he muttered.

Nate held up his hands. "Hey, I'm just telling you vhat we think of her. We spent a couple of days hangng with her and she's pretty awesome."

"Don't let her walk, Ryder. Don't you fucking dare," Chase chimed in.

Ryder took a deep breath and slammed his palms lown on the bar. If he was actually going to go through vith what he was thinking, he needed to let them in on t. There was no way he could do this on his own.

"That mean you wouldn't think I was crazy if I said was going to ask her to marry me?"

Neither Chase nor Nate said a thing. They both stared ack, mouths hanging open.

"You're serious?" Nate asked.

"Fuck yeah I'm serious."

Chase stepped forward to slap Ryder on the back. "Do t," he said, holding Ryder tight in a hug. "Do it now or ou'll regret it forever."

Ryder hugged Chase back, but he was watching Nate ow. For years he'd done his own thing, not worried bout his family or anyone else. All he'd cared about vas making his own mark on the world, having fun and

making money doing what he loved, but he'd alread
made one mistake since he'd been back and he wasn'
going to make another. Nate's opinion mattered to him
They were brothers, they had their grandfather's estat
to run and preserve, and that meant it was time for him
to start acting like he was part of the team.

"Nate?" he asked. "I know you like her, but . . ."

"Do it," Nate said, a grin spreading across his fac
as he reached for Ryder's hand and pulled in for anothe
brotherly hug. "There ain't no one I'd rather have as
sister-in-law than Chloe."

"It's not as easy as that," Ryder said, running a han
through his hair. Riding bulls and climbing onto wil
broncs had never fazed him, but what he had planned
Now that required balls. "If it's gonna work I need yo
guys to help me."

They both shrugged. "Shoot," Chase said. "Tell u
what you want and we'll do it."

Ryder turned and asked the bartender for a pen, jot
ting down some notes on a napkin. "Nate, I need you t
find a friend of Chloe's. Here's her address and if yo
can't find her there go to Joe's. She worked shifts with
Chloe. I need our jet back in Texas and returning with
her on it by tonight." He looked at Chase. "And I nee
you to buy suits, shirts, and ties for the three of us."

Ryder's brothers exchanged glances, but it was Nat
who narrowed his eyes and folded his arms across hi
chest. "Tell me you're not trying to pull off a weddin
in less than twelve hours."

Ryder laughed. "That's exactly what I'm doing. Now
get the jet to Texas and her friend on board, or I'll neve

ull this thing off. I've got a dress to organize, a chapel
o book, and a ring to buy."

"You're fucking crazy, you know that? Why can't you
ust propose like a normal guy?" Nate asked. "You could
et married back on the ranch next year or something."

"Because Chloe doesn't believe me that I can settle
own with one woman," Ryder told them, his voice low.
She's been let down all her life, and I want to show her
hat it's time she let someone take care of her. Starting
ow."

"And you think a quickie Vegas wedding's going to
rove that to her?"

Ryder shrugged. "It's a damn good start, and if she
as too much time to think about it she might run."

Chase laughed. "I hope for your sake you can pull
off."

"Me too." Ryder charged his drink and bought a bot-
le of water, taking the cap off and guzzling it. He still
ad a bit of a hangover from the champagne, and he
adn't exactly had a lot of sleep. Resting and playing,
ure, but not much sleep. "Keep your phones on and
on't let me down. Got it?"

Chase grinned and Nate just shook his head. Trust
is oldest brother to expect him to fuck it up.

"I'll meet you guys in the lobby in a few hours. And
f you see Chloe, don't say a word."

Ryder disappeared, checking his wallet to make sure
is Amex card was in his wallet. If memory served him
orrect there was a Tiffany store accessible through the
otel, and he wanted to make sure he had time to find
he perfect ring. And if they didn't have a big enough

rock in the store, he wanted them to have time to fly one in ASAP for him.

He was pulling out all the stops for Chloe—he didn't care how much it cost or what he had to do. There was no way she was walking away from him, not if he had a say in the matter.

Chloe stepped out of the elevator and glanced around the lobby, heading for the door. She'd half expected to see the boys at the bar or in the lobby, but she didn't see anyone she recognized. After trying Nate and Chase's rooms a couple of times, she was starting to feel like they'd all abandoned her.

"Ms. Rivers!" Chloe stopped and looked over her shoulder, hearing someone call her name. "Ms. Rivers!"

The concierge was running toward her, waving her hand to get her attention. Chloe frowned. "Is something wrong?" Why else would the concierge be chasing her through the lobby? The last time that had happened to her was when she was fifteen. Her dad had put them up in some extravagant hotel, then he'd promptly lost his money and they'd had to skip out on paying. Memories like that made her want to leave Vegas and never return.

"I have a message for you," the woman said, her smile genuine as she held out a card. "Mr. King left it for you. Three large boxes arrived for you just now, too, Ms. Rivers. Would you like me to have them sent straight up to your room?"

Chloe took the card and opened it. She wasn't sure which King had left it for her, but a quick scan to the bottom showed Ryder's name scrawled across it. She closed it and decided to read it in private.

"Yes, send them up," she instructed. "And would you mind ordering me a chardonnay too." Whatever the hell was going on, she needed a drink.

Chloe scratched her shopping plans and headed back up, embarrassed at the large boxes being ferried up with her. She craned her neck to read the words on the side and almost choked. *Vera Wang?* Why the hell were three boxes from Vera Wang being delivered to her?

"Can I just cross-check that these are definitely for me?" she asked.

The man smiled and pulled out a docket. "Chloe Rivers, care of Ryder King, staying in the Bellagio Suite. That sound like you?"

She nodded, leaning back against the wall and staring up at the changing numbers as they ascended. The card from Ryder was burning a hole in her pocket.

When they arrived at her floor she stepped out, opened the door for the parcels, and then tipped the bellboy. She eyed the boxes like they were full of bombs and sat down on the sofa, slowly opening the card again. It was the first time she'd seen Ryder's handwriting and it was more scrawly than she'd expected.

Chloe, meet me downstairs at 7 p.m. I'll be in the lobby waiting. I've sent up three dresses hoping that one will be right, and I need you to trust me. Wear your favorite one and I'll see you soon. Ryder.

A knock at the door made her jump. "Room service!"

Chloe crossed the room, tipped the waiter, and took her wine. Thank god she'd ordered it. She took a long, slow sip and eyed the boxes in the center of the living

area. She set down her drink and slid a nail under th
seal of the first one, sucking back a breath when she sav
the dress wrapped so carefully in tissue paper. It was th
softest dove gray color, and as she lifted it out she coul
see that it was strapless, the bust shaped and the soft fab
ric bolstered by structured stitching and a nipped-i
waist.

Chloe draped it over the chair beside her and opene
the second one, eyes almost popping out of her head a
she spied the off-white layers of tulle. The bust was
delicate symphony of tiny beads that gently caught th
light, the waist defined by a subtle strip of satin, befor
the tulle took over and made a princess skirt.

Tears pricked her eyes as she held it up. Was Ryde
serious? Did he actually expect her to wear one of thes
dresses without knowing what the hell he had planned
Was this some kind of test?

She reluctantly put down the second dress and opene
the final box, parting the tissue to inspect the dress.
was satin, the softest champagne color, and she imagine
it would hug all her curves like a second skin, flutin
out like a mermaid's tail at the back.

Chloe put it carefully back in the box and rose, tak
ing her glass and going to stand beside the window. Sh
looked out over Vegas and sipped her wine, her thought
full of dresses that didn't make sense to her. All sh
wanted was to rewind twenty-four hours, hell, eve
a few hours, and just stay there forever. But of all th
good things that had happened to her in her life, non
had lasted. Not one. Each great moment had been re
placed with one ten times worse than the last.

She picked up her phone and dialed Ryder. It rang, then went to voice mail, so she hung up, turning at the same time to survey the open boxes behind her. Here she was, surrounded by exquisite dresses that looked suspiciously like wedding gowns, all alone, and wondering what the hell was going on. All she knew for sure was that Ryder was expecting her to take a serious leap of faith, and as romantic as whatever he had planned for her might be, trusting anyone like that didn't come naturally to her.

Her phone vibrated in her hand and she glanced at the screen, swiping across to open it. "Shelly?"

"Would you like to tell me what the hell is going on?"

Chloe flopped down onto the sofa. "You're never going to believe it, but I'm in Vegas. I surprised Ryder at the rodeo here and I haven't left yet." She hadn't realized how desperate she'd been to talk to her best friend.

Shelly laughed down the line. "Oh, I believe you," she said. "Because one of Ryder's brothers personally escorted me onto a private jet about ten minutes ago, with the promise of a fun trip to Vegas."

Chloe put down her glass, goose bumps tracing across every inch of her skin. "He what?"

"I'm sipping champagne and looking into some seriously sexy brown eyes right now."

Oh my god. "Give Nate the phone," Chloe ordered. If Ryder had sent someone to get her friend on the jet, she'd bet hands down it would be Nate.

"So you want to tell me what's going on here?" Shelly asked.

"Honestly? I have no idea," Chloe admitted. And she didn't. Not the faintest damn clue and it was driving her insane.

"Hey baby." Nate's voice came on the line and she heard Shelly giggling in the background, no doubt in heaven traveling in luxury with Nate.

"Tell me what's going on," she demanded. "And don't give me any bullshit excuses."

"Sorry darlin'," Nate drawled. "Ryder told me he'd beat the crap out of me if I told you anything."

"Nate," she said, trying to sound less pissed off and ending up pleading. "I thought we were friends."

His laugh was loud through the phone. "No, sweetheart, you stole all my money in a card game and got me stupid drunk playing poker. I love you, but we're not friends."

She paused, looking at the dresses again and hating that she didn't know what Ryder was up to. She was always in control, never let anyone in her life just make decisions for her. At first it had been about survival, now it was just because she was stubborn as hell and liked her independence.

"Then what are we?" she asked, holding her breath as she waited for him to answer.

"Family," Nate said, the one word he uttered almost making her heart stop it held so much power. "Or at least we might be."

Chloe dropped the phone and crossed the room, never taking her eyes off the dresses. Her instinct was to pack her bags and run, but . . . this was Ryder. She was the one who'd pushed him to prove himself, and now she was going to have to sit tight and see what he had planned for her. She'd already run once and regretted it, so if she had to knock back a few shots and lock the door, then so be it.

Chapter 26

Chloe walked out of the elevator for the second time that day. Her pulse was racing, heart pounding as the doors opened. She expected something to happen the second she stepped out, but nothing did. She glanced around, pleased she'd been the only one traveling down. She smoothed a hand down her dress, the satin so smooth beneath her fingers it felt like a second skin. Part of her had wanted to wear the one with the beautiful tulle skirt, and a big part of her wanted to rush straight back up and slip into it, but the more sensible side of her brain wouldn't let her. Because what if it was all some cruel joke, what if it wasn't what she was thinking it could be, what if Ryder wasn't waiting for her like he'd said he would be.

She gulped and stepped into the lobby, her heels clicking on the polished tiles. It was always busy here and tonight was no different, except that tonight her nerves were jangling like wind chimes in the middle of a blustery storm, and she was checking out every single person.

"Chloe."

She stopped, took a big breath, and looked around. *Ryder.* He was standing waiting for her, dressed in a suave black suit, white shirt, and perfectly knotted tie. Chloe's feet didn't want to move, but she forced them to, walking toward his smile. Ryder's grin had always managed to get her—the way his eyes crinkled ever so much at the sides, his intense blue eyes like pools of the ocean as they fixed on her and never looked away. When she was in his gaze and transfixed by that smile, she was a goner.

Chloe went to call out to him, to tell Ryder that he had a lot of explaining to do, when the words promptly died in her mouth. *Oh my god.* What the hell was he doing? She slowed, feeling as if she were walking on a cloud as he dropped to one knee in the lobby. From the corner of her eyes she could see people stopping, knew they were being watched, but all she could truly see was Ryder before her, smile still fixed in place, bent on one knee, a hand extended out toward her.

She reached him, took his hand, and stared down at the man she was so stupid crazy in love with.

"Ryder, what's going on?" she whispered, not wanting anyone else to hear them. She knew there could only be one reason they were both dressed the way they were with him down on one knee, but still.

"Chloe, will you marry me?" Ryder's deep voice sounded like it had been dragged over gravel, his drawl husky.

Chloe choked. She couldn't say a word, didn't know *what* to say. All she could do was stare at him and focus on stopping her jaw from hitting the floor.

"Chloe?" he prompted, chuckling as he squeezed her hand, still on bended knee. "Don't leave me hanging down here."

"When I said I didn't think you'd commit, I didn't expect a proposal," she murmured, still trying to get her head around what was happening.

Ryder rose, still holding her hand as he reached into his pocket with the other and pulled out a blue Tiffany box. She gasped, hands to her mouth as he opened it to reveal the biggest diamond she'd ever seen, surrounded by an entire band of smaller ones.

"Chloe, I love you," he said, reaching for her left hand and tugging it down, slipping the ring onto her finger while she stared. "I've never loved a woman before so I know I have a crappy track record, but the one thing I do know is that I don't ever want you to walk out of my life again."

She raised her eyes from her finger, the dazzling diamond completely bewitching her until she stared into the bright blue gaze she'd grown to love.

"Will you marry me, Chloe?"

"Yes," she whispered, barely loud enough to hear herself. "Yes, Ryder, I'll marry you."

He threw his arms around her and pulled her in tight, kissing her like it was the last kiss of their lives. Ryder's hands found their way up to her hair, stroking her gently at the same time his mouth slowed. Clapping sounded out and Chloe glanced sideways, seeing a crowd had gathered. Ryder took a bow and then reached for her hand, raising it to his lips for a kiss and then slipping his arm around her waist.

"We have to go." He spoke directly into her ear, the same sexy voice she knew so well from the bedroom.

"Why?" Chloe would rather he dragged her back upstairs.

"I asked you to marry me, sweetheart. So let's go get married."

Chloe stopped, not taking another step and forcing Ryder to do the same. "What did you say?" she asked, heart racing at the same time as her breath caught in her throat.

"I said it's time for us to go get married. We don't want to keep everybody waiting, do we?"

She burst out laughing, incapable of words, staring at Ryder and waiting for him to tell her it was all a joke.

"Come on, baby. Your maid of honor has flown in from Texas, and I'm pretty sure she's wanting to get this over with so we can all hit the town."

"You're serious," she asked. "You've spent the entire day . . ." She was lost for words again, not even finishing her sentence.

"Planning our wedding," he finished for her, drawing her close again, his hands to her face, gently cupping her cheeks. Ryder dropped a soft kiss to her lips, then another. "I know Vegas might not have been your dream wedding destination, but I love you, Chloe, and I want to marry you. I have my brothers here and your best friend, and that's all we need." He touched his forehead to hers, somehow managing to calm her. "If you feel the same, there's a car waiting outside for us right now."

She laughed, it was all she could do. The whole day had been unpredictably crazy, and now here she was about to marry a man she'd once thought would never commit to her for their pretend relationship, let alone a real one.

Chloe stroked his face, admiring how handsome he was, then fiddled with his tie, playing with the knot. "You look damn fine all dressed up like this," she told him.

He chuckled. "Just because I'm not riding rodeo doesn't mean I'm trading in my Wranglers for suits."

She stood on tiptoe so she could press a kiss to his neck, inhaling his cologne and running her hands down his back and to his butt. "You look good in a suit, but I'll never stop admiring your ass in a pair of jeans."

Ryder made a growling noise and planted his hands on her butt, making her squeal. "It just so happens that you look damn fine in satin," he muttered. "Although you'd look even better out of it."

They stared at each other, the heat between them scalding, but it was Ryder who sighed and took a step back. "I've got all night to pleasure you. Come on."

Ryder waved away the driver and opened the car door for Chloe himself. He slid in beside her and took her hand, grinning as the vehicle pulled away and they headed for the chapel.

"Please tell me Elvis isn't marrying us," Chloe joked, dropping her head onto his shoulder.

"Damn, you don't want Elvis? How about Cher?"

She laughed as he draped an arm around her. "I can't

believe you did all this." Ryder watched as she held her finger out, admiring the diamond as it sparkled.

"Do you like it?" he asked. "If you don't, we can change it."

He'd never been so nervous buying a gift, but he wanted Chloe to have that ring on her finger for a long time, and it had sure put the pressure on.

"Ryder, I love it," she said, snuggling closer to him, tucked under his arm, cheek to his chest. "I just can't believe any of it, that we're going to get married, that we're even together right now."

"We've come a long way from meeting at the rodeo." He laughed. "Hell, we've come a long way from you offering to win back my ranch."

She gazed up at him. "What I want to know was why you trusted me."

Ryder stroked her hair, grunting as she slid one hand down his thigh. "Sweetheart, you had a glint in your eye that told me you weren't bullshitting, that you needed a way to make money for law school. You know, my granddad told me you were a keeper as soon as he heard what you'd done."

She laughed. "Does he know what we're doing right now?"

"No, but he will tomorrow when I fly you home as my wife." The vehicle slowed, then stopped, and Ryder removed Chloe's hand from his inner thigh. "As much as I'd like you to keep stroking me there, we have a wedding to attend."

"Shelly's going to be in heaven being looked after by your brothers."

"Last I heard she was drinking them under the table. We'll be lucky if she's coherent enough to sign as witness."

Chloe's smile warmed his heart, her eyes meeting his melting something inside of him that he'd thought would always stay cold. He'd never had a mom to care for him, never let any woman in his life close other than to warm his bed, and Chloe had only been in his life such a short time and she'd already changed him.

"You know, I was going to challenge you to a game of poker," he confessed. "I had this grand idea that if I told you the stakes, that if I won you had to marry me, that the only way for it to actually happen was if you *let* me win."

She shook her head. "You made me promise that I'd never let you win unless you were actually capable of beating me."

Ryder leaned across and kissed her, the tangy taste of her lip gloss as familiar to him now as her perfume. "And I meant it. Which is why I decided it was best not to challenge you."

She slipped a hand around his neck, giggling into his mouth. "Well, good. I would have hated to beat you and lose my husband in the process."

Ryder reluctantly let her go. "You ready?" he asked, pushing open his door to get out and holding out a hand to her so she could follow.

"As I'll ever be," she replied, smoothing down the satin of her dress to show off a perfect set of curves that he was desperate to explore some more.

They walked hand in hand toward the Vegas chapel, greeted by a guy dressed in a tacky sixties outfit. When they stepped inside it was Nate Ryder saw first, standing with his hands shoved into his suit pockets and a worried expression on his face that quickly turned into a smile. Chase was holding a beer and Shelly was saying something to make him laugh.

"The bride and groom are here," Ryder announced, just loud enough to get their attention.

Shelly turned first, eyes widening as she saw Chloe. She was rushing at them within seconds, arms around Chloe in a big hug. His brothers came closer.

"I take it your plan worked?" Chase asked.

Ryder grinned. There was no erasing his smile, not today.

"I never saw our baby bro being the one to wear the ball and chain first," Nate said, slapping Ryder on the back. "But if you're gonna have a chain attached, Chloe's a pretty nice ball to be dragging around."

"You calling my girl a ball?" Ryder joked, holding his fists up like he was ready to fight.

"Settle down, Romeo," Chase interrupted. "Your bride's waiting."

"And we only have about fifteen minutes left before the next bride and groom arrive," Shelly announced.

"Do you want to walk her down the aisle?" Ryder asked Shelly.

"No," Chloe interrupted, touching her friend's shoulder as she passed and reaching for Ryder. "I want to walk down the aisle with my husband. No offense, Shel."

Ryder stared down at Chloe, caught in the web of her gaze. She was beautiful, that was one reason he wanted her so damn bad, but there was a challenge in the way she looked at him, a desire there that he loved the most.

Hell, she'd beaten the pants off him at cards and as good as slashed Parker off at the knees when she'd played him, and then she'd managed to charm his brothers and leave him speechless when she left him. And now here she was standing beside him, demanding that he hold her hand and walk her to the altar. He'd thought it was enough doing what he loved for a living, working with horses every day, being on the land, but something had been missing, and that something was Chloe.

"You think I'll ever tame you enough to have you barefoot and pregnant?"

Chloe stood on tiptoe to wrap her arms around his neck, laughing as he held her around the waist and spun her around. "Not a chance."

He reluctantly let her down, interlinking their fingers. "Let's do this."

"I hope you don't have any vows prepared," she said.

Ryder winked at Chloe as they wandered down the aisle, a corny rendition of "Here Comes the Bride" bursting from the speakers. "Damn right I have."

They stopped when they reached their celebrant, dressed in flamboyant clothes and wearing a bad blond wig. She managed to get their names right and said the official words, then Ryder interrupted her.

"I don't actually have vows," he said, looking into Chloe's eyes, "but I do have some things I'd like to say."

Her eyebrows pulled together slightly, uncertainty written all over her face.

Ryder glanced at his brothers, then at Shelly. They were all gathered around them rather than standing on the sides. "I know you guys probably thought I was crazy this morning, but as you can see Chloe was just as crazy and agreed to marry me."

Chase cracked up. "Only because she didn't have time to think about what she was agreeing to."

Ryder scowled and Chloe nudged him in the side, laughing along with the others. "The truth is that this woman right here is amazing, and a wise old grandfather once told me that"—he grinned at Chloe—"if a woman is beautiful and smart, can beat you at cards, and you don't ever want her out of your bed, then only a fool would let her go."

"Your granddad told you that?" she asked, one hand on her hip.

Ryder laughed. "Yeah, he did actually. But he's not exactly your stock standard grandfather. Which is why he'll probably make us do this all over again when we get back."

"Come on, marry her already," Nate moaned.

"As I was saying," Ryder interrupted in a loud voice, "since this is my wedding and all. When it's yours you can, oh, hang on, no woman will ever be stupid enough to marry you." Now it was Nate scowling. "Anyway," he continued, turning back to Chloe, "you wanted proof that I was in love with you, that I was capable of commitment, and this is it. I'm yours for as long as you'll have me."

"And I'm yours," she whispered, leaning in for a kiss.

Ryder pulled away for a second. "This is the part where I kiss the bride, right?" He didn't wait for a response, but he did kiss the hell out of Chloe, dipping her back into a kiss for everyone to see.

"The new Mrs. King, huh?" he murmured against her mouth as he slowly brought her back up.

"Let's not get too carried away with this *missus* business, or me taking your last name," she murmured back. "But yeah, I'm yours, Ryder. Completely, totally yours."

"Now that's what I'm talking about."

"I can now officially announce you as man and wife," the officiant said, throwing a handful of colorful confetti over them. "And I would tell you to kiss the bride, but you've done that already!"

Nate and Chase let out whoops, clapping and whistling, and Shelly joined in, grabbing hold of Chase and planting a smacker of a kiss on his lips.

Ryder tucked an arm around Chloe and gazed down at her. "What do you say to an early night, just the two of us in that big bathtub?"

Chloe nipped his earlobe, teeth grazing his skin as she hugged him tight. "Sweetheart, we've been just the two of us for three nights straight. It's about time we hit the town, don't you think? Show these guys a good time."

He raised a brow, giving her his best impression of a sad puppy. When that didn't work he tried glowering, but she only laughed and kissed him.

"We can paint the town red and still have fun later," she murmured. "Besides, I have a rock to show off."

Chloe wiggled her finger in his direction, admiring her ring. "You got me," he said. "Three hours tops though, then you're all mine. Deal?"

"Hmmm, when you say deal . . ."

"I'm not betting *anything* against you, Chloe. Not now, not ever. I've learned my lesson damn good." In fact, he wasn't going near a betting table without her by his side and on his team. When it came to gambling Chloe had him beat every time.

"Deal, then," she agreed, looping her arms around his neck and leaning back when he picked her up and slung her across his arms. "But if there's space in the big game room at the Bellagio tonight . . ."

He chuckled and pressed a kiss to her lips. "It's our wedding night, darlin'. You want to play poker, then that's what we'll do."

"You know, I hated Vegas a few months ago, and because of you I love the place again." She sighed and gazed up at him. "And to think you were just a hot cowboy I checked out at the rodeo one afternoon, huh?"

"Happy to be of service," he told her, carrying her back down the aisle as his brothers threw way too much confetti at them.

"Oh, you can be of service to me," she joked. "You're all mine now, and I plan on putting you to good use."

Ryder put her to her feet and skimmed his hands down her body, getting hard just thinking about what she had planned for him. He wanted her dress in a puddle at her feet, breasts bare and cupped in his hands, mouth tracing across every inch of her skin. He wanted her moaning his name and naked in his bed for the rest of his life.

"You sound like the perfect wife," he muttered, running a finger down her chest and circling the top of one breast.

Chloe playfully smacked his hand away and put it around her waist instead. "Oh, I am, cowboy. Just you wait and see."

Epilogue

"Don't go," Ryder said, reaching up and catching Chloe's arm.

She gave in and let him pull her back down, lying over him, their naked bodies length to length. He stroked her hair, staring at her mouth and catching her lips in a kiss before she was able to say anything.

"Ryder," she attempted, giggling as he expertly flipped her. She was pinned beneath him now and she didn't bother to fight him, letting him hold her by the wrists.

"Why would you want to go to class when you could be here with me?" He waggled his eyebrows, stealing another kiss. "I could do all sorts of things to make it worth your while."

She craned her neck back so he could tease his lips across her skin, the sensation of his tongue sending goose bumps of delight over her entire body. It would be so easy to just give in to him, to say yes, but she wasn't going to.

"You make a compelling argument," she told him, running her nails down his back, digging them in hard enough to make him yelp. "But then so do I. Which is why I'm going to make such a great attorney."

"I know, baby, I know," he said, sitting up and tugging her up with him. "You know how proud I am, right? Dallas ain't gonna know what's hit it when you walk into the courtroom."

"You do know that I'm specializing in property law, right?" she asked, lips brushing his shoulder, tongue darting out to taste his salty skin. "I'm not going to be all *L.A. Law*, but I am going to be able to offer assistance to Nate with all your family's property deals."

"And here I was thinking your work was gonna be all role-play, like on the TV."

She swatted at him, trying to pull a frown and failing when he stroked her hair. He loved to tease her and try to distract her, but Ryder had been with her every step of the way when it came to finishing her law degree. She knew he'd have loved to have her on the ranch at his beck and call, but she needed to carve out a career for herself and he respected that.

"You know, this gorgeous guy I met lost a bet and ended up having to pay my tuition," she murmured, on all fours and nuzzling his neck this time, stroking his inner thigh and loving the sound of his groan. "It would be such a shame not to make the most of his generosity. Maybe I should move into a dorm so I can focus and not get distracted all the time."

"You," Ryder muttered, "are a witch." He grabbed her cheeks between his hands to plant a wet kiss on her lips before pushing her off the bed and slapping her butt.

"And that's for being such a tease. Any more smart comments and I'll have to punish you."

Chloe left him in bed, admiring his muscled, lean body as he stretched out. The man was insanely comfortable in his own skin.

"Want to go riding after class?" Ryder asked.

She called out over her shoulder as she gathered her clothes, "My inner thighs are still killing me from the last ride."

Ryder's laugh echoed into the bathroom as she turned the faucet on and waited for the water to run hot. "You sure that was from the horse ride?"

"As opposed to the two-legged beast I rode last night?"

"Come on, whadda ya say? Then I can show you the new bulls I have."

Chloe groaned. "Can't we just walk there?" It wasn't that she didn't like horses, but the riding was seriously killing her legs.

"I thought you wanted to be a real cowgirl? You can't live on the King ranch without being a pro on horseback."

Chloe didn't hear Ryder sneak up on her, his arms snaking around her waist and pinning her back against him, her butt rammed hard into him.

"Ryder, no!" she protested, squealing and thrashing to get away from him. Chloe pushed him back and leaped into the shower, closing the door and holding it shut tight. She burst out laughing as he flexed his biceps and made a play at forcing it open. "Go away. I'm serious."

"Is that any way to speak to your husband?" he asked,

spreading his hands against the glass and giving her a sad puppy-dog impersonation.

"Yes," she replied, slowly taking her hand off the door and rinsing her hair. "Now be a good boy and go make me breakfast."

Ryder's laugh was warm, his wink lazy as he gave her one final glance up and down before the glass fogged over completely. "Yes, ma'am."

"Never thought you'd be the one making breakfast in the mornings, did you?" she teased.

"Hey, if it means keeping you happy, I don't care if I have to scramble eggs every morning for the rest of my life."

He left her alone in the bathroom, massaging suds through her hair. Nothing beat living here with Ryder, and having . . . *the rogue.*

"Ryder!" she called, poking her head out of the shower and stretching to look into the bedroom.

"You change your mind about me joining you?" he asked, appearing in the doorway, jeans slung low and his golden-brown torso bare.

"You weren't going to call Nate's housekeeper over to cook breakfast while I was getting ready, were you?" she asked, not taking her eyes off him as she rinsed the shampoo off her long hair.

"Never crossed my mind," he said, "but that's a damn fine idea. Thanks!"

"Ryder!"

"I'm kidding," he said, poking his head in and snatching a quick kiss. "The one thing I know how to make is a mean breakfast. I promise it'll be all me."

Chloe couldn't wipe the smile off her face as she finished showering and reached for a towel. No matter how many times she pinched herself, she still couldn't believe that the sexy-as-hell cowboy cooking her breakfast belonged to her. Forever.

Coming soon...

Look for the next novel in this **HOT** Texas Kings series by
Soraya Lane

Cowboy Take Me Away

Available in January 2016 from St. Martin's Paperbacks